*Three Paths
to the Lake*

Modern German Voices Series

Ingeborg Bachmann
The Thirtieth Year
Three Paths to the Lake
Malina

Manès Sperber
Like a Tear in the Ocean

Peter Härtling
A Woman

Alexander Kluge
Case Histories

Eric Rentschler, ed.
West German Filmmakers on Film:
Visions and Voices

Wolfgang Koeppen
Pigeons on the Grass

Christa Wolf
Selected Essays of Christa Wolf

Three Paths to the Lake

STORIES BY
Ingeborg Bachmann

Translated by
Mary Fran Gilbert

WITH AN INTRODUCTION BY
MARK ANDERSON

HM

HOLMES & MEIER
New York/London

Published in the United States of America 1989 by
Holmes & Meier Publishers, Inc.
30 Irving Place
New York, N.Y. 10003

Originally published under the title *Simultan*
copyright © 1972 by R. Piper & Co. Verlag, Munich.

This book has been printed on acid-free paper.

Library of Congress Cataloging-in-Publication Data

Bachmann, Ingeborg, 1926-1973.
Three paths to the lake.

(Modern German voices)
Translation of: Simultan.
1. Bachmann, Ingeborg, 1926-1973—Translations, English. I. Title. II. Series.
PT 2603.A147s513 1989   833'.912   88-21243
ISBN 0-8419-1070-7 (alk. paper)
ISSN 0893-1143

MANUFACTURED IN THE UNITED STATES OF AMERICA

Contents

Introduction

Presented here for the first time in English, *Three Paths to the Lake* has already earned Ingeborg Bachmann a remarkable following not only in Germany and her native Austria but in the rest of Europe as well. This success was not immediate. The same critics who had once championed Bachmann's poetry during the 1950s and early 1960s were initially disconcerted, even dismayed, by her transition to a prose genre that seemed unsuited to her literary talents. Gone were the elegant hermeticism and high seriousness of her lyric work, replaced by what seemed to be trivial *Frauengeschichten,* "women's stories," with no apparent narrative energy, focus, or significance. One woman ruins her makeup and hairdo in the rain, another vainly refuses to wear corrective glasses, still another befriends her aging, reclusive mother-in-law. This was hardly the kind of subject matter one expected from a woman who had written a doctoral dissertation on Heidegger, inaugurated a series of influential lectures on modern European literature at the University of Frankfurt, and whose sophisticated verse had won for her—at an enviably early age—all the major German and Austrian literary prizes.

This ostensible poverty of content was only made worse by the language of *Three Paths to the Lake* which, in direct conflict with the bitingly laconic modernism of Bachmann's poetry, seemed embarrassingly subjective, digressive, colloquial, even chatty. For Bachmann had had the audacity to write not only about women, but about women with no stable voice of their own, no confident or effective relationship to the world through language. As a result, the stories themselves appeared to be prisoners of their protagonists' own stammering failures, gesturing toward but incapable of speaking a convincing language of truth and general human experience.

The opening of the first story, "Word for Word,"[1] is characteristic of this highly subjective, "insecure" voice, confronting the reader abruptly with the chaotic, multilingual stream of consciousness of a simultaneous interpreter named Nadja vacationing in the south of Italy.

Bože moj! were her feet cold, but this finally seemed to be Paestum, there's an old hotel here, I can't understand how the name could have slipped my, it'll occur to me in a second, it's on the tip of my tongue, but she couldn't remember it, rolled down the window and strained to see out to the side and ahead, she was looking for the road that should branch off to the right, credimi, te lo giuro, dico a destra. Ah there it was, yes, the Nettuno. As he slowed down at the intersection and turned on the headlights she spotted the sign immediately, illuminated in the darkness among a dozen hotel signs and arrows pointing the way to bars and beach resorts. . . .

This kind of beginning, which shifts abruptly not only between several languages, but between unspoken thoughts, dialogue and description of external objects, may well seem obscure, especially to English and American readers for whom translation has added an additional, inevitable register of complexity. Not a Joycean, virtuoso weaving together of diverse idioms into a common language, Bachmann's text offers a fragmented, stuttering diaspora of sound in which different national languages function as inadequate, incidental means of communication. What emerges is a strange cacophony of "surface noise," a buzzing of foreign or overly subjective phrases that block our access to Nadja and her story just as the neon signs and arrows obscure her way to the Nettuno Hotel. Nadja—whose own name in Slovene means hope—is searching for a name just off the tip of her tongue, and when it finally comes to her it proves useless, no longer in rapport with what it once signified.

Like the Italian landscape, however—itself a complex stratification of natural beauty, ancient Greek and Roman temples, Renaissance villas and the effluvia of a modern consumer society—Bachmann's text conceals layers of meaning persistently grouped around a sacred core. *Bože moj* means "my God" in Russian (one of Nadja's diplomatic languages), Paestum is the site of a Greek temple dedicated to Poseidon, the apparently offhand Italian phrases contain the verbs to believe *(credere)* as well as to swear *(giurare)*, "Nettuno" is the Italian spelling for the Roman sea god. The search for an old hotel, late at night, is also the search for its proper name, for primeval and sacred origins in language, for the one word that "lights up" in the dark among a welter of arrows and meaningless signs. Beneath Nadja's own "dead-tired" indifference, Bachmann's story displays a metaphysical, even mystical longing for a utopian state of being—a pure, primal language of origins.

Bachmann once considered calling the collection *Women from Vienna*, a title that recalls Robert Musil's *Three Women* while emphasizing the specific geographic locale her protagonists have in common. Although they share a regional identity, these women have in common few if any similarities in character or occupation. They are united rather by what is missing from their lives. Like Nadja, all of them are inhabited and controlled by a language that is not their own. All have in some way been robbed of their names, their childhood identities, their voices. And like Nadja they all unwittingly display some sign of revolt, longing, sickness, or anger that challenges the patriarchal logic of their society and cultural traditions. The difficulty but also the strength of these stories is thus the discrepancy between the "surface noise" of seemingly trivial, incidental, subjective details and a deeper but by no means completed or successful search for a more authentic language of experience. Casualties of a social order that is based on work, competition, exploitation, and war, Bachmann's "heroines" lack even the words that might begin to depict this condition.

Some sense of this paradoxical literary achievement has begun to assert itself among Bachmann's readers. The publication of her novel *Malina* in 1971 as well as the posthumous publication in 1978 of the unfinished novel cycle *Death Styles* (to which the stories in *Three Paths to the Lake* are directly related), have exposed the political thrust behind her "trivial" *Frauengeschichten*. Feminist readers now speak of the "other" Bachmann, rightly pointing to the importance of gender conflict in her later prose work and privileging it to the earlier poetry.[2] In tandem with this political interest, readers have also begun to discern a stylistic sophistication in Bachmann's "unmediated" prose. Jean Améry has insisted on the distinction between the linguistic failings of Bachmann's protagonists and her own quite accomplished and sophisticated prose style, which he characterizes in its "lightness" and "deliberate indirectness" as an "Austrian *parlando*," a spoken idiom that had been subjected to "musical principles of composition."[3] Recent critical scholarship on *Three Paths to the Lake* has also revealed a vast web of references to Bachmann's Austrian heritage: to Robert Musil, Joseph Roth, Hugo von Hofmannsthal and Karl Kraus; to Freud, Otto Weininger, Wittgenstein, and Schönberg; and finally to key events and places in Habsburg history—references supporting Améry's claim that Bachmann was attempting to "forge or revive a specifically Austrian literary language."

With Paul Celan, Ilse Aichinger, and a few others, Bachmann was one of the first poets to lift the German language from the rubble of the Nazi period into limpid, carefully wrought verse in a lyrical tradition stretching back through Rilke and Hofmannsthal to Hölderlin, Leopardi and Petrarch. Born in a rural province of southwestern Austria in 1926, Bachmann was twelve when the Nazis marched into her native Klagenfurt, nineteen when the war ended, twenty-seven when she first received public recognition for her poetry from the influential Group 47. From the beginning, this young Austrian displayed a charisma that quickly turned her into an object of fascination and cult-like devotion. Her two collections of poetry, *Mortgaged Time* (1953) and *Invocation of the Great Bear* (1956) received critical as well as public acclaim, eventually winning for her the Austrian State Prize for Literature and the prestigious Büchner Prize.[4] In 1954 the German news magazine *Der Spiegel* ran a cover story on the young poet then living in Rome, describing her as "lots of blond hair, soft brown eyes, quiet and shy," and animated by a "sharply trained intellect"—thereby establishing the alluring image of Bachmann that would haunt her all her life: a sylphlike, Undine figure, at once girlish, reclusive, and intellectually formidable.

It is to Bachmann's credit that in the midst of this public and critical acclaim she herself grew dissatisfied with the limits of her own work, abandoning its premises and methods in a turn so radical that one can legitimately speak of two distinct literary personae. This turn does not simply involve, as is often claimed, a rejection of poetry for prose, but a fundamentally different conception of what prose is for. Bachmann had already written a novel in the early 1950s, and all of the stories in *The Thirtieth Year*[5]—her first published prose collection—were conceived and written later in the same decade. This collection and the poetry comprise the bulk of Bachmann's first period, which she later saw as being limited by its hermetic aestheticism. *Three Paths to the Lake* and the novel cycle *Death Styles* occupied her from the early 1960s until her death in 1973, and represent a greater concern with what one might call the "politics of narrative," with a story told not for the formal beauty of its individual sentences but for its expressive totality, for what "needs to be said."

Introduction

I don't consider [the stories in *The Thirtieth Year*] to be narrated
. . . in the sense that I now understand "narration." Although
[my later prose work] is not narrated throughout and contains
some lyrical passages, I no longer attempt to make each individual sentence into an artwork. The only thing that matters
is what needs to be said.[6]

Bachmann's lectures at the University of Frankfurt, delivered during the winter semester of 1959-60, give us an un-
derstanding of the thinking that led to this change.
Although she had been invited on the strength of her lyrical
work, Bachmann devoted only one of the five lectures to
poetry, focusing instead on the modern novel. Indeed, the
first lecture can be read as an implicit autobiographical con-
fession of the crisis weighing on her own lyrical production.
Singling out the modern preoccupation with "silence, the
reasons for it and the return from silence," Bachmann cites
Hofmannsthal's Lord Chandos "Letter" as a paradigmatic example of the loss of trust between "the self, language, and
things themselves." "With this letter," she writes of her Austrian predecessor, "Hofmannsthal unexpectedly rejects the pure
magical poetry of his early years—he rejects aestheticism."[7]
At the end of the same lecture Bachmann returns to the
same point with even more vehemence. Quoting the "furious
sentence" by Hermann Broch (another Austrian) that "Morality is morality, business is business, war is war and art is art,"
Bachmann dismisses the doctrine of "l'art pour l'art" as un-
serious, a form of moral bankruptcy that endangers the per-
petually new dialogue between artist and society: "Merely to
stimulate one's aesthetic pleasure with a few difficult images,
to quicken one's aesthetic sensibility—this medicine against

art, which makes it harmless—cannot be the goal of this office."

At this juncture, in the highly charged political atmosphere of the early 1960s, Bachmann begins asking pragmatic questions that recall Jean-Paul Sartre's polemic against "bourgeois" literature in *Qu' est-ce que la littérature?*: Who writes? For whom? And to what end? What are the social and political concerns of writing? But for the writer who had grown up in Nazi Austria, these questions led to different answers, inevitably harkening back to the problems of fascism, the Holocaust, and collective guilt. Like other writers of her generation, too young to be directly compromised by the war but too old not to have been traumatized by it, Bachmann was an ambivalent prisoner of this heritage, a daughter of her mother and father, both symbolically aligned with "yesterday's hangmen." As the literary critic Christa Bürger has noted,

> Bachmann doesn't attempt to divorce herself from the destiny and spiritual dowry of her family. She knows that the family's truth is also her own. Yet she pays for this attitude with an excruciating emotional ambivalence: she hates the petty, everyday fascism experienced by her family and knows herself to be part of it at the same time. . . . This emotional ambivalence determines both her perception of reality and her attitude toward it. (*Text und Kritik* 13)

This conception of the ongoing force of a horrific past—manifest in colonial wars, exploitation of the Third World, poverty and social injustice, terrorism, or the degradation and exploitation of women in a patriachal society—led Bachmann to renounce the merely formal efficacy of her earlier poetry and lyrical prose as language games effective only within language. For the earnest, critical attention devoted to language, which Bachmann had praised in the 1950s as a moral force in Wittgenstein's work and which is also evident in her early writing, had culminated only in despair about the limitations of poetic language, not the awaited epiphany or miraculous breakthrough to a higher, alternative mode of being. One of her last poems, "No Delicacies," queries:

Should I
dress a metaphor
with an almond blossom?
crucify syntax
on a trick of light?
who will beat his brains over such superfluities—

I have learned to be considerate
with the words
that exist
(for the lowest class)

hunger
      disgrace
            tears
and
                darkness.

Yet this turn away from an aestheticist relation to language should not be confused with a rejection of modernism or literature generally. In fact, the bulk of Bachmann's Frankfurt lectures is devoted to a detailed examination of the problem of the self, the proper name, time, and narration in Proust, Svevo, Joyce, Kafka, Musil, Faulkner, Beckett, and other "high" modernist novelists. Rather than considering the obscurities presented by this work as merely formal literary problems, Bachmann treats them as symptoms of specific social and political conflicts, as the hard-won experience of human suffering in the present. Literature, a certain kind of literature, clearly had a social function:

> It was clear for me . . . that society could be brought to a new form of consciousness by a new kind of writing. Of course one can't change the world with a poem, that's impossible, but one can have an effect on something, and this effect can only be achieved with the greatest seriousness and from the new experiences of suffering, that is, not from the suffering of the great poets before us. (Interview, p. 139)

Put simply, Bachmann's response to this challenge was to formulate the status of women in contemporary Austria in terms of the modernist's aesthetic developed by Kafka, Musil, Faulkner, and Beckett. The effacement of the self, the relativity of narrative time frames, the tenuousness of proper names and heroic characters—to these formal issues Bachmann brings the content of Austrian women suffering from a particular kind of oppression at a particular moment in history.

The five stories in *Three Paths to the Lake* deal with five different Austrian women, all of them in some marginal or compromised relation to a social order that is largely defined by men. These women are by no means merely positive figures—one senses that Bachmann is both inside and outside them, describing (as a woman writer) the suffering of women from her own culture, and yet with sufficient distance and at times dislike to expose their character "type." One might well describe these stories as five case studies of women suffering from various psychic and emotional disorders—with the important provision that these "disorders" are experienced from the female protagonist's own point of view. Precisely because the stories are not narrated by an external, clinically objective observer, the psychological "disorder" takes on a different, more complex meaning.

Accompanying this shift to the question of women is the radical equation, on which all of Bachmann's later writing is founded, between fascism and personal relationships. For Bachmann, fascism begins in the family and carries over to the couple, in the subtle and not so subtle power relations between spouses and lovers, in the sado-masochistic rituals of sexual and social relations which rob a woman of her name, her voice, her feelings, her past—everything that is eliminated in the passage from childhood to womanhood. War doesn't begin, she maintains,

> with the first bombs that are launched or with the terror that one can write about in any newspaper. It starts in the relations between people. Fascism is the first element in the relation between a man and a woman . . . in this society war is constant. There's no such thing as war and peace, there is only war. (Interview, 144)

A polemical view, and one that Bachmann exaggerated when speaking with skeptical journalists, the equation between German fascism and the violence of interpersonal relations presents several historical problems. For some readers it can imply an objectionable trivialization of actual Nazi war crimes; others may counter that the origin of modern totalitarian states lies in specific historical, economic and social phenomena, not in the relationships between father and daughter or husband and wife. In short, Bachmann's conception risks emptying of their historical context the very historical events and problems that have given rise to her writing. These objections cannot easily be refuted. But to read Bachmann one must accept this equation as the basic analogy underlying all her later fiction, testing it case by case for the insights (or the limitations and historical distortions) it produces in the specific human stories at hand.

In the opening story "Word for Word," Nadja embodies the problematic status of a woman's voice in a patriarchal world. Given only a first name, she works for the Food and Agriculture Organization (FAO) in Rome as a successful simultaneous interpreter, her entire existence devoted to the mechanical reproduction of someone else's language: "What a strange mechanism she was, she lived without a single thought of her own, immersed in the sentences of others, like a sleepwalker, furnishing the same but different-sounding sentences." But this technical ability to transform words into their equivalent in foreign languages bars Nadja access to their meaning, thus keeping her outside her own language, an exile and mere manipulator of equal but empty phrases.

However, the opening search for the name of the Nettuno Hotel triggers a productive crisis in this conception of language. Nadja is initially overwhelmed by the huge stone Christ above the bay of Maratea, stretching herself on the ground in passive submission to this image of patriarchal authority. She later returns to the statue and reinterprets it in a subjective vision, not as Christ nailed to the cross but as an angel-like figure with outspread wings, "preparing for a grandiose flight, poised for flight or a plunge to the depths." Paradoxically, this creative vision coincides with the breakdown of Nadja's translating, merely reproductive faculty—she is unable to translate a simple Italian sentence chosen at random from the New Testament—a failure which forces her to acknowledge the limits of her multi-lingual but impoverished world. She returns to the hotel, transformed and apparently reconciled with her immediate surroundings, and is strangely moved by the incantatory cheers of a crowd hailing the winner of a cycling competition.

The hopefulness of this ambiguous opening is not always sustained in the subsequent stories. "Problems Problems" deals with the initially unengaging subject of a woman named Beatrix who does little more than visit a beauty parlor and lie in bed, the willing victim of a "perverse" and "fetishistic" desire for sleep. The repetition in the story's title is colloquial but also, in its mirror effect, indicative of the story's true subject: female narcissism. Looking into the "temple" of mirrors in René's beauty parlor after she has been cosmetically transformed, the heroine swoons: "I'm in love, I'm honest to goodness in love with myself, I'm divine!" The novelty here, however, is that female narcissism is presented from within. A bit like Georg Büchner's *Lenz*, which narrates madness from Lenz's own distorted point of view, Bachmann's text presents that paradigmatic object of male representation and desire—the "self-contained," elusively beautiful woman—as a subject, from inside her intelligent and by no means unperceptive consciousness. Intellectually, Beatrix is clearly the superior figure in this story: she sees through the self-comforting delusions of her chronically unhappy lover, and through the self-denying, compromising ambitions of her cousin Elisabeth Mihailovics (whose brutal murder by her husband will be related in "Three Paths to the Lake"). Yet morally she is unappealing, her indolent existence made possible by her manipulation of family and friends through language: "Beatrix was especially partial to words like conscience, blame, responsibility, and consideration because they sounded good to her and meant nothing."

This "trivial" subject is changed by the fleeting appearance of Franziska Jordan, the protagonist in "The Barking" as well as Bachmann's unfinished novel *The Franza Case*, whose husband has written a scholarly treatise on the psychoses of concentration camp inmates. Beatrix is led into a small massage room by a masseuse who begins to "torture" her with "two paws"; like the patients of Nazi doctors, she becomes the "victim" of crude "attempts" or "experiments" *(Versuche)*. She starts to cry and rushes from the beauty parlor into the rain, thus destroying the cosmetic illusion of her own formal perfection. The final scene leaves her literally speechless, incapable of responding to an old woman's friendly but uncomprehending commiseration.

"Eyes to Wonder" offers a parallel but reverse scenario of "Problems Problems."[8] Whereas Beatrix is finally imprisoned by her own sharp-sighted sensitivity, Miranda is literally short-sighted and willfully shields herself from the ugliness of her surroundings by refusing to wear glasses. More than a question of simple vanity, this refusal stems from a hypersensitivity to the "hellish" details of human existence: "With the help of a tiny optical correction . . . Miranda can see into hell. This inferno has never lost its terrifying effect." Yet Miranda's deliberately vague view of the world gives her an intuitive, creative capacity lacking in supposedly common, "photographic" perceptions. Normal vision is "sharp," immobilizing the world in a clinically precise but sterile reproduction, whereas Miranda "paints" the world of her lover in her own original way. The opposition here is not just between masculine and feminine ways of seeing but, as in "Word for Word," between an artistic and a mechanical language of perception, Miranda's "blindness" perhaps serving as a veiled allusion to Bachmann's own attempts to dissolve the limits of the factual, observable world, opening it up in time and space to the imagination.[9]

"Eyes to Wonder" is an elusive story, perhaps because Miranda's behavior seems to derive from Bachmann's reading the work of Georg Groddeck on the subjective nature of vision. In his "Seeing without Eyes,"[10] Groddeck emphasizes the necessarily distorting quality of all visual perceptions:

> Just as some people try with the help of short-sightedness to narrow down their field of vision, to exclude everything that is far away and also some unpleasant things which are near in space and time, so old people try to repress near and short-distance objects from their perception by presbyopia."[11]

Ultimately, Miranda cannot sustain her subjective reordering of the world: abandoned by the lover she has in fact pushed into the arms of a close friend, she finally runs into a glass café door, which shatters and leaves her bloodied, humiliated, symbolically blinded and, like Beatrix, incapable of articulating her suffering.

Groddeck's insight into the self-willed presbyopia of the elderly applies equally well to "The Barking," a haunting story about the friendship between Franziska Jordan and her aging mother-in-law, who lives alone in a suburb of Vienna, neglected by the son that she both fears and blindly admires. Unworldly, suspicious, socially pretentious, the older Frau Jordan has closed herself off from the present and is initially disinclined to speak about her past life. Through her own discreet, thoughtful attention, Franziska gains the woman's trust and comes to understand her full ambivalence toward her son, thereby gaining the first inkling of Leo Jordan's sadistic character. As death nears, the mother is plagued by hallucinations of barking dogs—mention of which coincides with the disclosure of Jordan's study of concentration camp psychoses—a sound which seems to give voice to her own long-repressed hostility toward her son. She grows indifferent to Jordan's presence, "the fear of an entire lifetime" suddenly abandoning her as she sinks into the barking of imaginary dogs.

"Three Paths to the Lake" is perhaps the most beautiful and moving piece in the collection, a deeply autobiographical meditation that dominates the other stories not only in length but in its capacity to transform the memories of a woman's life into an allegory of the "House of Austria." Elisabeth Matrei, a successful photographer working in Paris during the 1960s, returns to her native Klagenfurt to visit her aging, widowed father, often taking walks in the surrounding hillside on the three paths leading to the lake. Yet this familiar landscape of Elisabeth's youth gradually dissolves into the topography of her own memories and experiences, the "three paths" leading not to the lake but to the story of her relationships with three different men, all of whom symbolize some remnant of the Hapsburg Empire. The most important is Franz Joseph Trotta, a name and character Bachmann borrows from Joseph Roth's novel *The Capuchin Crypt* in which the old Trotta, knowing his world has come to an end with the Nazi occupation of Austria, sends his child into exile to Paris. Bachmann takes up this character at a later date, as an adult Frenchman without native country or language who imparts to the young Elisabeth her first sense of old Austria and the full, existential meaning of exile.

Elisabeth Matrei's three loves, her successful though ultimately compromising work as a news photographer in a world of men, her complex relation to her father, her place of birth, and "Austria" in the larger cultural, historical sense—this is only half the story. The other half, less prominent but perhaps richer in implications, concerns the vaguely incestuous love between Elisabeth and her younger brother Robert. Bachmann had already explored this subject in other writings. In *The Franza Case* brother and sister travel to Egypt in a semi-mystical retreat from contemporary Western civilization that owes much to Robert Musil's use of the same theme in his novel *The Man Without Qualities*. Invoking the Egyptian myth of Isis and Osiris, Musil's and Bachmann's novels explore the themes of incest and twin personalities to gain access to a mystical "other state" beyond conventional patriarchal relation.[12] Although "Three Paths to the Lake" eschews this mysticism, the latent sexual tension between brother and sister provides a suggestive contrast to the destructive, sterile relationships Elisabeth has with other men. But their professional life in foreign countries imbues the story with a sense of loss and decline. Their self-imposed exile signifies the death of their Austrian family, a microcosm of the "House of Austria," with Herr Matrei and Trotta recalling Franz Joseph, the last grand Habsburg Kaiser. The story's last words are ambiguously defensive. Waking from a dream that her heart has been cut open, Elisabeth insists: "It's nothing, it's nothing, nothing else can happen to me now. Something might happen to me, but it doesn't have to."

Three Paths to the Lake

Shortly before her death Ingeborg Bachmann traveled to Poland, where she visited Auschwitz and Birkenau, names that had hovered in the background of her writing for two decades. Yet the documentation she had read beforehand proved different from the camps themselves: "I don't understand how one can live with them nearby. . . . There is nothing to say. They are simply there, and it leaves you speechless."

Something of this experience—a memory that is an abyss, absent and yet undeniable—informs the lives of the five women in *Three Paths to the Lake.* Whether it is Nadja fumbling for the right translation of the New Testament, Beatrix and Miranda in their final humiliations, Franziska and her mother-in-law before the obliviously sadistic Dr. Jordan, or Elisabeth waiting anxiously by the telephone, Bachmann's stories trace the paths by which five different women are brought to an elementary state of isolation and speechlessness. Given diminutive first names in a powerful world of patronyms, they can at best, like Nadja and Elisabeth, reproduce the language and images of a world dominated by men, war, torture, economic and moral exploitation. Or, like Beatrix, Miranda and Frau Jordan, they can build a wall in front of this hell with cosmetics, blindness or insanity. For a moment the curtain of the mind is raised, the horror glimpsed. But the cry is choked in the throat, no sound emerges. In the end these woman have nothing to say, no language to say it with, no possibility of transcending a personal abyss that is as banal and horrifying as Auschwitz today.

Kafka once said that there was hope in this world, "an infinite amount of hope," but not for us. A poem by Paul Celan affirms that "there are still songs to be sung/beyond humani-ty." Writing within similar cultural and historical parameters, Bachmann gives an exact account of the hopelessly mired and isolated lives of five Austrian women—without herself giving up hope. "I have often been asked why I hold on to a notion of a utopian world in which everything will be good," she once explained in an interview, "when one is con-tinually confronted with a disgusting, quotidian reality. [But] if I didn't believe, I couldn't write any more." If the women in *Three Paths to the Lake* are denied a voice, denied transcen-dence, denied even the glimmer of a way out of their imprisonments, one can only respond that Bachmann fashioned a language in which the "principle of hope" is still present. To have looked this deeply into the well of history and personal relations without renouncing this principle is no small achievement. May these stories be read in the same unflinching spirit.

Notes

1. The original title of the story is "Simultan." This is also the German title of the entire collection, sometimes referred to in En-glish as *Simultaneous*.

2. See the particularly informative collection of essays devoted to the later prose texts (*Ingeborg Bachmann, Text und Kritik*, Munich, 1984). A recent issue of *Modern Austrian Literature* (vol. 18, 1985) also contains much useful material, including discus-sions of "Three Paths to the Lake" by Leo A. Lensing and Peter West Nutting.

3. Born in Vienna as Hans Mayer in 1912, a survivor of Ausch-witz who later committed suicide, Améry reviewed *Three Paths to*

the Lake for the Swiss newspaper *Die Weltwoche* on November 8, 1972. In her last story Bachmann directly refers to Amery and his essay on torture, which was originally published in German in *Merkur* in 1965. An English selection of his writings has been published as *At the Mind's Limits*, trans. Sidney and Stella P. Rosenfeld (Bloomington: Indiana University Press, 1980).

4. A comprehensive selection of Bachmann's poetry was published in English in 1986 as *In the Storm of Roses*, trans. Mark Anderson (Princeton: Princeton University Press, 1986).

5. First published in German in 1961, the stories appeared in English in 1964 in a translation by Michael Bullock and were reprinted by Holmes & Meier in 1987.

6. Bachmann is speaking here of *Malina*, the first part of the novel cycle called *Todesarten (Death Styles)*. But the remark pertains as well to *Three Paths to the Lake*, written in tandem with the cycle, as Bachmann herself explains. The quotation is taken from an interview of 1971 in *Ingeborg Bachmann, Wir müssen wahre Sätze finden*, ed. by C. Koschel and I. von Weidenbaum (Munich: Piper, 1983). Henceforth referred to as Interview.

7. The lectures have been printed in the four-volume set of Bachmann's works in German: *Ingeborg Bachmann, Werke*, edited by C. Koschel, I. von Weidenbaum, and C. Munster (Munich: Piper, 1978).

8. The German title of Bachmann's story, "Ihr glückliche Augen," derives from the last section of Goethe's *Faust*, Pt. II. The English title is by Marion Faber.

9. This utopian vision is particularly important in Bachmann's poetry, informing her notion of poetic landscapes and especially "Austria," which she insists "should not be thought of in geographic categories."

10. Considered the father of "psychosomatic analysis," Groddeck advocated deep massage and other non-medicinal treatments, and corresponded with Freud about the "sense" or meaning of illness. Even a broken leg, in his view, had a "causa interna." Bachmann

began a review of Groddeck's works but never published it.

11. From "Vision," in *The Meaning of Illness*, edited by Lore Schact (London: Hogarth Press, 1977), p. 190.

12. Musil, who was also born in Klagenfurt, hangs over "Three Paths to the Lake" like a local spirit, titles and themes from his work weaving their way into the fabric of Elisabeth's thoughts and her existence as the "friend of important men." Bachmann discovered Musil's writing at an early age and repeatedly referred to him as a major influence on her work.

Word for Word

Bože moj! were her feet cold, but this finally seemed to be Paestum, there's an old hotel here, I can't understand how the name could have slipped my, it'll occur to me in a second, it's on the tip of my tongue, but she couldn't remember it, rolled down the window and strained to see out to the side and ahead, she was looking for the road that should branch off to the right, credimi, te lo giuro, dico a destra. Ah there it was, yes, the Nettuno. As he slowed down at the intersection and turned on the headlights she spotted the sign immediately, illuminated in the darkness among a dozen hotel signs and arrows pointing the way to bars and beach resorts, and she murmured, it used to be so different, there was nothing here at all, absolutely nothing, just five six years ago, really, it doesn't seem possible.

1

She heard the gravel crunch under the tires and stones bounce up against the chassis and stayed slouched in her seat; she massaged her neck, then stretched, yawning, and when he returned he said, count this place out, they'd have to go to one of the new hotels, they didn't even bother to put sheets on the beds here anymore, these old hotels built next to temples, surrounded by roses and draped with bougainvillea, weren't in demand anymore, and she was both disappointed and relieved. Anyway, she didn't really care one way or the other, she said, dead tired as she was.

During the drive they hadn't been able to talk much: on the highway, the sharp hiss of the wind and the speed had silenced them both, except for the hour they had spent searching for the exit in Salerno, when there had been one thing or another to talk about: they had spoken French, then switched back to English, his Italian wasn't very good yet, and gradually she picked up the old singsong again, making lilting melodies of her German sentences and tuning them to his nonchalant German phrasing, how exciting that she was able to talk like this again, after ten years, she was enjoying it more and more, and now to be actually traveling with someone from Vienna! She wondered all the same how much they really had to say to one another, given that they had only this city in common and a similar way of talking, the same intonation, perhaps she'd just wanted to believe after that third whiskey on the roof garden at the Hilton that he would give her back something she'd lost, a missing taste, an intonation gone flat, that ghostly feeling of home, though she was no longer at home anywhere.

He had lived in Hietzing, he began, only to break off, there must have been something in Hietzing that was difficult for him to talk about; she herself had grown up in the Wicken-burggasse in Josefstadt, then came the inevitable *name-dropping,* they felt out the Viennese terrain but were unable to find any mutual acquaintances who might have helped them along, the Jordans, the Altenwyls, of course she knew who they were, but she'd never actually met them, no, she didn't know the Löwenfelds either, or the Deutsches, I've been away too long, I left at nineteen, I never speak German any more, I only use it when I have to, but that's not the same thing. At first she had had some difficulty at the convention in Rome, actually more like stage-fright, because of Italian, but then everything had gone very well after all, of course to him that must seem inconceivable, how someone like herself, someone with so many credentials could actually be nervous. She had just wanted to mention it because otherwise they never would have met and she had had absolutely no idea, not even the slightest inkling, after that strain, with her thoughts flying in all directions, under that pergola at the Hilton, and was it true, he only needed English and French in the F.A.O.?* He could read Spanish very well, but if he planned to stay in Rome now, then it really was advisable, and he was vacillating between private lessons and an Italian class organized by the F.A.O.

He'd been in Rourkela for several years, in Africa for two, in Ghana, then in Gabon, naturally he'd spent quite some time in America, that went without saying, he'd even gone

*Trans. note: Food and Agriculture Organization

to school there for a few years, when his parents had emigrated; they strayed over half the globe and in the end each had a rough idea of where the other had been periodically, where she had interpreted and where he had done research. Whatever on? she asked herself but didn't voice the question, and they left India to return to Geneva, where she had studied, to those first disarmament talks, she was very good and she knew it, she was very well paid, she would never have tolerated staying at home, not with her independent spirit, it's an incredibly demanding job, but I enjoy it nevertheless, no, marry? never, she certainly would never marry.

Cities swirled by in the night: Bangkok, London, Rio, Cannes, then unavoidably Geneva and, of course, Paris. Except for San Francisco, she sincerely regretted that, no, never, and that was just what she'd always wanted, after all those dreadful places there, Washington over and over again, how awful, yes, he too had found it awful and that was one place he could never, no, she couldn't either, then they fell silent, drained, and after a while she gave a small sigh, *please, would you mind,* je suis terriblement fatiguée, mais quand-même, c'est drôle, n'est-ce pas, d'être parti ensemble, tu trouves pas? *I was flabbergasted when Mr. Keen asked me, no, of course not, I just call him Mr. Keen because he always seemed to be keen* on something, on her, too, at that party at the Hilton, *but let's talk about something more pleasant, I utterly disliked him.*

Mr. Keen, who in reality had a different name and who stood in Mr. Ludwig Frankel's way in the F.A.O. hierarchy, was a topic of mutual interest at the railroad crossing in Battipaglia but, as such, was quickly exhausted because she'd actually only seen him once and Mr. Frankel had only worked with him and under him for the past three months, an American in shirt sleeves, un casse-pied monolingue, emmerdant, but, he was forced to admit it even to himself, in other respects really a disarmingly helpful and guileless man. She'd had to object once more and interrupted, I couldn't agree *more with you, I was just disgusted the way he behaved,* who did he think he was, he must be fifty at least, with that bald spot shining so obviously through his thin hair, and she ran her fingers through her Mr. Frankel's thick dark hair and laid her hand on his shoulder.

He wasn't divorced, no, but in the process, which he and a certain Mrs. Frankel in Hietzing were drawing out, he still wasn't quite convinced that divorce was the right thing. She had been on the verge of marrying once, but they had broken up at the last minute after all and she'd been wondering why for years but had never really gotten to the bottom of it, never been able to comprehend what had happened. As they stopped at the Lido in Paestum and she waited again in the car while he inquired at the new hotels, her thoughts drifted back: there hadn't been anyone else, the relationship hadn't disintegrated, she didn't believe in that kind of thing and never would have accepted anything of the sort for herself, although she knew people who'd been through horrible scenes, couples who conceived of life as a drama, or maybe they actually set the stage so it would happen that way, just so they could experience something, *how abominable,* what bad taste, never had she allowed anything degoûtant near her; it hadn't worked out simply because she had been unable to listen to him, only occasionally, as they lay side by side and he assured her over and over again that there were so many things about her, and he had little names for her which all began with: "ma petite chérie," and she had big names for him which all ended with: "mon grand chéri," and they clung to one another, passionately, perhaps she was still hung up on him, that was the best way to put it, on the ghost of a man, but back then when they'd finally emerged from bed late one morning or afternoon because it simply wasn't done, you couldn't just cling to each other all the time, then he would start telling her about something which didn't interest her, or he would repeat himself like someone already going senile, but that was impossible, he couldn't have been suffering from severe arteriosclerosis at the age of thirty, he would tell her about the three or four major events in his life and occasionally about other minor experiences, she knew them all by heart within the first few days, and had she, like others who surrendered their private lives to the courts of this world, had to appear before a judge to defend her rights or enforce them, then the court would have had no choice but to find that it was too much to expect from a man that he put up with a woman who didn't pay attention to what he said, but then again too much to expect from her, too, because she had had to listen: usually he had given her advice or lectured to her, about thermometers and barometers, how reinforced concrete and beer were manufactured, what rocket propulsion was and why airplanes flew, or what it was like in Algeria before and after, and all the while she had pretended to listen, with her eyes wide open like a child's, but she had always been thinking about something else—about him, about her feelings for him, about hours gone by or hours to

6

come—and had been unable to summon up anything in the present, least of all pay attention, and only now, years too late, when the question was moot, the why so faded as to be nearly imperceptible, the answer emerged. It finally came to her because she had not been searching in French but in her own language and because she was able to talk to a man who gave language back to her and who was, of this she was certain, *terribly nice,* only she hadn't yet once said Ludwig to him, because it was inconceivable that his family and friends could call him that. She wondered how she could make it through these next three or four days without using his first name, she would simply call him *darling* or caro or mein Lieber, and as he came to open her door, she had already understood and climbed out—he had two rooms on the same floor. He gathered up her bag, scarf and the car blanket and, before the hotel porter arrived, she grabbed him from behind in a clumsy embrace and burst out, I'm simply glad we've met, you are terribly nice to me, and I do not even deserve it.

They sat in the hotel restaurant, which was just closing, the last guests with the last of a lukewarm soup. Do you think this could be frozen cod, underneath the bread crumbs? She poked indifferently at the piece on her plate, don't they serve fish here anymore, with the Mediterranean a stone's throw away? In Rourkela you really had the feeling you could accomplish something, it had been the best part of his life, in India, in spite of everything; he traced the railroad line from Calcutta to Bombay across the white tablecloth with his fork, try to visualize it, just about here, we started with a bulldozer practically and built the first barracks ourselves, but three years of that strain is the most anyone can stand, I flew back and forth between Calcutta and Europe exactly twenty-one times, and then I had had enough. When the wine was finally served, she explained it carefully: they always worked two to a booth, not like pilot and co-pilot, no, it was only set up like that so you could switch after twenty minutes, that was a reasonable interval, you just couldn't translate longer than that, although at times you had to hang on for thirty or even forty minutes, utter insanity. Maybe you could stand it in the morning, but in the afternoon it became more and more difficult to concentrate, you had to listen so carefully, fanatically, totally immersed in another voice. A switchboard was comparatively easy to operate, but her head, just imagine, t'immagini! In the breaks she drank a mixture of warm water and honey out of a thermos, each of them had their own way of making it through the day, but in the evening I can hardly lift a newspaper, it's important that I read all the major papers regularly, I have to keep track of the latest expressions. But the terminology was the least of it, there were reports, lists that she had to memorize beforehand, she didn't like chemistry; agriculture was one of her favorites, refugee problems, that was okay as long as she was working for the United Nations, but the Union des Postes Universelles and the *International Union of Marine Insurance*, they had been her worst nightmares, it was easier for those who only did two languages, but she had to start working first thing in the morning while she did her breathing exercises and her gymnastics, once she had been in a hospital where a doctor had taught her relaxation and stretching exercises, and she had developed her own method, admittedly not quite orthodox, but it worked well for her. I was really going through a bad time back then.

Mr. Frankel, who evidently had never had bad times, didn't think twice about the fact that she often ended with the sentence: I was having a tough time of it. Or: Things were really bad then. *Actually, basically,* what people called perfectly, as though such a thing could exist! There was a Russian woman, an older woman to be exact, she admired her the most, she knew thirteen languages, *she really does them,* you see, I don't know how to put it, she confessed in a confused way, she planned to drop one language someday, Russian or Italian, it's killing me, I come back to the hotel, drink a whiskey, can't hear or see, I just sit there, wrung dry, with my files and my newspapers. She laughed, there was an incident in Rio, not with the Russian woman, with a young man from the Soviet delegation who had been supervising, her cointerpreter had translated that the American delegate was a *silly man,* and then they had been deadly serious in insisting that durak meant stupid, nothing more and nothing less, and they had all had something to laugh about yes, even laugh.

German—it's being used less and less, isn't it, he said, at least that's our impression, do you think the others have begun to notice it, too? As they were leaving, he asked again: what do you think, will there be a universal language someday? She wasn't listening or really hadn't heard, and on the steps she leaned against him and pretended that she could hardly walk another step, and he pulled her along. Tu dois me mettre dans les draps tout de suite. Mais oui. Tu seras gentil avec moi? Mais non. Tu vas me raconter un tout petit rien? Mais bien sûr, ça oui.

9

He looked again into her room, called softly: Nadja, Nadja? and closed the door gently, returning to his room which she had just left. The bed was still warm and bore her scent, she had told him when they first left Rome, she just couldn't anymore, not since a certain shock she'd had, it had ben quite some time now, she would explain it later, couldn't sleep in the same room with someone else, much less in the same bed, and he had been relieved upon hearing this story, he hadn't had the least desire either, was much too nervous and accustomed to being alone. In spite of its stone floors, the hotel began to creak: the balcony door whined on its hinges, a mosquito buzzed through the room, he smoked and reflected: it had been three years since something out of the ordinary had happened to him, with a perfect stranger, rushing off without a word to anyone. The weather was ominous and a terrible emptiness filled him, the mosquito bit him, he slapped his neck and missed again, I hope she doesn't want to see the temples tommorrow, she's seen them twice already anyway, best to move on early tomorrow morning, find a small fishing village, a quaint little hotel, get away from these tourist hordes, get away from everything, and if he didn't have enough cash then he always had his checkbook, but maybe they didn't even know what a check was in these holes, at any rate he had his diplomatic license plate, that never failed to impress, and the main thing after all was that they had a good time, nothing was complicated with her, and in a week's time she would disappear to Holland, he was disconcerted only by the thought of how he had fallen for her last week in Rome, on that Saturday, as if an old simplicity could be reinstated in his life, a forgotten, painful joy which had

so transformed him for a few days that even the people at the
F.A.O. had noticed something between *well well, okay okay,
you got that?* He put out his cigarette; the sleepiness which
had just barely come over him was dispersed by strains of
music drifting down the hallway, "*Strangers in the Night*," doors
were unlocked nearby, and in the confusion of his thoughts
the title merged to "*Tender Is the Night*," he had to make the
best of these days, in the sink the water gurgled abruptly
through the pipes, he started up again, now they were talking
next door in loud voices, this hotel was impossible, this trembling restlessness in the night, lo scirocco, sto proprio male,
it had begun in Calcutta or somewhere, and now in Rome
the anxiety attacked him with increasing frequency, *the
board, the staff*, the new project, tired, *I'm tired, I'm fed up*, he
took it after all, a Valium 5, felt for it in the dark, *I can't fall
asleep without it, it's ridiculous, it's a shame, but it was too much
today*, this hectic running around, the bank already closed,
but he had wanted to get out of the city with her, *she is such
a sweet and gentle* fanciulla, not all that young, but *girlish looking, I like it, with these huge eyes, and I won't have me hoping
that it's possible to be happy, but I couldn't help that, I was immediately happy with her.*

They walked quickly to the second temple and, after ex-
changing glances, turned back before the third. He held the
travel guide open in his hand and mechanically read a para-
graph aloud, but since she obviously didn't want to listen, he
decided not to elaborate. They strolled over to the garden at
the Nettuno which was full of deserted deck chairs, found a
spot with a good view of the temple, ordered coffee and
talked. This is such a bizarre year, he agreed with her, it was

surely the sirocco, it's so strange and depressing, it's always either too warm or too cold or too humid, no matter where I am, it's strange, it had been like that year in, year out. Tu es sûr qu'il s'agit des phénomènes météorologiques? some cosmic phenomena? moi non, je crains plutôt que ce soit quelque chose dans nous-mêmes qui ne marche plus. Greece isn't the same as it was then or even yesterday, there was nothing left ten, fifteen years ago, and when he tried imagine what had happened in two thousand years, all the while barely able to conceive of this short timespan and his own history and to keep it in perspective, then it seemed overwhelming and even crazy that they could simply sit here and drink coffee while gazing at Greek temples—come fosse niente, she interrupted, and he didn't understand how much of his train of thought she could have grasped. He hadn't put it into words and wasn't quite able to grasp it himself. Naturally it was none of his business with whom she had visited these temples before, but why did she have such a sudden aversion to seeing them? He couldn't be the reason, it must have been *something* else, but she talked about *everything* with the same superficiality, when she talked, and all he knew about her was something about a shock, and that she'd often had a tough time of it, but who cares.

Even when he had picked her up at the hotel in Rome, the departure had still seemed to her like part of a normal adventure, but the more distance she put between herself and her usual surroundings—which were more important to her than any home could be for others and leaving which was thus all the more delicate—the more unsure she became. She was no longer a self-assured presence in a hotel lobby, in a bar, step-

ping out of the pages of *Vogue* or *Glamour*, the right dress for
the right occasion. There was no longer any evidence of her
real identity, she could have been anyone in her faded jeans
and tight blouse, with a suitcase and beach bag. He could
just as easily have picked her up off the street. Because she
didn't want him to notice how afraid she was of being dependent on him she tried to convince him that her knowledge
of the geographical surroundings and her sense of direction
were indispensable. She paged through the maps, they were
all old and outdated, and at a gas station on the way she
bought a map of the coast which also turned out to be
wrong, but he wouldn't believe it and kept his left hand on
the steering wheel and his left eye on the road so that he too
could read the map, and she was forced to hide her aggrava-
tion, because he had no way of knowing that she could
decipher timetables, road maps and flight schedules better
than any porter, travel agent or clerk in an information
bureau. After all, her life consisted of connections and link-
ings and everything attached to them, and as he perceived
her irritation and annoyance, he pulled on her ear playfully,
non guardare così brutto. Hey, I need my ears, veux-tu me
laisser tranquille! She swallowed a "chéri," because that had
once belonged to Jean Pierre, and rubbed her ears at the spot
where she usually wore her headphones, where the switches
were thrown automatically and the language circuits were
broken. What a strange mechanism she was, she lived
without a single thought of her own, immersed in the sentences of others, like a sleepwalker, furnishing the same but
different-sounding sentences an instant later; she could make
machen, faire, fare, hacer and delat' out of "to make," she
could spin each word to six different positions on a wheel,

she just had to keep from thinking that "to make" really meant to make, faire faire, fare fare, delat' delat', that might put her head out of commission, and she did have to be careful not to get snowed under by an avalanche of words.

Later: the lobbies in the convention centers, the hotel lobbies, the bars, the men, the routine of getting along with them, the many long, lonely nights and the many much too short and still lonely nights, invariably the same men with their boasting and their jokes thrown in between boasts. They were either married and bloated and drunk or, as chance would have it, thin and married and drunk or quite nice and incurably neurotic or very nice and homosexual as one was in Geneva. Again she talked about her early days in Geneva, that unavoidable city, and to a certain extent she could understand, she said, what he had been thinking of that morning in the garden, if you considered a short span of time, or a long one, but admittedly her own lifespan didn't suffice for the latter, if alone what had happened and failed to happen in Geneva was indicative of her short existence, then it was impossible to grasp, and where do other people find the strength to grasp it, I only know that mine is fading, either I'm too close to it all, in my work, or when I leave and lock myself in a room, I'm too far away, I can't grasp it. He laid his hand between her legs and she looked straight ahead as though she hadn't noticed, but when he stopped and forgot her, concentrating on the road, she began teasing him and he hit her hand, *come on, you just behave, you don't want me to drive us into this abyss, I hope.* What was going on in the world these next few days basically had nothing to do with them, how everything changed and how hopeless it all

14

was; he only had to keep track of the road and make sure that they found the turnoff to Palinuro and that was all, and he had to keep track of this strange woman with whom he was driving out of the world, but he was irritated that his mind refused to suppress the things he wanted to leave behind, yes, he wanted to get away for a while, with an outburst of fury, because these days belonged to him and not to Food and Agriculture and because he could no longer conceive of any other plans for his life anyway since he had seen through the way the others more or less succeeded in acting as though they knew what they wanted, everyone he knew, with their stories, it didn't matter if they were half-truths or half-lies, pitiful, funny or crazy, just frustrated failures, all of them, who shoved their way up the ladder from rung to rung, from P 3 to P 4, only to eye P 5 ambitiously, or who got stuck or fell down; as though the act of climbing and falling could compensate for a position that was gone, for an energy that was gone, gone the joy, forever.

Now he left his hand resting on her knee, and it felt so familiar to her, driving this way, as in the many cars with a man, as with all men in a car, but still she had to pull herself together, had to, had to be here and now and not in some other past, not somewhere else on a road, not in this country another time: she was here now with Mr. Ludwig Frankel, study of International Economics in Vienna and then half the globe, diplomatic status and a diplomat's license plate which meant nothing at all on this steep coastline, at this, the furthest edge. Come on, just behave yourself! but what if she didn't want to and grabbed the wheel, if she just jerked on it a little, then she might turn over with him, establish their belonging once and for all and crash to the sea with him without regret. She drank a few sips from the thermos and took a pill, oh nothing, just this bothersome headache, she often got them, the entire coast was impossible, these places were unbearable, wherever they turned off to look there were camping grounds, fairgrounds, or small, inaccessible beaches, far below. I can see it coming, we'll have to spend the night in the car, she moaned. In Sapri it was the same story; then suddenly she let out a cry, but it was too late; on a treeless, dark, flat beach she had seen a cement block with the neon letters HOTEL, we've got to come back here if we don't find anything else. At ten p.m. he too was ready to give up. That must be Maratea, she said, it's ten after ten; if it was the last thing she knew, she would always be sure of the time and where she was. I'm telling you, drive down there, ti supplico, dico a sinistra, he turned and she gave him directions, something was suspended by a thread inside her, if only she could stay in control and not let her voice begin to break, and she said something very calmly, just to say something, before he stopped: sud'ba, Maratea, sud'ba.

She didn't wait in the car but staggered out, hungry for air, and as she climbed the stairs to the entrance she felt it, without seeing much, blinded by the lights, like someone sensing a familiar atmosphere: this was not a small or mid-sized hotel in a fishing village, but a completely different hotel, a comforting reentry into her world. She walked behind him with her eyes half-closed, instantly assuming the posture of someone who is not only exhausted but shows it brazenly, someone who can be neither surprised nor impressed—not even in faded dungarees and dusty sandals—

by a hotel lobby reeking its deluxe status from every pore, from the first-class, hushed transactions and voices to the categorical absence of anything conspicuous. She allowed a porter to take her beach bag, threw herself in an armchair in the lobby and watched him approaching from the reception desk. He looked at her doubtfully, she nodded, she had been afraid of that: there was only one room left. She yawned and then stared sullenly at the form the manager was handing her, scribbled an illegible signature on it, this was really too much, as if it couldn't wait until tomorrow. Upstairs in the room she pounced immediately on the bed next to the window; if she couldn't have her own room, then at least she should be able to sleep next to the window to preserve her peace of mind. The room-service waiter arrived, he shook his head, they didn't have Mumm, he'd never heard of Pommery, Krug or Veuve Cliquot; well, Moët Chandon, but then Dom Perignon brut, please, if that was all they had. In the bathroom he watched her shower, dried her off and massaged her awake. When the waiter returned she was sitting at the table, wrapped in a long white bath towel. How could he possibly know that today was her birthday, of course he had seen her passport, but the fact that he had thought of it, come sono commossa, sono così tanto commossa. They touched glasses, but there was no sound. She drank one more glass and he drank the rest of the bottle; it wasn't his year that was ending in Maratea. She lay there, more awake with each passing minute, squeezed into close quarters with a stranger as if in a sleeping car or on a plane, then sat up in bed and listened—either he was still awake, too, or he was an incredibly quiet sleeper. In the bathroom she spread out the two thick bath towels in the tub and tucked herself in, she

17

smoked and smoked, and only late into the night did she go back into the room. Her bed was two feet from his, she plunged her feet into the chasm between the two beds, hesitated, then carefully crawled up against him and, when he drew her to him in his sleep, said: just a little, you have to hold me just a little, otherwise I can't fall asleep.

The sun wasn't shining, small red flags fluttered on the beach and they sat debating what to do. He turned his attention to the sea; she watched a group of Milanese courageous enough to go in the water. He took his mask and fins and explained to her when he returned how she should go about getting in and swimming back. On one side the tide washed over the rocks; a white iron ladder reached down to where the water tore at its rungs with uncontrollable fury and waves danced madly on the rocks surrounding it. He taught her a complete alphabet of sign language and promised to meet her at the ladder. One signal meant: wait; another: a little closer; another: a little farther out; and then: quick, now, come on! and then she swam blindly with all her might toward the ladder where he stood, and she lost sight of him in the foam and he pulled her up or she lifted herself without his help. Most of the time it went well, once she swallowed mouthfuls of water, coughed, spat out, and had to lie down.

He swam more often and longer than she did, and while waiting she got annoyed and began to talk to him in her thoughts as though she'd known him for years. She would start in abruptly: I was terribly upset, you just disappeared, I've been looking everywhere for you, straining my eyes out of my head, I started to think you'd drowned, of course that upsets me, it's so inconsiderate, can't you understand that? She gave another glance out to sea and then at her watch, and when he still hadn't surfaced after fifty minutes, she began to wonder what one did with a drowned man at a hotel. First she would go to the management and establish the fact that she was not his wife, but they always guessed that immediately anyway, and then someone would have to be called, the F.A.O. of course, Mr. Keen, he was the only one she knew who knew him. Pronto, pronto, certainly a terrible connection, Maratea-Rome, *Nadja's speaking, you remember, to make it short, I went with Mr. Frankel to Maratea, yes, no,* pronto, *can you hear me now, a very small place in Calabria, I said Calabria,* it would be quite simple, Mr. Keen extremely upset and suddenly a *gentleman* who would refrain from disclosing with whom Mr. Frankel had driven to Calabria, and she wouldn't cry, oh no, she'd take those *tranquilizers* she'd seen with his things, a triple dose, the people in Rome could handle the problems, it was just too much for her, she'd pay any amount to have someone bring her directly to Rome by car, to the hotel, and then she'd still have three days until the IBM conference in Rotterdam, time to recover, to study, to bury and mourn, and to swim back and forth in the pool to get in shape again.

She threw a towel over his shoulders, rubbed him dry and launched in on her sermon, you're worse than a child, you're shivering, you're chilled to the bone, but then a huge wave crashed in, and she took the knife, the harpoon and the light he'd thrown to her and placed them on a higher rock before resuming her shouting. She couldn't hear herself speak anymore and signalled to him that she wanted to go in, she took his hand and clung to it, using the ladder was out of the question now. Come up as close as you can to the rim, put your feet on the very edge, and she clutched at the slippery stones with her toes. It's better if you stoop down and then dive right into the wave, there, where it peaks. Now. She dove a little too late and landed between two waves, she shouted: how was it? Not bad! Too flat, mais c'était joli à voir, tu es . . . What? What? Tu es . . .

She dove a few more times before lunch, always hesitating a fraction too long, her timing was off, her stomach hurt, then her head, but really, I feel it, really, he thought it impossible but held her head gently in his hands and comforted her until she realized she was hungry; she forgot her aching head and they walked back to the changing hut.

The stretch of afternoon until dinner, which she spent working, was strenuous and boring for him, he would so have liked to continue diving, but in the afternoon no one dared go in. He told her about a fish he had seen that morning, a wonderful specimen, last year, in Sardinia he had done a lot of shooting, but even there he had never seen such a beautiful cernia. We watched each other for a while, but I couldn't get the better of it, I was always in the wrong position, you have to hit them in the neck, it didn't make any sense just to shoot and maybe hit the tail, it was against the rules anyway, it was bad sportsmanship, at least he never did it. She said, oh, you're still thinking about it, I don't want you to kill it. But he insisted he would look for it the next day, and he told her how to catch this and that type of fish and where you could find them. She'd seen dolphins before and read how intelligent they were, and he had known a woman, it was his wife but he didn't say that, who had once been followed by a dolphin, it had just kept her company or been in love with her but she swam as though pursued by a shark, collapsing on the beach, she's never gone in the water since and can't swim anymore, either. Oh, she said as she slowly maneuvered herself under him and touched the corner of his mouth with her tongue, yes, ljublju tebja, oh that's a funny—she stopped herself—it's a sad story. Ljublju tebja. A single ship, or even a mine—it's horrible, not only for the fish who get hit, but for the ones far away, too—these violent tremors, these disturbances are horrible, not even fish can live in peace these days, and it's not their fault. Is it my fault? she asked, I didn't invent these atrocities, I invented something else, what? yes, I invented that, yes, you invented that, and she fought bitterly and wildly for her invention, speechlessly in the direction of the one single language, toward the only one which was explicit and exact.

He didn't want to return to Vienna, too much had been broken off, and what could he do, in his field, in Vienna? Nostalgia? No, something else, sometimes an inexplicable sadness. Usually he took a vacation only in winter because he preferred to go skiing with the children, his wife sent them to him for a month, this time it had turned out to be just two weeks, in Cortina, before they had always gone to St. Christophe; he always devoted his vacations to the children, who had already noticed that something was wrong, one day he would have to explain, it couldn't be hidden from them much longer. Just imagine, she said, once someone asked me point-blank why I didn't have any children and what the reason was, how does that strike you? you just don't ask things like that. Instead of answering, he took her hand. She thought, there's nothing easier than being with some-one from the same country, you always knew what and what not to say and how to say it, as though a secret pact existed between you, when she thought of the things she'd put up with from others, you couldn't constantly explain, look, this is my limit, don't overstep the line. Her indignation against Jean Pierre returned in full force; he had found something wrong with everything and anything she'd said or done, had wanted, without even attempting to understand her, to force her into the confines of an alien life, in a very small apart-ment with a large number of very small children. He would have preferred that she spend her days there in a small kitch-en and the nights in an admittedly very large bed where she would have been only a tiny creature, un tout petit chat, un petit poulet, une petite femmelle, but back then she defend-ed herself, had sobbed, cried, thrown dishes on the floor, pounded him with her fists and he had laughed calmly and watched her performance until she was beside herself, or he would simply hit her, never in anger but just because it was only natural for him to hit her occasionally, pour te calmer un peu, until she clung to him again and stayed.

Mr. Frankel asked, do you think that one day people will all speak the same language? What makes you think that, what a crazy idea! Her sandal straps kept slipping down and she pulled them back up over her heels. It's true, so many are disappearing, but you still have forty languages in India, even a country the size of Gabon has forty languages, there must be hundreds or thousands of them, surely someone has counted them all, you people are always counting something, she added spitefully, no, really, she just couldn't conceive of it but couldn't say exactly why. He on the other hand could easily envisage it, and she discovered that he was a hopeless romantic, and that pleased her more than her first impression of him as a practical-minded, successful man. It would be a great relief to me if languages disappeared, she said, but then I wouldn't be worth anything anymore. A romantic, oh what a child, and even if only in terms of Food and Agriculture, helicopters that had to be purchased for pest-control purposes, or fishing trawlers from Iceland for Ceylon; and when he finally stooped down to tighten her sandal, she asked, but then how would you say, "Wuerstel mit Kren," or: "Sie geschlenkertes Krokodil"?* Do you give up, t'arrendi? He nodded and looked up at her, amused; he had forgotten the Kren and the Krokodil. And again his thoughts returned to the cernia: and he had no idea of its German name.

The F.A.O. wasn't a new institution; it originated in a much older idea than the U.N., some kid from the American West had thought of it, a certain David Lubin whose name revealed his East European origins, probably where their own roots lay— if they took the trouble to trace them. He had ridden through his new country on horseback and discovered that, just a few miles away, the people were totally ignorant of the experiences their neighbors had accumulated in cultivating the land; each region had its own superstitions and ideas about grain, melons and cattle, so this Lubin began to compile these various ideas in order to exchange them throughout the world, and because no one understood him

*Trans. note: Roughly, "a hot dog with the works" and "you slimy reptile, you."

he took his idea all the way to the king of Italy; some things just started like that, like fairy tales, and that was the reason why today he had a position in the former Department for African Affairs in Rome, now there were these Mexicans, for example, with their wheat, which was better than any other, but she had stopped listening and exclaimed, what a nice story! And he said sternly, but it's not a story I'm telling you, it's true. Well, she said, usually when someone comes along and thinks up something adventurous and begins something new, you people come and administrate it to death, oh I'm sorry, please try and understand what I mean, I just can't see things any other way, when I hear all that gibberish between Paris and Geneva and Rome, when you listened in like she did and helped them to misunderstand and corner each other even more, you goddamn men are all the same, you always have to reduce everything to the ordinary, and that guy, what did you say his name was, that David, I like him, and I don't like the others. I bet he galloped around on horseback for real, not like you V.I.P's in a riding ring, taking lessons to stay in shape, no, he's different, I'm sure of that, you can take your whole damn pack of modern men and just go to hell.

He broke out in a laugh and let it go at that, he thought she was only too right for him to admit it so quickly, he thought she was pretty, even very pretty, when she lost her temper, much prettier than back at the Hilton with her false eyelashes and decorative shawl, holding out her hand at a slight angle to accept kisses. When she was angry, her eyes grew dangerous, moist and even larger, maybe she was only really alive when she went too far, went beyond herself and

her own limits. When we get back I'll show you what I do
there in the office, I don't only administrate things to death
and I don't cart files around all day long either, they're moved
in special elevators because they'd be much too heavy for me,
even for Mr. Universe or Atlas in person. For what atlas? she
asked suspiciously, and he thought it was so hilarious that he
ordered more wine. To Atlas, that he may bear the whole
burden! Ci sono cascata, vero? She pushed her glass away, I
don't want any more, I don't know why we have to talk about
this stuff, I don't want to do anything that I have to do every
day, before I go to sleep I usually read detective novels, but
only to escape from the reality of the daytime which is unreal
enough as it is, to me each conference seems to be just
another sequel in an infinite indagine—how do you say
that?—they're always searching for the reason for something
that happened long ago, for something terrible, and they
can't get through because it so happens that the same path
has been trampled by so many, because others have intentionally covered their tracks, because everyone tells only half-
truths to protect themselves and then you sift through mountains of inconsistencies and misconceptions, and you find
nothing, you'd have to have a revelation to grasp what was
going on and, at the drop of a hat, what you should do
about it.

Yes, he said distractedly, a revelation. Would you like some
fruit? That was another thing he liked about her, how she
reacted, said what she wanted, rejected or accepted things,
she was so presumptuous, so modest, so aggressive, or so simple: constantly changing, someone you could go anywhere
with; in a small café she would act as though all her life she

had drunk terrible coffee and subsisted on stale sandwiches; in a hotel like this she let the waiter know that she wasn't someone to trifle with, at the bar she gave the impression of being one of those women who, as a matter of principle, never lifted a finger, were impossible to please, who bore both boredom and entertainment with grace, who were prone to annoying whims, who got nervous because of a missing lemon rind, too much or too little ice or a badly mixed daiquiri. When he stopped to think, one of the reasons he felt smoldering aversion for his wife in Vienna was the way she walked down the street, clumsily, with handbags that were much too big, her head stooped over instead of proudly thrown back. A fur coat was wasted on her because she wore it with an air of patient endurance, and she never looked around disapprovingly with a cigarette in her hand like Nadja did, her frown saying: at least they could have ashtrays here, and for heaven's sake I don't want Vat, I said Dimple, and if they didn't understand instantly, an incredulous expression spread over her face, as if Dimple or not Dimple was decisive for the outcome of some extraordinary debate. During the drive she had harassed him no end, letting herself be dragged out of the car to Motta or Pavesi after a hundred kilometers as though she and not he had had to maneuver through the August weekend traffic, and of course she was the only one with cold feet, but it didn't occur to her to reach back for the blanket, she only mumbled faintly, would you *please,* grazie caro, God, I'm frozen stiff, and now when the sun finally came out and he was speculating idly about revelations, she laid her head on his feet, because naturally his feet where there to cushion her head and make her lie more comfortably, he bent over her, and their faces were distorted, their reversed features alarming and alarmed, but he said what she wanted to hear, and he had to kiss her because she wanted to be kissed, she turned and laughed, but no one's looking, because she'd seen him glance up uncertainly, she sank her teeth lustfully into his feet and his legs, and to stop her he bound her hands and pressed her to the ground until she couldn't move. Belva, bestiolina, are those the right words for you? he asked, and yes, she said happily, yes and, *well, that's a mild way to put it.*

They still hadn't been to see the village, and on the last evening he said he'd like to find out what Maratea was like because this hotel couldn't have much in common with the rest of Calabria, and she jumped up immediately, delighted, and got ready to go, d'accord, he had promised her that they would go for a walk together, and they hadn't taken a single step, tu m'as promis une promenade, she complained, I want my walk, so they left quickly with the car. The sun had come out from behind the clouds, but it was already sinking, and this sun, already beginning to display its late, rich hues above the sea, told them too that it would only then reappear in all its shining splendor when he and she were no longer there. I bet you can see the whole gulf from up there, we haven't seen a thing this whole time, tu te rends compte? She didn't want to see the gulf, she just wanted to take a short walk, ma promenade, I said, and as they drove higher and the curves followed each other in increasingly shorter intervals, she said but where is the village, I thought it was behind the hill, not up there, where are you going, no, please not up to the cliffs. She fell silent and planted her feet firmly against the floor of the car, heard him explaining about the Saracens, an advantageous position for defense, then more about the Saracens, look, I said, look! She said nothing, blinked, the sky blushed red, they were nearing the clouds, they would curve off into the clouds, she saw the first guardrail, then a second guardrail streaked past, she couldn't find her voice, yet another guardrail. He had not imagined finding it here, such a magnificent road, then bridges, one after the other, leading higher and higher, hovering free, and she looked down into her lap, at the pack of cigarettes and the lighter. The numbness started in her hands, she couldn't light a cigarette and couldn't ask him to do it, because she was at his mercy, hardly breathing now, and a feeling of emptiness began to fill her, it could have been the onset of speechlessness, or it was something establishing its presence within her, a fatal disease. Then the car stopped in front of a blue and white sign marked P, as if theirs was not only the first but also the last car to stop here on this desolate field of stone. C'est fou, c'est complètement fou. She got out of the car, didn't know where to look, put on his sweater, it was that cold, and huddled into the wool. They passed wretched, empty houses, and in front of a cloister stood a priest and three old women, all in black, who greeted them politely. She did not return the greeting.

S menja étogo dovol'no. He led her along a stony path overgrown with bunches of coarse grass that climbed upward to the highest cliff, toward the abyss. She skidded on her sandals and tried to keep in step, looked up and then saw it from behind, a gigantic, colossal figure of stone wrapped in a long stone cape, its arms outspread. Her tongue was tied, she recognized the monstrous figure she had seen on a postcard at the hotel, the Christ of Maratea, but now it loomed against the background of the sky, and she stood still. She shook her head, then shook off his arm, meaning: you go on. She heard him say something, stood there with her head bowed and then walked backward, she slipped again and sat down on a stone by the side of the path, and that meant: I'm not going another step farther. He still hadn't understood, she sat there and tore leaves off a bush, menthe, menta, mentuccia, and she managed to say, in her quietest and firmest voice: you go on, I just can't. Mareada. Dizzy. She pointed to her head and then sniffed at the crushed leaf as though she had found some cure, some drug. Aide-moi, aide-moi, ou je meurs ou je me jette en bas. Je meurs, je n'en peux plus. When he had gone, she could still feel it, against her ribcage, the presence of that insane colossus that someone had put on top of the cliff, these madmen, letting them do that, letting them do it, and in a wretched village that could plunge into the sea any minute, all that was needed was to tread heavily or make a single careless movement, and that was why she was sitting as still as possible, so that this cliff wouldn't crash down with both of them and the poverty of this village and the descendants of the Saracens and all heavy laden stories of all those weary times. If I don't move, then we won't fall. She wanted to cry and couldn't, how long has it been since I could cry, I can't have unlearned crying from traveling around in all those languages and places, but since crying won't save me, I'll have to get up, go down the path to the car, get in, and drive away with him. I don't know what will happen then, it will be my undoing.

She slid slowly off the stone and lay down on the ground with her arms outspread, crucified on this menacing cliff, and she couldn't get it out of her head, this grotesque presumption, given in commission, a resolution the town board passed at one time or another, and now it will destroy me. She didn't hear him return, it was nearly dark, she got up, held herself erect and walked at his side without looking back, they passed the cloister where the black figures had filed past, to the parking lot. It had been like nothing he'd ever seen before, he was so moved, he'd seen the entire gulf as the sun dissolved into a purple haze and then was soaked up by the sea. As he started driving, something occurred to him and he remarked casually, wasn't that an odd idea to erect such an awful statue up here, did you see it? When they were on the road she closed her eyes immediately and planted her feet firmly again, but still she felt the bridges, the precipices, the curves, a void she couldn't overcome. Further down she began to breathe more regularly. It seemed higher to me than in the mountains, it's higher here, and it's horrible. But my little fool, it's at most 600, 700 meters, and she rejoined no, no, it was even worse than landing in a Boeing. Will we land soon?

In the bar she asked for something, anything, like an invalid in dire need of an injection, usually she weighed her choice, but not now: just something that takes effect quickly, and she was given a glass, drank it in one gulp and tasted nothing, but the alcohol made her warm and her agitation melted away, the barrier separating her from him and the world. Trembling, she lit her first cigarette of the evening. In the room, when he embraced her, she began shaking again, didn't want to, couldn't, she was afraid of suffocating or dying in his arms, but then again she did want to, it was better to

30

be suffocated and undone by him and thus to undo everything which had become incurable in her, she no longer
resisted, let it come over her, and she lay there without feeling, then turned away from him silently and fell asleep.

In the morning when she awoke he had already packed,
and while listening to his razor in the bathroom she began
to collect her things. They didn't look at one another, and
after he had gone she walked down the path to the sea. She
couldn't find him, then he appeared at the ladder and held
out a large starfish to her. She had never seen a live starfish,
much less been given one, and she smiled, pleased and sad,
admiring the starfish and wanting to take it back as a sou-
venir, but then she suddenly threw it back in the water so
it could live. The sea was wilder than before, but no one
needed her anyway and knowing he was underwater didn't
frighten her anymore. She pointed to the cliffs, gesturing,
and then walked along the black, green and brightly mottled
boulders where the water roared furiously, and she climbed up
and down the cracked and jagged slabs, fearful in the midst
of the roaring sea.

They both looked at their watches at the same time. They
had two more hours, and tired from the meal, silently, lay
next to each other in deck chairs on the lowest terrace.
Originally they had thought that they would spend these
days immersed in talk and shared confidences, but things had
turned out differently and she wondered whether he was
thinking of someone else and if his train of thought led to
a multitude of faces, bodies, the broken and battered, the
murdered, the said and the unsaid, and suddenly she looked

at him with real longing, in the same split second thinking of Paris and imagining that not he but the other one should see her like this, and then Mr. Frankel looked at her and she at him with this urgency. Please tell me what you're thinking now, what are you thinking about right now, tell me, tell me, you've got to! Oh, nothing special, he hesitated, then said he'd been thinking about the cernia that he hadn't seen again, he couldn't get it out of his mind. So that's what he'd been thinking about, he wasn't lying, it was true, that alone occupied his thoughts, he had wanted to shoot it in the back of the neck. Her head suddenly started pounding and she put her hand on her own neck and said: here, I can feel it right here.

During the last hour she got up three times, once she went to the lifeguard, then to the bathroom, then to the changing hut where she sat and stared at the floor, and she thought, he must have noticed something by now, so she went back, knelt down before him and laid her head on his knees. Would you mind leaving me alone until we go? There's nothing wrong, she said, it's just a little difficult, forgive me. Can you carry our things back? Okay?

She went back to the rocks once more, not climbing carefully this time but jumping where she could from one to the other, once more close to tears that would never come, and she became more and more reckless, daring, and yes, now she crossed over to a black outcropping set far back, she just took the chance, risked falling, caught herself in a daze, and told herself it's an obligation, I have to, I have to live, and glancing at her watch out of habit she turned back so as not to

be late, correcting herself, what did I say there, what is that
supposed to mean, it's not an obligation, I don't have to, I
don't have to at all, I can. I can and I finally have to understand it, each and every moment, here too, and she sprang,
flew, ran on with what she knew, I can, a sureness her body
had never known propelling her every leap. I can, that's the
point, I can live. Only her jeans and blouse were left in the
changing hut, and she dressed quickly and sprinted all the
way back to the hotel, without losing her breath and practically weightless. Now I'll take a look back, it is the sea, not
the whole sea, of course, not the whole coast, not the whole
gulf—she stopped and stooped down, something was lying on
the path, his sweater, he must have dropped it. She picked
it up, pressed it to her face joyfully and kissed it. She looked
back at the water, her face burning, that's the sea, it's wonderful, and now I have the courage to look behind me, to
raise my eyes to the fantastic, high hills and to the cliff of
Maratea, the one jutting out over the sea, the steepest of all,
and her eyes focused on it once more, a small figure, barely
visible, with extended arms, not nailed to the cross but
preparing for a grandiose flight, poised for flight or a plunge
to the depths.

In the hotel lobby she paused, out of breath, not wanting
to see him yet and ran hastily up to the room. The suitcases
were gone, the beds still unmade, she stood in front of the
mirror and tried to comb her long tangled hair, to give some
life to the dry, salty strands. Ripping open all the closets and
drawers, she threw out empty cigarette packs, scraps of paper
and kleenex, checked under the beds and, as she was leaving,
discovered a book in the drawer next to his bed. It was a good

33

thing she had come back a last time. She tucked it in her bag and then took it out immediately, this book couldn't belong to him. Il Vangelo. It was only the Bible, part of the standard equipment in these hotels. She sat down on the unmade bed and, just as she often flipped open her dictionaries to search superstitiously for a word to help her through the day, consulting them like oracles, she now opened this book. For her it was only another dictionary, she shut her eyes, tapped the upper left-hand corner with her finger and opened her eyes to a single sentence which read: Il miracolo, come sempre, è il risultato della fede e d'una fede audace. She returned the book to its place and tried to digest the sentence, to let it pass over her lips and be transformed.

A miracle

A miracle is as ever

No, a miracle is the result of faith and

No, of faith and of a bold, no, more than bold, more than that—

She began to cry.

I'm not all that good, I don't know everything, I still don't know everything. She couldn't have translated the sentence into any other language, although she was convinced that she knew what each of the words meant and their usage, but she didn't know what this sentence was really made of. She just couldn't do everything.

She stopped at the bar, where he was already waiting for her, but he hadn't seen her come in and didn't notice her

34

presence; he, the other guests and the boy behind the counter were watching the television set in the corner. Bicycles, a group of them at first, rode across the screen; the picture switched to a single cyclist curved over his handlebars, then to a roadside crowd. The broadcaster's words rushed out in a whirlwind of excitement, he blundered, corrected himself, then tripped over a word again, there were three kilometers to go, he talked faster and faster as though he were pedaling, as though he could no longer stand it, as though his heart could stop beating, now his tongue was sweating, she asked herself, how long can this go on, two kilometers, she turned to the boy at the bar who was staring at the screen in a trance and asked agreeably: chi vince? The boy didn't answer, one more kilometer to go, the broadcaster panted and gurgled, incapable of ending this last sentence and broke the tape with an inarticulate cry. In that instant the TV exploded in a roar from the roadside crowds who had begun screaming until their chaotic outbursts crystallized into distinct staccato cries of

A
    dor
        ni
A
    dor
        ni

She listened with horror and relief and, in these staccato cries, heard all the staccato cries from all the cities and countries she had ever been to. Hate in staccato, joy in staccato.

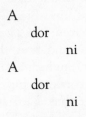

He turned and looked at her, embarrassed because she must have been in the bar for some time. Smiling, she pointed to the sweater draped over her arm. The boy behind the counter came back to life, gazed at her stupidly and stammered, commandi, Signora, cosa desidera?

Niente. Grazie. Niente.

But in leaving, when she had already taken his hand, she turned around, the most important thing having just occurred to her, and she called it out to the boy who had seen Adorni triumph.

Auguri!

Problems Problems

"All right, at seven. Yes, dear. I'd rather. Hochhaus Café. Yes, it just so happens I have to go to the beauty parlor every once in a while. About seven, I imagine, if my appointment . . . What, really? It's raining? Yes, I think so too, it just never seems to stop raining these days. Yes, me too. I'm looking forward to it."

Beatrix breathed a few more words into the mouthpiece and replaced the receiver, rolled over onto her stomach with relief and buried her face in the pillow again. While she had been straining to sound lively, her glance had fallen on the old travel alarm that no one ever traveled with, it was only 9:30 after all. The best thing about Aunt Mihailovics' place was that there were two phones and she had one of

37

them at her bedside and could talk anytime. She liked to pick her nose while pretending to wait intently for a reply; or, better still, late at night she preferred doing bicycles with her legs in the air or even more strenuous exercises; then she would go back to sleep the minute she' hung up the receiver. She just happened to have a knack for answering the phone as early as nine in the morning with a clear, bright voice, and good old Erich believed that she, like he, had been up for a long time, maybe even been out already, prepared for anything the day might bring. It had probably never occurred to him that she always fell asleep again instantly, hoping that she might even be able to reenter a pleasant dream, but only if it was pleasant, although that was seldom the case; she didn't really dream much and then nothing special: the most important thing to her was really just going back to sleep. If anyone had ever asked her: What is your favorite thing, how do you most like to spend your time, what is your dream, your desire, your goal in life? and if she had answered, which was even more improbable, she would have had to say with drowsy enthusiasm: Nothing but sleep! But Beatrix was on her guard not to tell anyone about this because she had realized some time ago what the others were driving at, Frau Mihailovics and Erich, for instance, or even her cousin Elisabeth: namely that she must finally decide to do something, get a job once and for all, and you had to make a few concessions to these people and drop occasional hints about future plans and interests.

But this morning she didn't go back to sleep immediately; she lay there, relaxed and happily buried under the covers, thinking: How awful. She had a numb feeling that something was unbearable but didn't know what it was, it must have to do with the fact that she'd made a date for tonight after all instead of putting it off until tomorrow or the day after. She had only promised to meet Erich in order to pay a small tribute to the world; a date with Erich was meaningless, just as all dates were probably meaningless, even if Beatrix had actually had the chance to go on other dates at the moment, but right now she didn't have any, and that again was due to the fact that she simply didn't feel like doing anything. Erich or another man, Erich or a lot of other men, that wasn't the point at all, and she let out the loud, healthy groan of a beast in agony. How awful.

Of course she couldn't tell Erich how awful she thought it was, he was such a nice person, he had a difficult enough time as it was, and was it his fault that she wasn't supportive or inspiring for anyone, was at best an imagined oasis in his life.

Beatrix carefully eased herself out of bed and immediately fell back exhaused: first things first, she needed to decide what should happen next. After a while she squinted at the alarm clock as if she had fainted and was gradually regaining consciousness, she needed that alarm clock to get her bearings but hated it just as much for the same reason. It was already after eleven. It puzzled her that she couldn't remember having fallen asleep again: either she had spent all her energy in the first quarter of an hour or hadn't really surfaced at all, remained submerged in a place deep inside her, where a silent cry sounded a retreat, summoning her to withdraw again and again. Beatrix decided not to force herself to do anything: when she tried to force something, it never worked at all, and at exactly one p.m. she was standing in front of the wardrobe, bewildered, and began pulling out drawers and opening doors. She rummaged around in the underwear drawer, then in the one with stockings, unearthing a pair of thin pantyhose and dragging them out as though she were hoisting a lead weight. She surveyed them critically, carefully easing her hands inside and slowly rotating them against the light, but she already knew it was no use, she wouldn't be spared: she never discovered the runs until she had put the stockings on. This agonizing effort, every single day, a whole life long, always having to hunt out a pair of stockings and never knowing whether it happened to be one of those days for good underwear or a day for the old, washed-out things. That alone was awful enough, and then after finally taking a lukewarm shower—there was never enough hot water to go around—she succeeded in avoiding both Frau Mihailovics and that awful Elisabeth so that no one in the house noticed when she really got up, and that was a terrible nuisance, a real burden. "Awful" was Beatrix's favorite word, and it came to her mind whenever she preferred not to dwell too deeply on something but didn't want to lose sight of it entirely, either. She had already laid out two dresses but kept her nightgown on while the coffee was heating in the kitchen. Posing in front of the bathroom mirror with the two dresses, she tried to establish a connection between them and herself. She was almost transparent, her face waxen, and during her inspection a small gleam touched its reflection in the mirror. She was close to finding something out for herself, something fundamental about getting dressed and what made it such a strain and why there were days on which, even two or three times, such difficult decisions had to be made as, for instance: dark blue, or beige with white? She looked out the window, oh no, not that, too, it was raining, of course it was raining, she'd almost given herself away on the phone but recovered in time to pretend that naturally she, too, had already noticed how horrid the weather was. This stupid rain, where everything was up in the air and you even had to debate which coat and shoes to wear although things could change completely by seven in the evening! Beatrix dropped the clothes on the rim of the bathtub and began the process of cleansing her face; it was too early to make decisions and consider consequences, but she could put her makeup on now just in case, only a hint of blush, no lipstick, just in case, because very little had been decided until now, and then when she had rescued the last of the coffee and taken a few sips, curled up on the bed, her spirits rose somewhat, she had simply gone too long without coffee, but even a second cup couldn't release her from the lifelong burden she had taken on and couldn't yet deal with because, as she thought now with increasing confidence, she was simply still too young.

She liked to say to people: That must be a terrible burden for you! Or: My dear, I understand, the whole thing must really weigh you down, I know, I've been through it, too!

Today, Beatrix's second favorite word, crossed her path. The slightest movement, the most insignificant thought seemed to send her colliding with these key words, and she noticed that everything was awful and complicated and that she had a burden to bear. Two of her bras were too tight and the other two were baggy, that could only happen to her, because she had so often cut corners to save money without using her common sense, but at least now she had those delicate bikini panties that fit perfectly, she owed that to Jeanne, that and the advice about the bras, although after that short and stormy friendship with a Frenchwoman, a genuine Parisienne, she had come to the conclusion that there were things you couldn't learn even in Paris and that it was hardly worth the effort to learn anything at all, if that was all you got out of it. Jeanne had hitchhiked to Vienna but hadn't really known what she was doing there, and Beatrix of all people was in no position to know what was worth doing in Vienna. That enterprising Parisian spirit had, however, had one lasting effect on Beatrix: all her life, when referring to a slip, she had used "combinaige" or "combinaison" like many Viennese women, but now she simply called it a "slip," having learned that the world "combinaison" must have been a casualty from some linguistic accident between Paris and Vienna, and she didn't want to make a fool of herself in those matters like the Mihailovics women did; they surely still abided by the rule that it was more genteel to use a French word. In other respects she hadn't gotten along very well with Jeanne, whose curiosity and childishness had been nothing but a strain, particularly on her nerves. They were both the same age—to be exact, Jeanne was almost twenty-one already—but Beatrix had come to the conclusion that Jeanne was digustingly hyperactive and wanted everything at once: to know where you could get hash, to meet guys, go dancing, rush to the opera, then afterward to the Prater amusement park or to a Heurige wine cellar, and it had always been on the tip of her tongue to tell Jeanne that her Parisian head was full of confused ideas and nothing more, you couldn't be a hippie and go to the opera at the same time, ride the ferris wheel and revolutionize the world, at least not in Vienna, and then to top it, sit arrogantly in Café Sacher, although once Jeanne had gotten nasty and told her that she was nothing but a *dropout*, which she pronounced with a funny accent. She had a family, a father who was a lawyer and a mother who was also a lawyer, and of course that could be a burden of sorts for her, but it was a horrible burden for Beatrix to be forced to accompany Jeanne through a Vienna she didn't know very well herself. After all, she'd lived here all her life, and to be forced to pay those astronomical prices for coffee at Sacher because Mademoiselle wasn't satisfied with a normal, smaller coffeehouse: nothing could be Viennese enough for her. Most embarrassing of all had been the problem of meeting men, because Beatrix hardly knew any. She had made obliging phone calls, but hadn't wanted to admit to Jeanne that she only met one man on a relatively regular basis, a married man who was already thirty-five, and though she didn't actually conceal Jeanne from Erich, she gave him the impression that, for her aunt's sake and because her cousin had to work, she had had to take on a delightful French student, father a lawyer, mother a lawyer, and that they wanted to see all the sights—in short, a very educated girl. And as always whenever it was in any way possible she asked Erich innocently for advice: My dear, you know I'm not that sure of myself, if you could only give me some sensible advice! Erich brought up the Albertina and the Museum of Art, and Beatrix gazed at him gratefully, thinking all the while: How awful. Of course Beatrix was far ahead of good old Erich in this type of thing, he had no idea how direct Jeanne was and how she really lived, although he might have read about that kind of thing in the paper, but it was certainly an incomprehensible world to a married man who was employed at the A.U.A. and wore himself to a frazzle between the office and a miserable home life, and, more for these reasons than out of discretion, she prevented the two from ever meeting. Jeanne would certainly have wanted to know and would have asked about everything at once and besides, for a Parisienne who was dropping out of somewhere it would have been a severe shock to find out what wasn't happening between Beatrix and Erich, she might even think that Viennese girls didn't go to bed with men or some other stupid nonsense, although the whole point of the matter was, quite simply, that it was too exhausting for Beatrix. Erich on the other hand would have considered Jeanne an unsuitable companion for his little girl, while Jeanne would have considered Erich philistine and bourgeois, and the opinions of both would have hurt Beatrix, but fortunately that episode with Jeanne was over now; Jeanne had "picked up" two young Englishmen with whom she'd hitchhiked to Rome; Vienna she'd found lacking, not rigolo enough, a boring city, although Café Sacher of all places had been chic, as though it wasn't just another café, just as a slip by any other name was just a slip after all, even if neither she nor Jeanne ever wore one.

In any case, the weight of that burden and the strain of lying were unimportant now, because Erich's wife had made another suicide attempt shortly before Jeanne's departure, but since it was already the third attempt in the course of Erich's acquaintance with Beatrix—and of which she was therefore immediately notified—she had already acquired practice in listening with a sort of attentive absentmindedness and she was free to dwell on Jeanne's departure with an inward sigh of relief. Nevertheless, it was a strain to sit in the remotest corner of Café Eiles with Erich, even though she liked the café and happily stayed when Erich rushed off in haste, it meant being subjected once again to the narrated annals of

his marital situation through the ages, the whole time knowing and feeling that Erich, who was much too decent and
scrupulous, would never bring himself to divorce his wife.
Beatrix was always sympathetic, even though Erich's mar-
tyrdom had nothing to do with her. They weighed the pros
and cons of the matter over and over again, and each time
they discussed it down to the last detail; Erich admired
Beatrix's saintly patience; the poor man couldn't understand
that Beatrix had no interest in a divorce—for that matter
neither did he—and when he talked for hours on end to this
patient, undemanding child, he was filled not with some vul-
gar, commonplace desire, but rather a desperate wish to finally live in peace and see that unsolved, unsolvable problem
with Guggi solved at last. The fact that Beatrix was so sympathetic was, in fact, somewhat odd, but her lack of interest
was not: for minutes or sometimes a half-hour at a time, she
found it amusing to play the role of an extra, and sometimes
she thought that, after they had split up, she would tell him
one day what had occurred to her, because she was simply too
fond of the expression, namely that there must be a "pyrami-
dal telepathy" between himself and Guggi. He always arrived
home in the nick of time, once he had just happened to take
the train back from a conference in Graz three hours ahead
of schedule, out of annoyance that his proposals for domestic
air traffic had been rejected, and once again he had promptly
saved Guggi, who would have been beyond saving three
hours later; he had rushed around like a madman, called the
ambulance and taken her to the hospital; immediately afterward he had called Beatrix, his one "ray of hope," the "oasis
of peace" in his botched-up life, and had fervently assured
her, his voice still shaking, that he couldn't go on without

her, how much he admired her courage and her composure, her strength and that common sense that surely no other twenty-year-old girl had. In his fits of admiration, he sincerely wished her a man different from himself, someone who could really give her what he never could. Beatrix didn't like it when Erich praised her or talked about her admirable maturity; she laughed and laughed as soon as an opportunity arose when laughter was allowed and merriment no longer out of place: My dear man, you keep forgetting that I was born on the 29th of February! Just figure it out for once, I'm still a child and I'll never grow up! I need you so, you're the only support I have! She gave him a grateful look, and Erich thought, preoccupied of course with Guggi, that he undoubtedly gave her needed support, the child was practically alone in the world, and now he had two responsibilities, Guggi and Beatrix, and he never noticed the deception since she deceived him so unintentionally in every respect that he had no choice but to believe in his own importance, which meant believing in his sense of responsibility. During the few fleeting moments when Beatrix felt any affection for Erich, she would sigh inwardly thinking that the one thing she sincerely wished this poor nice man was that, once and for all, he would arrive home too late when Guggi again deigned to attempt suicide. He really didn't deserve a woman like Guggi—and another one like herself in the bargain.

But that was just the way this stupid man was, always confounded by his catastrophically bad luck, like someone who had landed in a trap from which there was no escape. So she sat out her hour with him, certain that she couldn't help him—no one could—trying to get his mind off himself. It was better if Erich believed he was responsible for Beatrix, too, because then he was distracted from his Guggi for a while at least. Anyway Beatrix didn't really contribute significantly to his misfortune, but she had to magnify the importance of these things so that he wouldn't be totally overwhelmed by the real catastrophe.

Occasionally, in fact rather seldom, they went to the movies and held each other's hands. It meant nothing to Beatrix, but sometimes, when he had talked enough— although he rarely stopped talking, because he had no one else to confide in—he would become affectionate, nibble gently on her ear or touch her breast or her knees, but she preferred discussions and alarming phone calls. Beatrix found this physical contact embarrassing, she was simply too old for it. A lot more than that—which was quite enough, as far as she was concerned—had happened during the last years at her first school, but since she had grown up and staunchly refused to go to college or train for any profession, it no longer occurred to her to become involved with a man, and her aversion to this awful normality to which people subjected themselves had coincided with the discovery of a perversion: her sleeping fetish. Granted, it was perverse, but at least she was something special in the midst of all these normal fools. Genuinely perverse. Everything else was such an absolute waste of time, the simple task of getting dressed and undressed was a real strain, but nothing could compare with her addiction to deep sleep, a sleep she had found her way into, could find her way into even fully dressed on the bed with her shoes on. When she considered that childish nonsense in the past, largely provoked by curiosity, and all the rest, which she today believed to be nothing but gross exaggeration, then sleep was the only real fulfillment: it made life worth living.

The few times when her Aunt Mihailovics had left and Elisabeth been told to shut up—after the affair involving Marek, Elisabeth forfeited any right whatsoever to tell her what to do—she let Erich come to the Strozzigasse, to her room. Of course it was a burden for her to consider that he might want to have a drink or at least a cup of coffee, but then they lay next to each other and she let him continue talking. When he unfortunately stopped talking, she broke into exuberant laughter at each of his timid attempts, because Guggi's unrelenting shadow lay over him, and an unbrideed desire to play provocative games took hold of her and she was seized by an even wilder resistance, and Erich had said once, not in the least disappointed, that he liked it, he liked her like that. That meant it wasn't his patience with her that kept him in bounds; once, when his mood of disaster had lifted and he had actually laughed, he had said, chuckling, that she was just a demi-vierge. Beatrix, who hadn't understood the word at the time, had looked it up in the dictionary she had often used in the days of Jeanne, and she had been pleased, because at least she was something half. She would not have liked to be something whole, but Guggi was presumably one of those passionate women who loved hysterically, and there you had it again, where these women were headed in the end, even with someone like poor Erich.

The only thing that bothered Beatrix was when Erich brought up the subject of her future, because of course there was no concealing the fact that she didn't want to go to school anymore and didn't have a single diploma and just claimed vaguely and in passing that she was looking for the right job. Erich, with his sense of responsibility, became extremely tedious when he went into it, that it was in her best interest, he'd thought it over too, what the best job for her would be, maybe training to be an interpreter or maybe a job in a boutique or a bookstore or a gallery. She just had to do something, he'd say, it worried him so much, because—under the given circumstances—he couldn't marry her. But Beatrix knew very well that there were no jobs, not even the most pitiful office routine—she wasn't even qualified for that—and that no one would allow her to sleep until late in the afternoon because these ill-advised people all around her let themselves be squeezed into schedules; that she would never work, least of all learn a trade, because she had no ambition whatsoever to earn a single shilling, become self-supporting and spend eight hours a day with people who smelled bad. Women who worked were especially awful: they surely had some defect or suffered from delusions or let themselves be exploited by men. She for one would never allow herself to be exploited, would never sit down at a typewriter, not even for her own sake, or ask meekly in a boutique: My dear madam, may I have the pleasure of showing you something else? Perhaps this blouse in green?

No, she protested, but only once, in order not to upset good old Erich; I don't worry about it in the least, and what future, anyway? She added tenderly: Why should we worry about the future? Just look, the present is already a big enough burden for you to bear, and I don't want you to have to think of me, too, let's try to think of Guggi instead. What does Professor Jordan say? Please don't conceal anything from me, there shouldn't be any secrets between us. And with that she had Erich back with Guggi again, back with the prolonged treatments, the new hopes, and the old fears. Her mother, the late Herr Mihailovics' sister who had married and gone to South America, regularly sent her a small sum which accrued from an ancient dilapidated apartment building in the tenth district, and even though it wasn't much, a kind of pension which always remained the same and continually decreased in value because of inflation, to her aunt's chagrin she depended entirely on this pittance; she didn't need much and her room and board were practically free. Never did it occur to her to give the Mihailovics women something for the room and the other expenses, her share of which was paid without a word. She never went out, or, when she did, only with Erich or, rarely, to a coffeehouse. She was too exhausted to plunge into life, and the only expenditure more important to her than anything else, even more important than food, was the money she spent for the beautician and makeup. For some time now she had been saying: I'm running a little low on makeup. This was the only reason she had once, unmoved and without reservation, accepted a five-hundred-schilling bill from Erich. She couldn't expect anything from him for her birthday anyway, because she never had birthdays with her strange February 29th. One thing Erich did not and could not know, because he had too little time for her, was a thing she would never confess to any other man, perhaps the very reason she didn't want one: it was simply that she was only happy when sitting in the beauty parlor, that René's was the only place in the world she felt at home. For René's she sacrificed almost everything, even regular meals, and she was glad to be slim, as fragile as a china doll, and weigh so little, less than 50 kilos. She liked Herr Karl best, and Gitta and Frau Rosi, she even preferred the little clumsy Toni to Erich and her anxious, unsympathetic Aunt Mihailovics. The people at René's, every single one of them, understood her better than other people, and that was why she only felt comfortable there on the second floor in the Rotenturmstrasse, and people should finally stop coming and expecting that she follow her cousin Elisabeth's example, who had mastered and doctored and slaved herself to death, a model child, and now she'd gotten what she deserved with all her education: she was already thirty years old and, in spite of all her self-sufficiency, the humiliations she'd borne and her hopeless battles for survival, she hadn't been able to find her niche anywhere and moreover didn't dare to go to the beauty parlor and for that reason really looked thirty. If there was anyone Beatrix avoided it was Elisabeth, although her cousin was quiet and retiring and never interfered or uttered a reproachful word. Her mere presence provoked Beatrix to rebellion, and had her peace and her sleep in the Strozzigasse been any less valuable to her she would have enjoyed telling her in so many words how stupid she was, just plain stupid, and she just couldn't stand that much stupidity, at least not in a woman. With Erich it was different and touching, no matter how ridiculous she found his opinions and anxieties. A man could afford to be stupid, a woman never, she should never waste herself away and even cause her mother sleepless nights because she wasn't earning enough money, because she had become involved with something as esoteric as art history in the first place, and what good did it do her, knowing everything about that Dürer and all those other painters, memorizing all that stuff about Florence to the letter; the scholarship to Florence hadn't worked out either, and Beatrix had guessed enough to know that the Mihailovics women were at a loss and it was true after all that the stupid woman had fallen in love with Anton Marek just to take on one more burden. And if anyone had ever asked Beatrix, she for one would have grasped it at the age of fourteen. This Marek didn't care one iota about anything or anyone except himself and had no intention whatsoever of marrying the Mihailovics woman only to divorce her after a prudent and carefully calculated marriage for some sentimental woman with no money or prospects. Erich, on the other hand, was simply doomed: regrettable for him, admittedly, but advantageous for Beatrix. An Erich who was divorced or widowed would never have induced Beatrix to drag herself to René's only to spend hours between washing and highlighting and manicure and epilation treatments, happily lost in thought and gazing at her reflection in those huge mirrors that were lacking in the Strozzigasse, where there was only one tiny mirror in the bathroom, too high and inadequate for her needs. At René's all the walls were covered with those wonderful mirrors, and there were some of those three-paneled mirrors that let you see yourself from all sides, and in the end Gitta brought the hand mirror so that nothing escaped her. Everything she took seriously was taken seriously at René's, and when she mounted the stairs to the second floor once a week and sometimes even before the week was up, excited and expectant, she breathed differently, her fatigue fell away, and in no time she was transformed and could step radiantly over the threshold into this temple. Even before she registered with Frau Yvonne her eyes took in the many reflections: she was one with herself again and had come home. Even before she posed critically in front of a mirror she was happy to see herself arriving in the glass and to be able to stop thinking about her burdens. So that's me, one Beatrix said to the other in the mirror and stared at herself, deeply moved, even while they began to call out, back and forth, where is Herr Karl, Gitta, Rosi; and Frau Yvonne smiled, she almost always remembered her customer's every desire, but she asked anyway, wrinkled her forehead because Gitta wasn't free yet and Frau Hilde, it was just a shame, a real shame that she was expecting a child and wouldn't be back in for a while yet. Yes, what a shame, thought Beatrix with discontent, that would have to happen just now. She put on a vague, sad smile: all the same, it was inconsiderate, especially if you were as used to Frau Hilde as she was. In a trance, Beatrix already had a brush in her hand and began stroking her hair into disarray with a grimace on her face, remarking flippantly: Just take a look at me, I need to be completely redone, da capo, from head to toe, I hardly dare go out, it's hideous, the way I look . . . Herr Karl, please save me, take a look at this! She ran her fingers through her long brown hair: Go ahead and admit it! Things can't go on like this, I was here just last week! Lifting strands of her hair with a comb, Herr Karl said that it was tolerable to a certain extent, to some extent, but on the other hand he strongly recommended that she undergo the bio-intensive Chev-09 treatment developed by the Oréal Laboratories, and he urged even more strongly that she take the whole treatment, only ten applications were required. Beatrix interrupted him briskly: As far as I'm concerned, one sample application, I can see that, but to decide to take a whole series, no, Herr Karl, today is just not the day for me to make decisions like that, I've got an unbelievable day ahead of me, you just can't imagine, and then with this weather! She looked around helplessly: her umbrella was dripping on the wall-to-wall carpeting; Gitta ran to her with a nervous glance at the wet spots and deposited the umbrella in a stand which Beatrix hadn't seen; after all, the most important thing was the decision for or against a bio-intensive treatment, which was simply too expensive for her at the moment.

Humming, she crossed two René rooms, already savoring her disappearance into the side room full of pink smocks which led into the pink changing rooms, and she undressed confidently even though another woman had come in—it was a good-underwear day—she draped the pink smock slowly and deliberately around her shoulders and hung her dress and coat on a hook. Outside in René's rooms, she wandered around indecisively for a while: everyone had disappeared all of a sudden, she didn't see Herr Karl or Gitta, but she enjoyed listening when the women were on the phone or when someone came in and was greeted. So that was Countess Rasumofsky. But which one? She had had a completely different picture of her; it was less important to her to know who the others were because most of them were accommodated with an all-encompassing, charming "My dear madam." The names only had to be revealed when the bills were collected and paid, and then these women were called something or another, Jordan or Wantschura, wait, the name Jordan did suddenly sound familiar, she must be the wife of that brilliant psychologist who was treating Guggi, but she had envisioned her differently, she looked so modest, but pretty, as pretty as a picture, and so young, but the other women really left her cold, the ones who were embraced by an anonymous title like "Frau Doktor" or were the wives of

Ph.D.'s; Frau Yvonne did her best to find some sort of title for each of the women, depending on her mood or instinct, or because she'd been briefed. It had never struck Beatrix that all of the women here were at least thirty, on the average around forty, with the exception of the petite Frau Jordan, but she couldn't be all that young anymore either, and at any rate Beatrix was the youngest by far, because as a rule young girls in Vienna washed their own hair and filed their own nails, and they certainly looked it, too. Beatrix would never do that, it would have been unbearable for her to give up these afternoons, it would have been as bad as being stricken with some horrible disease. Paralysis, for instance. To her it would mean being paralyzed, if she were deprived of her René world. The attention here was a demanding challenge to her, as was the fact that everything she was entitled to was given serious consideration. In the Strozzigasse, in that eternally provisional home, there was no one who even made her bed, now and again her aunt dropped a gratuitous remark provoked by the fact that, for days on end, Beatrix would leave her bed tangled and rumpled. This was because rummaging and hunting around in the messy wardrobe had robbed her of her last ounce of energy, and only Erich's extremely rare visits made her capable of straightening everything up in a flash, once again to keep up appearances, but otherwise nothing could have induced her to scrub and clean up a room, and it remained her secret that she could nevertheless give the impression, on the street or at René's, that she lived in one of those high-class, well-aired residences managed by legendary housekeepers, the kind of place these other women here probably came from, and she alone was able to keep her few dresses and articles of underclothing in such flawless condition in the midst of such chaos. For the sake of this impression and her appearance she was even willing to wash and iron once a week, groaning and feeble, but it couldn't be avoided. But here Gitta washed her hair for her and massaged it dry so gently, and Beatrix pleaded: Please don't let the water get too hot! Gitta knew that already, of course, but she nodded appreciatively and let the lukewarm water flow over her hair for a long time. But then Gitta disappeared and they sent a new one who was now tugging at her hair with a comb, and Beatrix eyed the mirror, searching for a familiar face. No, this was just unbearable, this goose who was trying to comb out her long hair, only Gitta could do it right, sometimes Herr Karl even did it himself, and she suggested, stammering, that it might help to pre-dry her hair a little, oh Jesus, do I have to say it again, either put me under the dryer or use the blowdryer! Beatrix had never understood why they all imagined for some reason that hair should be combed out when it was still damp. She had a headache and looked in the mirror, her hair hung down stringy and wet on each side, she opened her eyes wide and examined this alien, distorted, utterly strange skull, just imagine how awful a naked skull must be, but she was immediately distracted, because she noticed that the eyeshadow on her left lid had worn off slightly, and she blinked her eyes, inspecting her eyelashes critically. The woman was finally done, and Beatrix reached for a magazine. There were always German magazines lying around here, *Vogue* was extremely rare; who wanted to read German magazines, anyway? Twin Murders in Stuttgart. Certainly an awful place, it even sounded like murder. Sex in Germany. That was probably even worse. Jacqueline Kennedy, now Mrs. Onassis, had dozens of wigs for every occasion.

At least that sounded more interesting, debatable, although that Kennedy woman—Herr Karl was standing behind her at last, she closed the magazine hastily and asked: What are the new hairstyles this winter? No, basically she wasn't really interested, and didn't care what was piled on other women's heads, hopefully we've seen the last of postiches, after all, there were more important things in the world, for instance she was much more interested in knowing what he, Herr Karl, thought of wigs. For her part, Beatrix still had her doubts. This was Beatrix's opinion mainly because of the price, but that Kennedy woman was still pretty convincing, even if she wasn't as young as she used to be. Herr Karl had begun to expertly wind one strand after another onto rollers with nimble fingers which never touched her head, talking to her at the same time as though it were the simplest thing in the world to attach long strands of hair to rollers. He exclaimed: But this isn't the first time I've said it, you definitely need one, actually two, you absolutely need two wigs, if you do winter sports and then head south! Beatrix made a face, she didn't do winter sports, because first of all, she didn't have the money; and then sports in general—even if you didn't really do any when you "did" winter sports—required getting up at a certain hour in the morning; and third, there were so few places she would have liked. She could do without those ski huts and the whole business, not to mention those people in the Alpine Clubs. Camping out on straw mattresses: that was how she imagined it. Yodelers and unheated rooms. She said judiciously to Herr Karl: Speaking of summer, now that northern Italy is out of the question, I would rather stay at the Wörthersee, that's why I'm asking you. I just can't run to the hairdresser's every time I go for a swim, expecially not to one down there in the wilds, it would be too much for me. Herr Karl explained that if he wasn't mistaken, he had already gone into detail with her three times this authum about his reasons for recommending these new wigs to her and why they were really waterproof this time but still of the highest quality. Beatrix had understood this very well and stopped listening. She sat completely absorbed in the mirror while Herr Karl spread a pink net over the rollers, placed cotton balls in her ears, pulled down the hood of the dryer, and switched on the machine. Yes, she wanted a black sweater, men's cut, with a V-neck and a white blouse underneath, it looked girlish, and Erich was bound to like it, so demivierge. Pulling the hood up once more, she asked gravely, although this phase of the procedure was over: Herr Karl, I forgot, I mean I've been thinking about it the whole time, whether I should have these mèches done, you know how difficult it is for me to make decisions. I simply can't decide. Herr Karl said firmly, but not without empathy: Then we'll just have to start from the very beginning.

No, you have to tell me what to do, you know very well that I can't take a single step without you. I just want to think about it a little longer. But what am I going to do if I'm at a lake or the ocean and they can't do the mèches there, that's the point! You know I'm like an amputee without your help, I can't pack you and take you with me, I'm not the Queen of England.

At the close of this successful sentence, she bestowed a special smile upon Herr Karl and thought how much prettier and younger she was than that woman who had even had to sign death sentences. Jeanne, who knew something about politics, had reproached her forcibly with this fact. Well, she was thankful for that; that crown-bearing Elizabeth could probably never sleep late, in fact, she had a worse time of it than a beggar, for all her diadems and her money. But still, she could take her hairdresser everywhere with her, that was something, but when you wore hats like that and had grown children, not even a private hairdresser and private cosmetician could do any good, but Beatrix did not necessarily want to dwell on death sentences during these precious hours, and she dismissed Herr Karl, who had already written off the two wigs and pulled the hood of the dryer back over her head.

She whispered to Gitta: Tell me, that lady over there, the pretty one, relatively young, she must be one of your regular customers, is she really the wife of that Jordan? Gitta said with an eager nod: An enchanting woman, and yet so simple! That didn't make much sense to Beatrix: how "simple" could a woman like that be, maybe it was a trick and she just made herself interesting with all that simplicity. Chacun à son goût. Of course she couldn't tell anyone why she was so exceptionally interested in Frau Jordan, she usually had no interest whatsoever in these women.

Frau Rosi appeared with the small bowl for her feet and Beatrix had to stand up again, take off her pantyhose in the back room and change into the pink-and-white René slippers. Then she went back under the hairdryer and submerged her feet in the warm soapy water. Thank goodness it was the right temperature, and she nodded her thanks to Frau Rosi, who was already spreading out her instruments; she took one of Beatrix's feet on her knee and began to trim the toenails. She would like to have been called Elfe, wasn't there an actress at the Burgtheater, of course, Lombardi's first name was Elfe, she was still around, but she didn't look like the name fit her. All sensitive people should be allowed to choose their own names after a certain age, but of course no one had ever thought of that; Beatrix would have been glad to relinquish her right to vote, she would be eligible soon, but she didn't care one bit about politics; it was bad enough the way all those politicians looked. As she glimpsed the slight figure of Toni hurrying by in the mirror, she called out: it's too hot, I can't stand it anymore, oh, please turn it down to 2.

She would have liked to be an ash blond; she might have looked too old as an auburn blond with red highlights, but an ash blond, unobtrusive at first glance . . . Then she would have to change her makeup, apply a very pale fond de teint and simulate the appearance of being sickly, because everyone was so crazy about looking healthy these days, although hardly anyone was healthy, except for her. Still, she thought she was kind of cute after all, with that light brown tinge to her face, most of that rose-brown shade wasn't real, but Frau Hilde had taught her how to apply the blush, and now the woman had to go and get pregnant, although you had to admit she really knew how to apply makeup, and however you looked at it, Vienna was a thoroughly backward city, because so few women had their makeup done in beauty parlors, apart from those who had something to do with TV and the movies. Thanks, but no thanks, she had never given a thought to the movies and didn't have any illusions, either. Katti—who had once been her best friend for a short time when Beatrix still believed that there was such a thing as a best friend—had become so tense about the whole thing, a real bundle of nerves. But there again Katti had already been twenty-five at the time, and everything she'd reported had seemed to indicate that it wasn't exaggerated after all, that sleeping around among the movie people, how awful. And then Katti had reappeared with yet another fresh hope, this time of getting into a German movie. The things Beatrix had heard about Rome from this ex-girlfriend, whether they were true or not—it really was no laughing matter, although she felt indifferent to her having caught a case of the jitters, it could have been worse, maybe she herself was moody too, but at least she was never depressed or disappointed; she never let things upset her. Katti had been the kind of person who drove Erich up the wall; unfortunately, she had brought the two of them together once—never again. And à propos girlfriends, they were something you simply no longer had once you grew up.

She conducted a private dialogue with Erich: You know, I don't care what the rest of mankind does, if they're clean or dirty, take LSD or don't, whether they keep struggling again and again for no reason whatsoever, or just drift around; I think they're all, the rest of mankind, yes, all the rest, they're just a joke, the whole bunch of them, I can't put my finger on it. I don't care one bit, you know what I mean. Me? Me, not able to express myself—you're quite right, I can't express myself. It's a fault. I know it, and you're absolutely right. But it is strange, don't you think, that I can't express myself?

But out loud she would say something completely different to Erich today: I'm really crazy about myself sometimes, and she would squeeze the remark in quickly, before he had a chance to start in on Guggi and his problems. Incidentally, Erich had said something quite funny recently, something about relationships between men and women, and that you could never solve the basic problem, in any case he was beginning to capitulate and that was certainly the right thing to do, although he retained this mania for deliberating every-thing and analyzing himself, his predicament in general, then his predicament with Guggi, and then his predicament with her, and at the same time he claimed that the most im-portant thing was not to analyze the situation but rather to allow the predicaments to work themselves out; then the so-lution would come on its own. A man full of contradictions, but she didn't give two hoots about the whole thing, namely each of the predicaments individually and in relation to one another. Predicaments had nothing to do with her. But perhaps that was a false conclusion on her part. Erich was constantly drawing her attention to all sorts of false conclu-sions, and Beatrix found that very stimulating because the predicaments were so monotonous, and for that reason she often said, while gazing at him with a despondent and help-less expression on her face, I think I've jumped to another false conclusion, don't you? And when she even took the blame herself for something or other, he became the nicest, most considerate person, but it had to be some sort of blame he had thought up, it made him feel so good to forgive some-one for something, and from now on Beatrix would always remember to take the blame for something at least once a week. One of the rollers was really uncomfortably tight to-day; that had never happened to Herr Karl before. She would ask Erich to forgive her for all the unbelievable and insignifi-cant things: Please, Erich, you have to forgive me, I was so inconsiderate last time, no, really, I notice it myself, in retrospect, and I realize it, I'm afraid I, oh dearest, I was so on edge. And that would have to happen on a day you were so on edge, too; I was inconsiderate, really inconsiderate, and I have to change. Erich, please, I have to be able to be honest with you, otherwise there's no sense in it for me, and losing your trust would be the worst thing that could happen to me.

Beatrix looked at her toenails, which were nearly finished and only needed to be painted, cute, maybe there was nothing special about her, but she had to admit her feet were enchanting, and she wasn't even sorry that no man ever had the chance to see them like this; even when Erich came to the Strozzigasse and she took off her stockings to excite him, he never gave her feet a second glance. But the fact that she knew it was enough. Pretty feet were rare, and Frau Rosi in particular could sing a song about that. But Frau Rosi wasn't singing a song today, she removed the tub, disappeared and then returned with an entire battalion of manicure utensils. Beatrix called out toward the back: Herr Karl, how long do I have to languish today? What? Another ten minutes, that's downright inhuman of you, and if you say ten minutes, that really means twenty. But I won't get my hair cut in spite of it, I won't do you that favor, I'd rather languish.

She held out her left, damp hand to Frau Rosi and sank her right hand into the water. Then she reached for the magazine again. When she was fifteen, someone had fallen in love with her turtleneck sweater, the green one, and that was before she had found out her neck was too short for turtleneck sweaters. The things you learn over the years! Never again turtleneck sweaters, that was for sure.

The yacht Christina. Headed for a Greek island. Ari on deck, that was what this person had looked like, only younger. There was a gruesome eyewitness account about Africa, but she preferred steering the yacht toward the islands, she stood on deck and the wind caught her hair, but she was standing alone, without guests on board and without any superfluous Aris around. For heaven's sake, she shrieked, Toni, it's too hot again, how many times do I have to say 2, that's not 2, that's 3!

Erich was constantly overworked and overtired, he didn't know how to fight this latest staff cut and had even taken on the work load of a certain Herr Jakob who had been fired, that was just like Erich, although "staff cut" didn't mean much to Beatrix, just some kind of additional burden. Then the fact that Erich, who would have had every right to do so, didn't take advantage of the free tickets for wonderful trips sponsored by the A.U.A. was typical, too, because in spite of his complaints about the management, which she thought justified, ultimately he identified with the upper echelons who doubtless took those trips, and today she'd have to suggest that he try to get tickets, just as a joke: It would be so easy for you, and then we could finally be together, far away, in Karachi or Bombay. At least he could get her a flight to Istanbul, or even better to the Canary Islands. You and I, alone, together, in the sun on one of those magnificent beaches on the Canary Islands, Erich, you must be able to do that much! Hopefully the flights to those fabulous locations didn't leave early in the morning or at noon, surely there were evening flights, but could you sleep comfortably on a plane? She wasn't so sure. Just a little chat about far-off places in the sun couldn't hurt, Erich had to pull himself together one of these days, get up some initiative, make it possible for them to go away together. Forget this gray Vienna and the strain of it all, just think, Erich, it would make me so happy! She wouldn't fly, though; she imagined these glorified places as being horribly uncomfortable, and Erich would hardly have the nerve to wheedle two flight tickets out of his

boss for just a pleasure trip, but she'd give him some incen-
tive to devote at least some thought to having fun, it was
high time he did that.

The dryer was probably set on 2, but today 2 felt like 3, and
she called out: Please Toni, put it on 1, it's unbearable, I can't
stand 2!

If she got done in time, including all the extras, she could
go to the movies before her date with Erich. On the other
hand, the entire length of the Kärntnerstrasse in the rain and
then back again to the Hochhaus Café—that would be too
devastating, and a taxi was too expensive. She sighed. She'd
have to wait an hour and a half for Erich in the café after all.
Still, some new aspect of the drama might be revealed, not
every man had a wife like Guggi, and she really would like
to see Guggi just once, from a distance, she'd rather not get
too close. She for one would never kill herself, although she
was probably much more scared of life, simply scared to
death. Beatrix reflected that, when she left René's, she could
leave a quick message for Erich in the coffeehouse and then
go home to the Strozzigasse where she could lie down with
her freshly-done hair. My hair is just the prettiest thing about
me, the rest is relatively run of the mill, except for my feet,
of course. At home she would lie down, relaxed and happy,
spread out her hair, contemplate her feet—at the movies they
were probably showing another one of those stressful films
with blood and guts and sometimes even war, and even
though everything was merely acted and invented it still took
a lot out of her for the simple reason that in reality things
happened differently. In her reality Guggi was the sole
problem, but she was only a borrowed problem after, and
Erich was nothing but a weak person who allowed himself to

be bullied in the office, too, and he knew it; she would have given his boss a piece of her mind long ago, she would have laid out the pills and razor blades for that pinnacle of instability with her own two hands long ago, intentionally, so that she might come to her senses once and for all.

She drew her compact out of her purse and examined her teeth—not bad, although a bit irregular, she absolutely had to go to the dentist, and soon. And they really needed to be cleaned again, not this week, next week. A horrendous burden. She was glad that she'd finally almost half-decided to go.

I am a girl-woman. Or am I more of a woman-girl? She debated, dozing off, whether there was a dangerous difference between the two terms, but it was better to say something completely different to Erich today, so that he didn't have too easy a time of it. One thing finally had to be said. You know, I'm a woman, she would say, because that was the point everything revolved around and which he didn't understand—that, in spite of everything, she was a woman. Demi-vierge was one thing, but she couldn't always give him the satisfaction of regarding her as so unproblematic. I'm a woman—that should be a problem for him, at least it would be a small thorn in his side, but then, because it became too complicated for her to keep thinking about, she sank into near-unconsciousness under the roar of the dryer. Her hands were finished and painted now, she'd barely noticed that Rosi had packed her things and was standing up, and she begged to turn off the dryer. It had been at least twenty minutes. An unspeakably long twenty minutes, to please Herr Karl.

She followed the new chubby assistant who was substituting for Frau Hilde into a booth and lowered herself onto the hard, narrow cot, already beset by a vague suspicion, and after this "substitute's" first few strokes, her mood darkened. She had the distinct feeling that this was not going to work out. She couldn't explain why, admittedly there was nothing that could go wrong with the cleansing and massaging, but this woman's hands, two paws, she could sense it, she had this instinct when hands touched her, the woman was dabbing gingerly at her face with a kleenex—how sluggish could you get! Beatrix kept her eyes closed so that at least she didn't have to see that red-veined, doughy face bent over her own, but now the creature was plucking at her eyebrows with a tweezers, oh no, not this slow-motion routine again, this was supposed to be done at lightning speed so that it wouldn't hurt. (Stop it, I can't stand it any more, please stop it!) Beatrix didn't have the courage to say anything out loud, she'd never been subjected to such treatment at René's, to this degree of torture; apart from running away or insulting this woman, she didn't know to escape, how, with these ridiculous rollers in her hair, to find her way out of this predicament. This was surely a predicament! Herr Karl would have understood instantly, but he never came to the booths, that wasn't his domain, no one ever came, not even Gitta, and she couldn't just burst into tears and scream out loud in this torture chamber. The new, clumsy cow kept plucking away and Beatrix, with great effort, asked what time it was. Oh—it was already too late for the movies, it was too much, and the rollers were pinching her, this creature hadn't even thought to put a pillow under her head, she didn't know the first thing, Beatrix didn't come to René's to sacrifice herself to the fledgling experiments of a dilettante with those hands who would never develop into a cosmetician, she could sense it. The first tears began to trickle from the corners of

Beatrix's eyelids. What would it be like when she started putting on the makeup, you needed to be fully relaxed for that, and she had always been relaxed with Frau Hilde, completely relaxed and even drowsy. She couldn't even stay still at this point; the eye makeup was doomed to be a catastrophe. Weren't the tears enough already, why hadn't this clumsy cow noticed, one tear was sufficient to make it impossible to work on makeup, and Beatrix said in her despair: A glass of water, please, I feel sick, bring me a glass of water. The creature stopped in surprise, and left the booth. Beatrix sat up immediately, trembling, and looked for a mirror.

How idiotic to choose today of all days to meet with Erich, who had no idea what she went through. It would be the most sensible thing to tell him soon, today would be best, that they shouldn't see each other any more, or rather were not allowed to see each other, perhaps because she had confessed everything to her Aunt Mihailovics who then, with her narrow-minded views, had considered this relationship to a married man scandalous, and then naturally Beatrix, dependent on her aunt as she was and frightened to death by her aunt's outburst ... No, that wouldn't work. But she could cite Guggi as the reason, and her own guilty conscience, which just gave her no peace of mind anymore. Beatrix was especially partial to words like conscience, blame, responsibility, and consideration because they sounded good to her and meant nothing. On the whole, people should really limit their vocabularies to meaningless words when they were talking; because otherwise it was impossible for them to understand each other, and "conscience" would carry true credibility with Erich: a brilliant example of how well this could work—you could feed a man the most nonsensical words because those were the only ones he understood. If confronted with Beatrix's secret words and clandestine thoughts, Erich would have plunged into an abyss or at least become fully disoriented. He needed a little guidance, that was all.

Her eyes fixed on the mirror, she loosened a few rollers at the back, then two at her temples, and was amazed that the corkscrew curls dangling on her cheeks gave her face such a different appearance than when her hair was combed out. This was how she should look! That was it! Slender, doll-like, with these two curls in front that looked fake, maybe a whole head of these corkscrew curls, framing a mask-like face drained of all expression, like this one. Fascinated, she unwound one roller after the other, she didn't care what Herr Karl would say, her heart began to pound, she wet her lips and whispered something to herself. She looked so improbable, like out of a fairy tale, mysterious, she was such a mystery, and who would ever see her like this, this mystery of a passing instant, revealed? I'm in love, I'm honest to goodness in love with myself, I'm divine! Beatrix only hoped that the woman would take her time finding a glass and water, because she was in love for the very first time, and now she knew it was possible after all, so powerful a feeling that, with laughing and crying, between laughing and crying, you couldn't find the word, but this was unbelievable, just like in the movies, or a novel, an earthquake was inside her, and because she didn't know more words than anybody else, this had to be love.

She hastily suppressed a swell of emotion: she heard footsteps, the door to the booth would open in a second, and everything would be awful again, life outside would go on miserably, a life where stockings ran, where there were stuffy, run-down apartments like the one in the Strozzigasse, where clothes got dirty, where after you had been looking forward to going to the hairdresser's it rained, and where your hair got greasy again in no time. The short interval of perfection when she was immaculate, with rosy feet and hands and still feeling the tremors following a quake—this moment was already slipping away, and she would be consumed once more by life, by Erich; that self-pitying fool consumed her, too, having no idea how valuable she was and how much she wore herself out, all for nothing, just so he could muster up a little courage and regain his balance after each fall, while she was destroyed in his presence and by his presence and wasted away for no reason at all. Erich could never have known moments like this, could never have experienced anything as ecstatic and enchanting; he was the type who was made for having and creating problems, all this nonsense, instead of just opening his eyes for once and seeing what a jewel had been bestowed upon him, what was special about her, unique, and that she was not some "cute little thing" or a "little cute thing" but rather that she, with or without brains, was a lonely, misunderstood work of art, unattainable and fortunately misunderstood, because she had once heard from her encyclopedic cousin that the essence of a painting was that one could never understand it, because there was nothing to understand and the meanings had no meaning. Not all of what stupid people rattled on about was so stupid after all.

She drank the glass of water because the woman had brought it, and then lay down in surrender; the creature didn't have anything better to say than that she shouldn't have taken out the rollers, Herr Karl wouldn't be too happy about that. Beatrix made no reply to this remark, it wasn't worth the effort. She merely murmured what Frau Hilde did with her makeup and how Frau Hilde did her makeup and she would just like to suggest... The woman bent over her again and began applying eyeliner which she wiped off again instantly, this was just her lucky day, then she closed in again on the other eye which had begun to twitch, but Beatrix hadn't intended her eye to twitch. It was caused by this clumsy creature, now she closed in again, and Beatrix stopped the twitching so that the woman wouldn't be able to talk her way out of it, and finally, after what seemed like an eternity, the eyeliner and eyeshadow had been applied. Beatrix said only once: Not too heavy, please don't make it too obvious, just a hint, I'm not an actress. The new woman had stopped talking altogether, but the silence was ominous, and it required an enormous amount of patience—of which only Beatrix was capable—to bear this questionable wiping-off, these repeated corrections. Finally she was released and stood up in gloomy silence, no, she didn't want to see anything, she said, no mirrors, she just wanted to go straight to Herr Karl to have her hair done. The charged atmosphere in the booth was already unbearable, and Beatrix fled. In the past hour she had completely lost the affectionate spirit and the fun of gossiping she usually enjoyed at René's, and she sat down in the front room to wait for Herr Karl.

She first looked up when he rushed over—they were already preparing to close—and called out to Toni to come and hold the dryer, and she gave him a look of stern reproach. Beatrix hoped that he would understand her instantly. But Herr Karl was furious only about the missing rollers, and that was really the limit, but no, there was more to come, because even before she could answer she looked in the mirror after all, steered by some uncontrollable force. She was at a loss for words and said so: Herr Karl, I'm at a loss for words. Look at this makeup, I don't want to say what I look like, you can see for yourself!

Herr Karl was already working with the brush, he combed and dried each strand as though he hadn't noticed anything, and that was her most bitter disappointment of all. It was as though her secretive face had never existed. But my dear young woman—thank God he hadn't said "My dear madam" to her, that would have stretched her strained nerves to the breaking point—I know that you're so accustomed to Frau Hilde, but in my opinion, this new makeup isn't bad at all. Beatrix controlled herself and thought this is just too much to bear, at least he could have said she looked ghastly and her eyes were a catastrophe. She wasn't blind, she saw it clearly: irregular lines, too thick, too much black, it was a downright catastrophe. Herr Karl said merely to distract her: Unfortunately, it's pouring again, you always come when it's raining. Beatrix still hadn't answered, she was debating feverishly what to do, she couldn't possibly meet Erich like this, couldn't risk arriving at the Hochhaus Café at the same time he did; the only thing she could do was dash into the Linde Restaurant, go to the ladies' room and wash off this paint, but water wouldn't do the job, and so she grabbed one of the cotton balls lying around, saw a jar of cream standing in front of her that said *leave on overnight,* but she couldn't understand that damn English, and while he asked her to hold her head straight, she desperately began rubbing her eyes with the cotton balls and the cream, she just had to get this stuff off, she looked like a whore and Erich would think she'd gone crazy, but this wasn't the right cream, and Herr Karl was aghast and said something but she wasn't listening, she kept wiping and rubbing her eyelids, and suddenly just couldn't go on, broke into uncontrollable sobs, the mascara ran from her eyes, and as the black and blue tears flowed down her cheeks she jumped up and screamed: Leave me alone, have someone bring me my coat right now. But because her dress was in the back, too, she ran to the dressing room, flung the René smock to the floor and pulled on her dress, the coat, and she sobbed and sobbed, she just couldn't negotiate with Frau Yvonne now and distribute the tips, and Herr Karl, who had run after her but wasn't allowed to go into the "Ladies," was waiting and addressed her: My dear young woman, please allow me, what's wrong, I can't just let you . . .

Beatrix didn't even look at him and only called out as she was leaving: I'll pay next time, I'll be late! She dashed out and down the steps, but Herr Karl caught up with her; she had forgotten her umbrella and it was raining outside, pouring, and he wanted to say something else, but Beatrix, who had taken the umbrella but didn't open it, was already outside the door and said, with the rain whipping at her face: And I've been sitting around here the whole afternoon, I've lost an entire afternoon, I don't have all that time to waste! By the time she had hurled the entire afternoon in his face, her head was dripping wet, the hairdo dissolved, but she categorically refused Herr Karl's proffered handkerchief.

Don't you understand! My whole day is shot!

She crossed the street, and in the Linde, in the powder room adjoining the ladies' room she resumed her helpless sobbing and then remembered Erich who was already waiting, but today he'd wait in vain. Hopefully Guggi had committed suicide and he wasn't waiting. All of a sudden she was certain that Guggi had committed suicide; she stopped crying and looked in the mirror. A catastrophe.

To the old women who looked after the restroom she said: It's a catastrophe. I've lost everything. People are just so inconsiderate. The old woman took her in her arms and said comfortingly: There, there, child! And Beatrix said, with monumental composure: I'm not a child, it's just that everyone is so inconsiderate. I have to get this smeary mess off my face right now.

Ah yes, those men, said the old woman, in a knowing, sympathetic tone. Beatrix didn't understand at first, but then, for the sake of an old woman who still believed in fairy tales, she let out another loud sob. She could do an old woman a favor, leave her illusions intact.

Ah yes, those men!

Eyes to Wonder

In Memory of Georg Groddeck

At first her left eye had been 20:80 and her right eye 20:140, Miranda remembers, but now both eyes are in harmony at 20:1200. The near point in her range of vision has come abnormally close, and the far point is closing in, too. Once she had wanted to memorize the prescription for her glasses so that in case she ever had an accident—for instance on vacation—she could have new glasses made immediately. On second thought she had decided against it because her astigmatism had also complicated the prescription, and this additional abnormality frightens her, because she will never really understand why her meridians are impaired and their refractive power will never coincide. The expression "distorted vision" does not bode well for her either, and she says to Josef with an air of self-importance: Having distorted vision, you know, that's worse than being blind.

But there are times when Miranda views her defective optical system as a "gift from heaven." She is always armed with this kind of maxim attributing everything to the will of the heavens, God and the saints—yes, a gift from heaven, that's what they are, although perhaps only an inherited gift after all. She is astonished at how other people can stand it day after day, seeing what they see and have to witness. Or do the others suffer less from it because they have no other way of system viewing the world? Perhaps normal vision, including normal astigmatism, completely dulled people's senses, and in that case Miranda would no longer have to reproach herself for living with a privilege, a mark of distinction.

Miranda certainly would not love Josef any less if she had to see his yellow-stained teeth every time he laughed. She knows what these teeth are like close up, but the possibility of "always seeing" makes her uneasy. It probably wouldn't bother her, either, to be startled by the network of lines etched around his eyes when he's tired. Nevertheless, she is grateful to be spared such precise vision and that her feelings cannot be influenced or diminished by it. Anyway, she notices at the blink of an eye—because she receives signals on other wavelengths—whether Josef is tired, why he's tired, whether his laughter is presumptuous or pained. Unlike others, she doesn't need to see him in a sharp outline, doesn't fix anyone with her eyes, doesn't photograph people through her glasses, but rather paints them in her own style, relying on other impressions, and now Josef is her masterpiece and has been from the very beginning. She fell in love with him at first sight, although any eye doctor would have shaken his head at that, because Miranda's first glances only result in catastrophic errors. But she holds fast to her first glance and of all the men she has known, Josef is the one with whose early sketches and the subsequent, more detailed drafts, in light, in darkness, and every conceivable situation Miranda is truly satisfied.

With the aid of a minute correction—that of the dispersing lens—in a gold frame perched on her nose, Miranda can see into hell. This inferno has never became any less frightening to her. That is why she is continually on the alert: she scans a restaurant cautiously before putting on her glasses to read the menu, looks up and down the street when she wants to hail a cab. If she isn't careful things might enter her field of vision which she can never forget: a glimpse of a crippled child or a midget or a woman with an amputated arm, but those are merely the most glaring, conspicuous apparitions in the midst of a mass of unhappy, malicious and damned faces marked by humiliations and injustices, nightmarish faces. And their emanation, the all-pervading ugliness they exude, forces tears to her eyes, makes her lose her footing, and to avoid this she reads through the menu hastily and tries, in a split second, to differentiate between a taxi and an ordinary car, then puts her glasses away, needing very little information. She is not interested in knowing more. (Once, as a form of self-punishment, she walked all around Vienna with her glasses on, through district after district, and she feels it wouldn't be right to repeat that walk. It would go beyond her strength, and she needs all her strength to cope with the world she knows.)

Some people do not take Miranda's apologies seriously when she fails to say "hello" or respond to greetings; others dismiss them as dumb excuses or find them to be a peculiar brand of arrogance. Stasi says, almost spitefully:

Then put on a pair of glasses!

No, never, never again, Miranda replies, it's no use, I can't bear it. Would you wear them?

Stasi counters:

Me? Why me? My vision is decent.

Decent, Miranda thinks, why decent? And she inquires somewhat meekly: But can you understand that I don't do it out of vanity?

Stasi leaves Miranda without an answer, and that means: Not only fabulously conceited, she's vain as well, and to top it off the fabulous luck she always has with men—if it was true—but that damn Josef was so reserved, it was hard to get any information out of him.

To Josef, Miranda says:

Stasi has calmed down a lot, she never used to be so nice, I think she's in love, at least something must be doing her good. What does he want from her anyway, a divorce and the child? The whole thing is beyond me.

Josef is distracted, as though he doesn't know who she's talking about. Yes, he thinks so, too, Stasi has become much more pleasant, he says, almost sociable, maybe that was due to Berti's feat of medical expertise or maybe even Miranda or simply their joint effort; Stasi had simply been worn to a frazzle, had become embittered from all that bad luck, but now she's been awarded custody after all. That is the first Miranda has heard of this, and she hears it from Josef. She wants to call Stasi right away and rejoice, but then suddenly feels cold; she checks to see if the window is open, but it's shut. Josef looks back down at his newspaper, Miranda at the roof across the street. How gloomy it is in this street; all these buildings are so gloomy and expensive, an execution site from the good old days.

Miranda has been waiting in the Arabia-Espresso, now it's time to go, she pays and leaves, banging her head against the Espresso's glass door. She rubs her forehead, there'll be another bump, and the old one has just barely disappeared, she should apply ice immediately, but where would she to get ice now? Glass doors are more hostile than people; in this respect Miranda never stops hoping that people will take care of her as Josef does, and in no time she is smiling trustfully again, on the sidewalk. She could be mistaken, though, because Josef had wanted to go to the bank first and then to the bookstore or the other way around, and so she waits in the Graben and tries to spot him among those crossing the street, and then she stands in the Wollzeile with her eyes open wide and blurry. She glances back and forth between the Rotenturmstrasse and the Parkring, convinced that he is close by, then that he is far away, oh there he is, coming down the Rotenturmstrasse after all, but she is happy about seeing a complete stranger who is abruptly dismissed from her affection as soon as he is recognized as Not-Josef. Then the expectation sets in again, builds up, and in her nebulous world there is a sunrise of sorts after all, if somewhat belated, for the veil of haze is torn open and Josef appears. She slips her arm through his and walks on cheerfully.

The overcast world in which Miranda wants only one thing in particular, namely Josef, is the only one in which, in spite of everything, she feels at home. A more focused world is made possible by Vienna's Studio of Optometry or their foreign competitors Söhnges and Götte. But whether it is seen through leaded glass, lightweight or plastic lenses or

through the most modern type of contact lenses, Miranda
will never accept it. She makes a real effort, meets sudden
and unexpected resistance, gets a headache, her eyes water,
she is forced to lie down in a dark room. Once, before the
Opera Ball, but really only to surprise Josef, she had sent to
Munich for those expensive German contact lenses and read
the advertising slogan on the bill: Never lose sight of the best
things in life. Bent over a black cloth, she had attempted to
insert the tiny things, reciting the directions from memory,
blinded by pain-killing eyedrops, and then she had lost one
in the bathroom, never to be found again, it had leaped
down the drain in the shower or been smashed on the tiles,
and the other was under Miranda's eyelid, high up on her eye-
ball. Nothing could be done until Berti arrived, in spite of
a flood of tears, then another hour, in spite of Berti's
knowledgeable hand, still nothing could be done; Miranda
does not want to remember how and when Berti finally
found and removed the contact lenses, but now and again
she maintains: At least I tried my best.

Sometimes Josef, too, forgets when he talks to her that he
is dealing with a person who is not exactly blind but who
moves in a twilight zone between two worlds. It slips his
mind that Miranda doesn't necessarily know the things that
are common knowledge, but that her insecurity is nevertheless productive. Although she looks timid, she is by no means
weak: she's independent for the very reason that she knows
what's brewing in the jungle she lives in and is prepared for
anything. Because Miranda is incorrigible, reality is forced to
tolerate her modifications for the time being. She enlarges,
reduces, she directs shadows of trees and clouds, she admires
two moss-green lumps because she knows they must be the

Church of St. Charles, and in the Vienna Woods she doesn't see the trees but the forest, breathes deeply and tries to get her bearings.

Look over there, Mount Bisam!

It's only Mount Leopold, but that doesn't matter. Josef is patient. Where are your glasses this time?—Oh, you left them in the car. And why couldn't it just this once really be Mount Bisam? Miranda asks herself and begs Mount Leopold to do her the favor some day of being the right mountain.

Tender and trusting and always half-snuggled in Josef's gaunt frame, she takes the next hurdles of roots on the pathway in stride. "Tender" is not only the way Miranda feels at the moment; everything about Miranda is tender, from her voice to her groping feet, including her only function in the world, which might simply be to be tender.

When Miranda boards a streetcar in Vienna and sways between the passengers on the Ring line, she fails to notice that naked hate reigns between the conductor and the old woman with the wrong ticket and that the pushing-to-get-in shovers are rabid and the shoving-to-get-off pushers have a murderous glint in their eyes. When she succeeds in making her way to the exit mumbling a series of "excuse-me's," glad that she has recognized the Schottenring in time, and finds her way down the two steps unaided—then Miranda thinks that everyone is just "tremendously kind." The other passengers moving off in the direction of the university fail to realize why the atmosphere has brightened and the air is breatheable again; only the conductor has noticed that someone has forgotten his change, probably the woman who got out at the Stock Exchange or at the Schottenring. Good-looking woman. Nice legs. He pockets the money.

Whereas things are usually stolen from others, Miranda loses them, and she passes people by untouched instead of bumping into them. Or she does in fact have a collision, but then it was only a mistake, purely accidental: she was to blame. Miranda could have Masses said for all the drivers who didn't run her over or dedicate candles to St. Florian for all the days her apartment didn't go up in flames from the cigarettes she lights and puts down, searches for and then, thank goodness, finds, even if a hole has already been burned into the table.

Sad though, yes, a little sad, the number of stains, scorch marks, overheated burners, and ruined saucepans in Miranda's apartment. But things always turn out all right in the end, and whenever Miranda opens the door because the bell has rung and, unexpectedly, a perfect stranger is standing there, she is persistently lucky. It's Uncle Hubert, it's her old friend Robert, and she hugs Uncle Hubert or Robert or whoever it is. Admittedly it could have been a salesman or a burglar instead, Novak the Killer, or the "Womanslayer" still at large and terrorizing the streets of the first district, but only her best friends come to visit Miranda in the Blutgasse. There are others whom Miranda doesn't recognize anyway, at larger gatherings, at parties, in the theaters and concert halls; and these people, with their effervescent presence or doubtful absence, encounter a Miranda who is not unsociable. She just isn't quite sure if Doctor Bucher has said hello from across the way or maybe not said hello, though it could be, when she considered height and breadth, that it was Herr Langbein. She can't decide. In a world composed of alibis and double checks, Miranda is puzzled—naturally not by some global enigma, but rather by things of no great significance. But still: Is that Herr Langbein's outline or isn't it? It remains a mystery. When everyone else strives for clarity, Miranda retreats, no, she just doesn't have the ambition for that, and whereas others suspect some sort of secret to be lurking behind anything and everything, Miranda has only one secret: in front of her. A distance of two meters suffices to make the world or a person impenetrable to her.

Hers is the most relaxed face at the Musik-Verein, an oasis of peace in a hall where she can be seen by at least twenty gesticulating people, while she herself sees no one. She has learned to refrain from being nervous in rooms when people look around and take stock of one another, write each other off, avoid or eye one another. Miranda doesn't dream, she simply rests. When Miranda's eyes are at ease, her mind is at peace. Her gloves steal quietly away and slip under her chair. Miranda feels something on her calf, she is afraid that she has accidentally grazed her neighbor's leg and murmurs, "Excuse me." A chair leg has fallen in love with Miranda. Josef retrieves the program, Miranda smiles uncertainly and tries to hold her legs straight and still. Doctor Bucher, who is not Herr Langbein but rather Herr Kopetzky, sits offended three rows behind her, searching for reasons why this woman is so fickle, this woman for whom he once would have given anything, everything—

Josef asks:

Do you have your glasses?

Of course I do, Miranda says and digs into her purse. She has the feeling she brought her gloves, too, but better not tell Josef that, no, her glasses, that's odd, well then, maybe they're in the bathroom or right next to the door or in her other coat or, Miranda doesn't understand, but she says swiftly:

No, I don't have them with me. But I don't need to see anything at a concert.

Josef says nothing, moved by his refrain for Miranda: my innocent angel.

In Miranda's eyes, other women have no defects; they aren't plagued by hairy legs or mustaches sprouting on their upper lips; they are creatures of perfection, consistently well-groomed, without pores or rough skin, free of pimples and nicotine-stained fingers, no, she alone fights a lonesome battle against her imperfections in front of the shaving mirror that once belonged to Josef, seeing what she hopes Josef can mercifully overlook. But afterward, when Miranda has finished her bout of self-criticism, she poses before the more lenient Biedermeier mirror in the bedroom and judges herself "presentable," "okay," it's not all that bad, and she deceives herself here, too, but then Miranda lives with a dozen possibilities for self-deception, and every day of her life she tries to maintain a balance between the most and least favorable.

In good times, Miranda has three pairs of glasses: prescription sunglasses with gold rims inlaid with black; a cheaper model with see-through frames for the house; and a pair in reserve which has a loose lens and supposedly doesn't suit her. Besides, it seems to have been made from an old prescription, because everything is out of focus when she is forced to resort to her "reserve" pair.

There are times when all three pairs of glasses have vanished or been lost or misplaced, and then Miranda really doesn't know what to do. Josef comes over from the Prinz-Eugen-Strasse before eight in the morning and makes a thorough search of the entire apartment, scolds Miranda, ac-

cuses the cleaning woman and the workmen, but Miranda
knows that people don't steal, it's just all her fault. Because
Miranda doesn't tolerate reality but can't get along without
some reference points, reality occasionally takes its revenge.
Miranda understands this, she nods conspiratorially at the
objects, the props which serve as the scenery surrounding her
life, and on days like these the funny furrow deepens, the one
that shouldn't be there yet, but which comes from the intensity with which she opens and shuts her eyes. Josef promises
to go to the optician immediately, for Miranda cannot get
along without glasses, and she thanks him, clinging to him
in sudden fear and wanting to say something, not only because he's come and helped her but because he helps her to
see and to see ahead. Miranda doesn't know what's wrong
with her; she wishes she could say: "Help me, please!" And
the disjointed thought occurs to her: She's just more beautiful than I am.

During the week when Miranda has to wait, when she
can't go out and loses her perspective, Josef has to go out to
dinner twice with Anastasia to counsel her about the
divorce. After the first time, Stasi calls the next morning; the
second time she doesn't call anymore.

Yes, we were at the "Roman Emperor." Awful. It had been
bad, the food, and she had been freezing.

Miranda is unable to reply; to her the "Roman Emperor"
is the nicest and best place in all Vienna, because it was
there that she and Josef ate dinner together for the first time,
and now all of a sudden it was supposed to be the most
awful—Miranda, can you hear me? Well, like I said. Afterward the Eden Bar. Horrible. The clientele at that place!

There surely must be something to Stasi's idea of clientele, but what could it be? Miranda breathes more easily again. She's never been to the Eden Bar with Josef, that's a slight comfort. Is she just acting or is she really like this?

After another half-hour of details, Stasi reassures her: At least you didn't miss anything.

Miranda wouldn't have put it like that, "didn't miss anything"; she's afraid she's missing everything these days. The week just won't come to an end, and every day has an evening when Josef is unable to come by. Then the glasses are done, he brings them over from the optician just a few hours later, but it happens again immediately. Miranda is in a daze and has to lie down, to wait and figure out when Josef will arrive in his Prinz-Eugen-Strasse. When she finally reaches him, she doesn't know how to begin to tell him that the new pair has fallen into the sink.

Yes, you know, into the bathroom sink. I feel like an invalid, I can't go out, I can't see anyone. You understand.

Josef's voice reaches her from the fourth district:

This is a nice mess. But you've gone out often enough before without your glasses.

Yes, but. Miranda is unable to produce any convincing arguments. Yes, but this is different, because I usually have them in my purse.

No, you don't. Come on now, just stop it.

But we don't have to, just because of this, Miranda says in a whisper, why do you sound like that?

What do you mean, how do I sound?

Different, just different.

And because he doesn't answer, she rushes to say:

Okay, dear, I'll come anyway, I just feel so insecure, yesterday I almost, yes, almost but not quite fainted, really, it's terrible, I tried my "reserve" pair, but everything was out of focus, distorted, you understand what I mean.

When Josef is quiet this way, it means he hasn't understood.

I regret to say I fail to see the logic in that, this different-sounding Josef says and hangs up.

Miranda sits in front of the telephone, guilty. To make things worse, now she's even given Josef a reason, but for what? Why do my glasses have to fall into the sink, why does Josef have to and why does the world, oh God, this can't be happening. Aren't there any other restaurants in Vienna? Does Josef have to go to the "Roman Emperor" with her? Does Miranda have to cry, does she have to live in a gloomy hole, walk the length of the bookshelves, her face pressed against the bindings, and chance upon a volume entitled *De l'Amour*? After laboring through the first twenty pages, she gets dizzy, slumps further down in her chair, the book on her face, and topples over onto the floor with the chair. The world has gone black.

Because she knows that her glasses didn't fall into the sink by accident—she will have to lose Josef and would rather lose him voluntarily—she sets herself in motion. She takes the first steps toward an end she will one day discover, blinded by fear. She mustn't allow Josef and Anastasia to guess that she is letting them drift toward each other, Stasi in particular, and thus she must invent a story for all of them which is more bearable and better than the real one: Josef has never really mattered much to her, that was the main thing. She is already practicing her role. Josef is a good, dear old friend and nothing more, and she will be happy for them, she knew it, suspected it all along. What she doesn't know is what the two of them are really doing and planning, how far they've already gone and how they will bring about her downfall. Miranda calls Ernst, and after a few days he is encouraged and begins calling her again. To Stasi she drops a few incomprehensible hints, then half-confesses: Ernst and I, you can't see it like that, no, who says that? no, it was never really over, after all, that's, well, you're one person I can, always been more than just another one of those affairs, you know—

And she mumbles something else, as though she has already gone too far. A confused Anastasia learns that Miranda is still hung up on Ernst, and no one in the entire city has had the slightest idea, although here supposedly everyone knows everything about everyone.

Miranda goes so far as to arrange to meet Stasi, in time to be seen standing in the doorway with Ernst, where she begins to kiss an indecisive, embarrassed Ernst and asks him, between kisses and excited laughter, if he still remembers how to unlock her door.

Stasi discusses the doorway scene in detail with Josef. She saw it all very clearly. Josef doesn't say much, he doesn't feel like dwelling on the picture of Miranda in Ernst's arms in the doorway. Josef is certain that he is the only man in Miranda's life, but the next morning, after he has made breakfast for Anastasia, his mood has improved. He thinks it's not so bad after all, even a relief, and in any case, Anastasia is a very intelligent woman gifted with keen insight. He will get used to the idea that Miranda needs other men, that Ernst suits her better after all, if only because of their common interests, and he could even see her with Berti or with Fritz, who talks about her in such atrocious terms because he's never had any luck with Miranda but would still jump at the chance if she

wanted him. Josef perceives in Miranda a new power of at-
traction, which he has never been aware of before, and when
Anastasia brings up the subject again, he almost proudly believes her quite capable of causing real devastation.

Fritz, the poor guy, he's been drinking ever since.

Josef isn't as sure about that as Anastasia: Fritz drank before, too. And once he even defends her, feebly. Stasi dissects
Miranda's character and claims that, above all, she has none:
she's constantly changing. One day she makes an elegant appearance at the theater, the next she's unkempt, her hem is
uneven, or she hasn't been to the hairdresser's for weeks. Josef
says:

But you don't understand. It all depends on whether she's
found her glasses or not, and then it depends on whether she
puts them on or not.

The silly goose, Stasi thinks, he's still attached to her, no,
I'm the one who's the silly goose, because I'm raising my
hopes about Josef, and now he doesn't know what he wants,
what does he want? But that's clear as glass, the cunning,
slovenly, silly, the—at this point Stasi is at a loss for words—
she has him eating out of her hand with her helplessness,
Josef wants to play the protector, but who's going to protect
me?

And two teardrops fall from her pretty blue eyes with their
decent vision and land in the orange juice, and she swears
that she will never cry again as long as she lives, at least not
this year and not because of Josef.

Josef's holy Miranda, patron of all those living in a border-
line world, is led to the stake by Stasi: roasted, carved, ske-
wered, and burned to death, and Miranda can sense it physi-
cally, although she will never hear a word of it. She doesn't

dare leave the house, just sits around with her new replace-
ment pair, not wanting to go out on the street. Ernst comes
over for tea and they make plans for a visit to the Salzkam-
mergut, and Berti comes over to check on her, he thinks she
is suffering from a vitamin deficiency. Miranda looks at him
trustingly, that's her opinion exactly, and she volunteers to
eat large quantities of raw carrots. Berti says, writing out a
long prescription:

They're good for your eyes, too.

Miranda says gratefully:

Of course, you know, my eyes are the most important thing.

But she can hardly look at Josef any more. She always looks
to his left or to his right or past him somehow so that her
gaze drifts into the distance. She wishes she could hold her
hand in front of her eyes because she still has the strongest
temptation to gaze at Josef in rapture. It hurts her eyes, this
act he's putting on for her, she doesn't have the aches other
people do: it's not her heart, her stomach or her head. Her
eyes alone have to stand all the pain, because seeing Josef
had been the most important thing in the world for her. And
now every day is full of seeing-Josef-less, seeing-less-of-Josef.

Miranda puts ice in Josef's glass, and Josef sprawls there as
he always did, as if it were the most natural thing in the
world, but he is talking about Stasi as though they had always
talked about Stasi. Sometimes he says ceremoniously:
Anastasia. Miranda, with Josef constantly in her way, looks
down at her manicured fingernails. "Porcelain," that was the
polish which had accompanied her Josef-days, but now that
Josef only fleetingly kisses her hand when he comes and goes
and no longer admires and pores over the porcelain, perhaps
she can do without this polish, too. Miranda jumps up and

closes the window. She is hypersensitive to noise. Lately this city seems to be made of noise: radios, TV's, young yapping dogs, and those small delivery trucks, wait, Miranda stops short at that: she can't wish to lose her hearing on top of everything else! And then she would still hear noise just as peristently but no longer be able to discern that voice, the voice she most likes to hear.

Miranda says pensively:

With me everything depends on my sense of hearing, I have to like a person's voice, otherwise it won't come to anything.

But doesn't she profess to liking only beautiful people? No one knows more beautiful people than Miranda, she attracts them because she places more emphasis on beauty than on any other quality. If she is abandoned—and Josef is now in the process of leaving her—then it will be because Anastasia is more beautiful or especially beautiful. This is the explana- tion for all the vicissitudes of Miranda's life.

(Do you understand, Berti? She was simply more beautiful than I am.)

What was Josef talking about all the time, ah yes, about her again, if she wasn't deceived.

It's very, very rare, Josef is saying.

Oh, you think so?—Miranda still hasn't grasped what he's said. She pays less and less attention when he talks.

Yes, he says, with you it's possible.

So that's what he's aiming at, and now Miranda looks at him for the first time in weeks. Oh yes, she will transform this terrible, pious lie into a truth. Doesn't he understand? Good friends—she and Josef, good friends?

Well, Miranda says, good friends aren't all that rare. And

an inner, different Miranda who is less sublime is beside her-self: My God, is this man an idiot, he's a real idiot, can't he understand a thing, is he never going to wake up, and why oh why does the only man I like have to be like this!

Naturally they'd go to the Sunday concert together, Josef states matter-of-factly. Miranda doesn't think it's all that natural anymore. But because Stasi has to see her husband on Sundays to debate the question of the child again, one Sunday is left over for her.

What, Mahler's Fourth, not again? she says.

No, it's the Sixth, I said. Do you still remember London? Yes, Miranda says, her confidence has returned, she'll listen to Mahler once more with Josef, and Stasi won't be able to ruin a single note, not even to dispute her right to Josef on the staircase at the Musik-Verein, as long as she's busy on Sunday with the "Great Debate."

After the concert, Josef goes home with Miranda after all, acting as though it isn't the last time. He can't just come out and tell her, in a few weeks she'll have realized it, she seems so reasonable. Slowly he puts his shoes on and then hunts for his tie; he knots and straightens it with an absent expression, not once looking at Miranda. He pours himself a Sliwowitz, stands at the window and gazes down at the street sign: 1. Blutgasse. Blood Lane. My innocent angel. For a moment he takes Miranda in his arms and presses his mouth to her hair; he is incapable of seeing or feeling anything but the word "Blutgasse." Who is doing this to us? What are we doing to each other? Why do I have to do this? and he wishes he could kiss Miranda, but he can't, and so he only thinks, executions are still taking place, it's an execution, because every-thing I'm doing is an undoing, the deeds themselves are just misdeeds in the end. And his angel is watching him with her eyes open wide, their openness asks a question, as though there were some last thing about Josef to be understood, but ultimately they have an even more devastating expression for him, for it sets him free and forgives him. Because Josef knows that no one will ever look at him this way again, not even Anastasia, he closes his eyes.

Miranda doesn't notice when the door closes, she hears only the sound of a garage door slamming from below, brawls from a distant bar, drunks on the street, the musical prelude to a radio program; she no longer wants to live imprisoned in this noise, this cell of light and darkness, her sole remaining access to the world by way of a droning headache that forces her eyes closed: they have been open too long. Now what was the last thing she saw? She saw Josef.

They meet again in Salzburg, in the Bazar Café. Anastasia and Josef enter as a couple, and Miranda is trembling only because Stasi looks so angry or unhappy, what's wrong with her anyway, how am I of all people supposed to—and Miranda, who has always flown to Josef, now hears him say something derisive, joking, then Stasi darkens and leaves him, coming over to her. While Josef—fleeing, but not from her?—pays his respects to old Court Counsellor Perschy and then to the Altenwyls and the rest of the clique, Miranda stands up, slipping on her sandals with a jerk, and flies clumsily at a pale Stasi, a tinge of red coloring her face when she kisses Stasi on the cheek and mumbles, blushing out of hypocrisy and the strain of controlling herself:

I'm so happy for you, and for Josef, too, of course, yes, the card, thanks a lot, I got it.

She holds out her hand to Josef fleetingly, laughing, hello, and Stasi says magnanimously: Come on, Josef, give Miranda a kiss.

Miranda pretends not to have heard, she steps back, pulling Anastasia with her, whispering and chattering, her face a deeper shade of red with each word, you know, sorry, this Salzburg is one confusing place, no, no, nothing serious, but right afterward I have to, Ernst, who suddenly, you know what I mean. Break it to Josef somehow, you'll know how to handle it.

Miranda is in a hurry, she catches a final glimpse of Anastasia nodding that she's understood and all at once she seems "nice" but her face is suddenly flushed, too. But it could also be that only she is so feverish and that her impression of a tawdry world is getting the better of her. Surely she'll make it to the hotel with this scarlet fever, this burning shame on her face and in her limbs, and she sees the swinging doors but doesn't see that the doors don't want to swing in her direction, one of them is coming at her and her last thought, even as she is hurled to the floor under a shower of broken glass, even warmer now from the impact and the blood that is streaming out of her nose and mouth, is: Never lose sight of the good things in life.

The Barking

Old Frau Jordan had been called "old Frau Jordan" for the past three decades because there had been first one and now another young Frau Jordan, and although she did live in Hietzing, she had only a one-room apartment in a dilapidated villa, with a tiny kitchen and no more than half a tub in the bathroom. From her distinguished son Leo, the professor, she received 1,000 schillings per month, and somehow she managed to make do, although those 1,000 schillings had depreciated so much over the last twenty years that she was just barely able to pay an older woman, a certain Frau Agnes who "looked in" on her twice a week, to tidy up a little, just "the bare minimum." She even saved some of the money for birthday and Christmas presents for her son and grandson from her son's first marriage, whom the first young wife sent over punctually every Christmas to pick up his present. Leo on the other hand was too busy to notice, and since he had become famous and his local prestige had blossomed into international renown, he was busier than ever. Things only changed when the latest young Frau Jordan began to visit the old woman as often as she could, a really nice, likable girl, as the old woman soon admitted to herself, but at each visit she said only: But Franziska, it's not right, you shouldn't come so often, it's such a waste. You two surely have enough expenses as it is, but Leo is just such a good son!

Franziska always brought something with her, delicacies and sherry, some pastries, because she had guessed that the old woman liked to take a sip now and then and, moreover, attached great importance to having something in the house "for the company." After all, Leo might drop by, and he mustn't notice how much she was missing and that all day long she wondered how to allocate her money and how much she could put aside for presents. Her apartment was meticulously clean, but gave off a faint "old-woman" smell which she was not aware of and which put Leo Jordan to flight, apart from the fact that he had no time to lose and no idea what to talk about with his eighty-five-year-old mother. Sometimes, seldom, he had been amused—that much Franziska knew—namely, when he was having a relationship with a married woman, because then old Frau Jordan had gone without sleep and made strange, convoluted allusions, trembling for his safety: she believed that the married men whose wives Leo Jordan was living with were dangerous and jealous and bloodthirsty, and she wasn't able to calm down until he married Franziska, who did not have a jealous husband lurking in the bushes but was young and cheerful, an orphan, admittedly not from an educated family, but at least with a brother who had gone to college. Families of the educated classes and educated men in general carried great weight with Frau Jordan, although she didn't do much socializing; she only heard about things. But her son had the right to marry into an educated family. The old woman and Franziska talked almost exclusively about Leo, because he was the only productive topic the two of them had, and Franziska was shown the photo album over and over again, Leo in a stroller, Leo at the beach, and Leo through the years, taking hikes, pasting stamps in his collection, and so on until his military service.

The Leo she came to know through the old woman was a completely different Leo from the man she had married, and when the two women sat drinking their sherry the old woman would say: He was a complicated child, a strange boy, actually you could tell all along that he was destined for great things.

For a while Franziska was happy to hear these assertions, that Leo was so good to his mother and had always done everything conceivable to help her, but then she noticed that something was wrong, and with dismay she realized—the old woman was afraid of her son. It began with the old woman saying, sometimes hastily and parenthetically (she believed it to be a clever tactic that Franziska would never see through because she was blinded by admiration for her husband): But please don't mention a word of it to Leo, you know how concerned he is, it might upset him, whatever you do, please don't tell him that something is wrong with my knee, it's such a little thing, he might get upset about it.

Although Franziska had since learned that Leo never got

upset at all, certainly not because of his mother, and only listened to her reports with half an ear, she suppressed this first realization. Unfortunately she had already told him about the knee but swore to the old woman she wouldn't say a word. Leo had reacted with annoyance and then, to placate her, had explained that he really couldn't drive out to Hietzing because of such a trifle. Just tell her—he rattled off some medical terminology—she should buy this and that and do and walk as little as possible. Franziska bought the medication without further comment and claimed in Hietzing that she had secretly spoken with one of her husband's assistants without mentioning any names and that he had given her this advice, although she was at a loss as to how to keep the old woman in bed without the help of a nurse. But she no longer had enough courage to approach Leo about it, because a nurse cost money, and now she was caught in the middle. On the one hand Frau Jordan didn't want anything to do with it, and on the other Leo Jordan—albeit for completely different reasons—simply didn't want to hear about it. When Frau Jordan's knee was swollen, Franziska lied to her husband several times: she drove quickly to Hietzing, allegedly to the hairdresser's, and straightened up the little apartment, bringing all sorts of things with her. She purchased a radio but was uneasy afterward: Leo was bound to notice the expenditure, so she quickly transferred the money back and broke into the meager savings she had set aside for some sort of emergency which would hopefully never arise and could only be a minor emergency at any rate. She and her brother had divided what little remained after the death of their entire family, with the exception of a cottage in southern Carinthia which was slowly falling into disrepair. In the end she called a general practitioner in the neighborhood and asked him to treat the old woman for a while, paying him out of her own savings. More importantly, she didn't dare reveal to the doctor who she was and who the old woman was, because that would only have hurt Leo's reputation, and protecting Leo's reputation was also in Franziska's best interest. But the old woman thought much more selflessly: there was no way she could ask her famous son to go so far as to come and take a look at her knee. She had used a cane before on occasion, but after this knee problem she really needed it, so Franziska sometimes drove her to town. Shopping with the old woman was a somewhat laborious undertaking: once she had only needed a comb, but there were no combs like the ones "in her day," and although the old woman was polite, standing in the store with erect dignity, she annoyed the little saleswoman by eyeing the price tags suspiciously, unable to refrain from telling Franziska in a clearly audible whisper that the prices here were outrageous, they'd better go somewhere else. The saleswoman, who was in no position to judge how important buying this comb was to the old woman, replied rudely that they wouldn't find this comb cheaper anywhere in town. Franziska launched into embarrassed negotiations with the mother, took the comb the old woman wanted but looked on as costing a fortune and quickly paid for it, saying: Just consider it a Christmas present from us, a present in advance. Prices have really gone up horrendously everywhere. The old woman didn't say a word, she sensed her defeat, but still, if prices really were so outrageous—a comb like this used to cost two schillings and nowadays it cost sixty—well then there wasn't much left for her to understand in this world.

After a while the topic "the good son" had been exhausted

and Franziska repeatedly steered the conversation to the old woman herself, because the only thing she knew was that Leo's father had died young of a heart attack or stroke, quite suddenly, on a staircase, and that must have been a long time ago, because if you stopped to figure it out this woman had been a widow for almost half a century. First she had worked for years to raise her only child, and then she was suddenly an old woman nobody cared about anymore. She never spoke about her marriage, only in connection with Leo who had had a very difficult life, without a father, and she was so preoccupied with Leo that she failed to see the parallel to Franziska, who had lost both her parents when she was young. Her son was the only one who could have had a difficult time, and then it turned out that it hadn't been so bad after all, because a distant cousin had paid for his education, a certain Johannes about whom Franziska had heard very little, merely a few derogatory, critical references to some eternal—now aging—loafer who was swimming in money and supposedly led a life of idleness with all its ridiculous affectations. He dabbled a little in art, collected Chinese lacquerware, and was just another one of those freeloaders found in every family. Franziska knew also that he was homosexual, but she was really amazed how someone like Leo, whose very profession obliged him to uphold a neutral and scientific attitude toward homosexuality and phenomena of a quite different magnitude, could go on and on about this cousin as though he had somehow, through his own negligence, fallen prey to works of art, homosexuality, and an inheritance to boot, but at that time Franziska still admired her husband too much to be more than irritated and hurt. With relief she heard from the old woman, in discussing those hard times, that Leo was infinitely grateful and had been a big help to this Johannes, who was then in the throes of a number of personal crises—which were better left untold. The old woman hesitated and then added, because she was, after all, sitting opposite the wife of a psychiatrist: I think you should know that Johannes is sexual.

Franziska controlled herself and suppressed a laugh, it was surely the most daring revelation the old woman had roused herself to in years, but with Franziska she was opening up more and more. She told her how Leo had often given Johannes advice, naturally free of charge, but Johannes was a hopeless case, and if a person didn't have the willpower to change it was understandable that he would be at his wits' end, and from what she heard, Johannes just kept on with it, the same as always. Franziska carefully translated this naive story into reality and understood even less why Leo talked about this cousin in such a disparaging and malicious way. At that time the obvious reason escaped her, namely, that Leo was reluctant to be reminded of his mother and his former wives and lovers who were nothing to him but a conspiracy of creditors from whom he could escape only by belittling them to himself and others. His tirades about his first wife were similar: she had been the epitome of everything diabolical, unappreciative and spiteful, traits that had not been revealed in depth until the divorce when her aristocratic father had hired a lawyer for her to secure some of the money for the child, money she'd given him when he was a young doctor and hard times had struck again. It was an alarmingly large sum to Franziska but, as she was told, one could expect nothing less from the "baroness," as Leo ironically called her, because the family had always treated him like an upstart, without having the slightest idea who was dwelling in their midst. It amused him to note that the "baroness" had never remarried and lived in total seclusion. After him she hadn't been able to find another fool—young and gullible and poor, as he had been—who would have married such a deserving Fräulein. She had understood nothing about his work, absolutely nothing, and although she behaved fairly in respect to the agreement about their son, sending him for regular visits and teaching him to respect his father, she obviously did it for no other reason than to prove to the world how generous she was.

The brilliant doctor's rise to fame along the thorny path of suffering had already become Franziska's religion at that time, and again and again she reproached herself with the image of him making his way, against indescribable odds and despite the obstacle that dreadful marriage posed, all the way to the top. And the cross he was forced to bear because of his mother, the financial and moral burden, was no light one for him, but that at least Franziska could take off his shoulders. Although it otherwise might not have occurred to her to spend her free hours with an old woman the time became something special when she thought of Leo: a helping hand, evidence of her love for him, allowing him to devote his undivided attention to his work.

Leo was just too good to her, he told her that she was overdoing it, the way she took care of his mother, a telephone call now and again would have sufficed. For the past few years the old woman had had a telephone which she feared more than loved: she didn't like to talk on the phone and always shouted into the mouthpiece and couldn't hear what the other party said, and besides that, the phone was too expensive, but of course Franziska wasn't to mention that to Leo. Once the old woman—prompted by Franziska and a second glass of sherry—did in fact begin to talk about the old days, the very old days, and it turned out that she wasn't from an educated family, her father had knit gloves and socks in a small factory in Lower Austria and she had been the oldest of eight children, but then she'd had a wonderful time when she took up employment with a Greek family, immensely rich people with a little boy, the most beautiful child she had ever laid eyes on, and she was his nursemaid. Being a nursemaid was a really good job, nothing degrading about it, and the Greek's young wife had had servants aplenty, oh yes, she'd had a real stroke of luck, such a good position had been hard to find back then. The child's name was Kiki, at least everyone had called him Kiki. When the old woman began talking about Kiki more and more frequently, remembering every detail—what Kiki had said, how cute and affectionate he was, the walks they'd taken together—her eyes lit up as they never did when she spoke of her own child. Kiki had simply been a little angel, never naughty, she stressed, never naughty at all, and the separation must have been terrible, they hadn't told Kiki that the Fräulein was leaving, and she had cried all night long, and once, years later, she had tried to find out what had become of the family. First she'd heard that they were traveling, then that they were back in Greece, and now she had no idea whatsoever what had happened to Kiki, who must be over sixty by now, yes, over sixty she said pensively, and she had been forced to leave because the Greek family had planned their first major trip and couldn't take her along, and when they left the young wife had given her a wonderful present. The old woman stood up and rummaged in a jewelry box, then showed her the brooch from Kiki's mother, it was the real thing, with diamonds, but she still asked herself today if they hadn't let her go because the wife had noticed that Kiki was more attached to her than to his own mother, she could understand that all right, but it had been the hardest blow of all, and she had never completely recovered from it. Franziska regarded the brooch thoughtfully; perhaps it really was quite valuable, she didn't know much about jewelry, but she was beginning to realize something else: this Kiki must have meant more to the old woman than Leo. She often hesitated to talk about Leo's childhood, or she began only to break off in fright saying abruptly: It was just childish nonsense, you know boys are so hard to raise, he didn't do it on purpose, he was just having such a bad time and it was all I could do to make ends meet. But you get everything back a hundredfold when a child has grown up and made his own way and become so famous, he takes after his father more than me, you know.

Franziska carefully handed back the brooch, and once again the old woman started in fear. Please Franziska, don't mention a word of this to Leo, it could annoy him. I have my plans, you know, if I get sick I could sell it so that I won't become even more of a burden to him. Franziska embraced the old woman with a hug that was both timid and fierce. Don't ever do that, promise me you'll never sell this brooch. You're not a burden to us at all!

On the way home she made one detour after the other, in a state of inner turmoil, this poor woman shouldn't sell her brooch while she and Leo spent money freely, went on trips, entertained. She kept debating what she should say to Leo, but a first, faint alarm sounded inside her, because even though the old woman had her quirks and exaggerated things, she must be right about something, and so in the end she didn't say a word about it at home and only reported cheerfully that his mother was doing very well. But before they left for a conference in London she arranged a contract with a garage which ran a private taxi service, made a down-payment, and said to the old woman: An idea has occurred to us, because you shouldn't walk too far by yourself. Just call a taxi when you want to go out, it hardly costs a thing, it's just a favor from an old patient, but don't say anything about it, especially not to Leo, you know how he is, he doesn't like it when you thank him and everything, and you just ride to town when you need something, and have the taxi wait, but always have Herr Pineider take you, the young one. He doesn't know that his father was one of Leo's patients though, that comes under professional secrecy, you know, I was just there and talked to him, and you have to promise me, for Leo's sake, that you'll take the taxi, it would ease our minds. In the beginning, the old woman made little use of the taxi, and Franziska scolded her for it when she returned from England; her leg had worsened and the old woman had naturally done all her shopping on foot, once even going so far as to take the streetcar into town because one could hardly get anything in Hietzing, and Franziska said firmly, as if to a stubborn child: This is definitely not to happen again.

They exhausted one topic after another: Kiki, the life of a young nursemaid in Vienna before the First World War and before her marriage, and sometimes it was only Franziska who talked, especially when she had just returned from a trip with Leo, a brilliant talk he'd delivered at the conference, and that he had given her this offprint for his mother. The old woman labored through the title with an effort: "The Significance of Endogenous and Exogenous Factors in Connection with the Occurrence of Paranoid and Depressive Psychoses in Former Concentration Camp Inmates and Refugees." Franziska assured her it was merely the groundwork for a much larger study he was working on, and he was even letting her help him with it. It would probably become the most significant and the first really important book in the field. A work of incalculable impact.

The old woman was strangely mute, surely she didn't understand the implications of these studies, maybe nothing at all of what her son was doing. Then she said, surprisingly: I hope he won't make too many enemies with it, here in Vienna, and then there's that other thing . . .

Franziska grew agitated: But that's exactly the point, that would be a very good thing, it's a provocation, too, and Leo isn't afraid of anyone, for him it's the only thing that counts, that has a purpose far beyond its scientific significance.

Yes, of course, the old woman said quickly, and he knows how to defend himself, and if you're famous you always have enemies. I was just thinking about Johannes, but that's so long ago now. Did you know that he was in a concentration camp for a year and a half before the war ended? Franziska was surprised, she hadn't known, but she failed to see the connection. The old woman didn't want to say any more but then continued: It meant a certain amount of danger for Leo, having a relative who, well, you know what I mean. Yes, of course, said Franziska, still somewhat confused; sometimes the old woman had such a roundabout way of saying things without really saying them, and she couldn't make head or tail of it, although suddenly she was bursting with pride that

106

a member of Leo's family had been through something so terrible and that Leo, in his tactful, modest way, had never said anything about it to her, not even about the danger he must have faced as a young doctor. That afternoon the old woman didn't want to go on talking; she merely asked disjointedly: Do you hear it, too?

What?

The dogs, the old woman said. There were never so many dogs in Hietzing, I've heard them barking again, and they bark at night, too. Frau Schönthal next door has a poodle now. It doesn't bark much though, it's such a nice dog, I see her almost every day when I go shopping, but we only say hello, her husband doesn't have much of an education.

Franziska drove home as quickly as she could; this time she wanted to ask Leo if there was anything to the fact that his mother had suddenly begun talking about dogs, if it was an alarming symptom, maybe it had something to do with her age. She had also noticed that the old woman had been upset once about ten schillings which had been lying on the table and then disappeared when Frau Agnes left, all this excitement about ten missing schillings, certainly she had only imagined it anyway, weren't those all signs of the process of aging? It couldn't possibly have been the cleaning woman, she was what people in certain circles—that is, in better circles—called a "God-fearing" woman who came more out of pity than for the money, which she didn't need anyway—she did it as a favor and nothing more. And old Frau Jordan's pitiful presents—an ancient, threadbare purse or some other useless paraphernalia—would hardly have induced Frau Agnes to come; she had realized long ago that she had nothing to expect from the old woman or from her son, and she know nothing of Franziska's enthusiastic plans for improving the situation; Franziska had chided the old woman as though she were a child, because she didn't want to lose this valuable help over a bout of senile obstinacy and an unfounded suspicion.

More and more often she found the old woman at the window when she arrived, and they no longer sat together when Franziska came to drink sherry and nibble on pastries. The business with the dogs continued, although at the same time her hearing problem grew worse, and Franziska was at a loss. Something had to be done, and Leo, whom she bothered with none of this, was not going to avoid devoting some attention to his mother one of these days. Only then things started becoming complicated between Leo and herself, and she discovered that he had so intimidated her that she was afraid of him. But at least once, in a fit of her old courage, she overcame her inexplicable fear and suggested at dinner: Why don't we invite your mother to come and stay with us, we have enough room, and then our Rosi could always be with her and you would never have to worry, besides, she's so quiet and undemanding, she would never disturb you, and certainly not me, I'm suggesting it for your sake because I know how much you worry. Leo was in a good mood that evening and secretly happy about something. She didn't realize what it was but had decided to make use of the opportunity, and he answered, laughing: What an idea, you have no feel for the situation, my dear, you can't uproot an elderly person after a while, it would only depress her and she needs her freedom, she's a strong woman who has lived alone for decades. You don't know her the way I do, she would die of fright here, just from the kind of people who come over.

She'd probably debate for hours on end whether to use the bathroom, out of fear that one of us just might want to use it. Come on, my little Franziska, please don't make such a face, I think your impulse is touching and admirable, but that wonderful idea of yours would be the death of her. Believe me, it's just that I happen to know more about these things.

But this business with the dogs . . . ? Franziska began to stutter, she hadn't wanted to talk about it and would gladly have immediately taken back what she'd said. She was no longer capable of putting her apprehension into words.

What, her husband asked in a completely different tone of voice, she doesn't still want a mutt, does she? I don't understand, Franziska answered. Why should she—you don't mean she wants to have a dog, do you?

Of course I do, and I'm more than glad that this childish interlude has blown over so quickly, at her age she just couldn't handle a dog, she should take care of herself, that's more important to me, a dog is such a nuisance, she has no idea what that would mean, with her advancing senility. She never said anything about it, Franziska replied half-heartedly, I don't think she wants a dog. I wanted to say something entirely different, but it's not important, sorry. Would you like a cognac, are you going to work later, should I type anything for you?

At her next visit Franziska didn't know how to persuade the old woman, who was always on the alert, to give her answers she needed to know. She approached the subject in a round-about way, remarking casually: Incidentally, I saw Frau Schönthal's dog today, really a cute dog, I like poodles a lot, actually all animals, because I grew up in the country, you know, we always had dogs, I mean my grandparents and everyone in the village, and cats too, of course. Wouldn't it be good for you to have a dog or a cat, now that you have trouble reading. I mean, certainly that kind of thing passes, but I for one would absolutely love to have a dog. But you know, in the city it's just a bother and not really fair to the dog, but here in Hietzing, where it can frisk around in the yard and you can go for walks. . .

The old woman exclaimed in agitation: A dog, no, no, I don't want a dog! Franziska realized she had done something wrong, but felt at the same time that she hadn't offended the old woman as she might have had she suggested a parrot or canaries: it must have been something else entirely that had put her in such a state of agitation. After a while the old woman said very quietly: Nuri was a really nice dog, and I got along well with him, that was, let me think, it must have been five years ago, but then I had to give him away, to a home or a place where they resell them. Leo doesn't like dogs. No, what am I saying, it was different, there was something in that dog I can't really understand, he couldn't stand Leo, he always jumped at him and barked madly whenever Leo made the slightest move toward door, and then once he almost bit him, and Leo was so indignant, of course that's understandable, when a dog is that wild, but he was never like that otherwise, not even with strangers, and then naturally I gave him away. I couldn't let Leo be barked at and bitten by Nuri, no, that would have been too much, Leo should be able to feel at home when he visits me and not have to get angry about some poorly-trained dog.

Franziska thought that, although there was no longer a dog who jumped at him and disliked him, Leo came seldom enough as it was, and even less often since Franziska came instead. How long had it been anyway since his last visit? Once the three of them had gone for a short ride along the Weinstrasse and into the Helenenthal and lunched at an inn with his mother; othewise Franziska always came alone.

Be sure not to say anything to Leo, though, that business with Nuri really hurt his feelings, he's very sensitive, you know, and to this day I can't forgive myself for being so selfish as to want to have Nuri, but old people are very selfish, dear Franziska, you can't understand that yet, you're still so young and good, but when you're very old you get all these selfish desires, and you can't just let yourself give in to them. What would have become of me if Leo hadn't taken care of me, his father died all of a sudden like that and there was no time to make any arrangements, and there wasn't any money, either, my husband was a little careless, no, not a spendthrift, but he had a hard time of it and didn't have much of a knack with money, Leo doesn't take after him in that respect. In those days I could still work, the boy was a reason to keep going, and I was still young, but what would I do nowadays? My one fear has always been having to go to an old people's home, but Leo would never stand for that, and if I didn't have this apartment I'd have to go to some home, and I guess a dog isn't worth all that. Franziska listened to her, clenched up inside, and she said to herself: So that's it, that's it, she gave her dog away for his sake. And she asked herself: What kind of people are we?—because she was incapable of thinking: What kind of a man is my husband!—we're just so cruel, and she thinks she's selfish, and all the time we have everything we want! In order to hide her tears she quickly unpacked a small package from Meinl, little things, and acted as though she hadn't understood. Oh, by the way, I'm so scatterbrained today, I've only brought you the tea and coffee and a little smoked salmon and Russian salad. Actually it doesn't go together all that well, but I was really flustered at the store because Leo is leaving and one of the manuscripts isn't finished yet. But he'll give you a call tonight, and he'll be back in a week anyway.

He needs a break, the old woman said, see to it that he gets one if you can, you two haven't had any vacation at all yet this year. Franziska said brightly: That's a good idea, I'll convince him some way or another, I just need to think of a strategy, but thanks a lot, that's really a good piece of advice, he's constantly overworked, you know, and at some point I have to make him slow down.

What Franziska did not know was that this was her last visit to the old woman and she no longer needed the strategy, because other things came to pass, events of such hurricane force that she almost forgot the old woman and a great many other things as well.

In her fear, the old woman didn't ask her son on the phone why Franziska had stopped coming. She was worried, but her son sounded cheerful and unconcerned, and once he even came over and stayed for twenty minutes. He didn't touch the pastries, he didn't finish the sherry and he didn't talk about Franziska, but he did talk quite a bit about himself, and that made her ecstatic because it had been such a long time since he had spoken about himself. So he was leaving on vacation now, he needed a break, but the word "Mexico" gave the old woman a mild shock, wasn't that the place where they had scorpions and revolutions and savages and earthquakes, but he laughed reassuringly, kissed her and promised to write. He sent a few postcards, which she read religiously. Franziska hadn't added her regards. Once Franziska called her from Carinthia. Really, the money these young people throw out the window! Franziska had only called to ask if everything was okay. Then they talked about Leo, but the old woman kept shouting at the most inappropriate times: It's getting too expensive, child, but Franziska kept talking, yes, she had finally succeeded, he was finally taking a break, and she had had to go to her brother's, there was something to settle here, that was why she hadn't been able to accompany Leo. Family matters in Carinthia. Because of the house. Then the old woman received a strange envelope with a few lines from Franziska. She didn't say anything, just sent her regards and wrote that she would like her to have this photo she had taken herself, the photographs was of Leo, apparently on the Semmering Pass, laughing in a snowy landscape in front of a large hotel. The old woman decided not to say anything to Leo; he wouldn't have asked her anyway. She hid the photograph under the brooch in her jewelry box.

She could no longer read books and was bored by the radio; newspapers were all she wanted, and Frau Agnes got them for her. It took her hours to decipher them, she read the obituaries and always felt a certain satisfaction when someone younger than herself had passed away. Well, look at that, Professor Haderer too, he could hardly have been more than seventy. Frau Schönthal's mother had died, too, of cancer, she wasn't even sixty-five. The old woman stiffly offered her condolences in the grocery store and didn't even look at the poodle, and then she went home and stood at the window. She slept more than old people are said to sleep, but she often awoke, only to hear the dogs again. She was startled whenever the cleaning woman came: since Franziska's visits had ended, it bothered her when anyone came over, and she had the impression that she was changing. Now she actually was frightened of suddenly collapsing in the street or losing control of herself when she had to go to town for something, and so she obediently called young Herr Pineider, who drove her around. And she became accustomed to this small precaution for her own safety. She completely lost her sense of time, and when Leo once came by to see her, deeply tanned, she no longer knew if he was returning from Mexico or when he had been there at all. But she was careful not to ask, and gathered from something he said that he had just arrived from Ischia, back from a trip to Italy. Confused, she said: Good, good. That was good for you. And while he was telling her something the dogs began to bark, several of them, all at once, very near, and she was so completely encircled by the barking and a very gentle, gentle terror that she was no longer afraid of her son. The fear of an entire lifetime suddenly left her.

When he said on his way out: Next time I'll bring Elfi over, you have to meet her one of these days! she had no idea what he was talking about. Wasn't he married to Franziska anymore, how long had it been, how many wives was that now anyway, she could no longer remember how long he had lived with Franziska and when, and she said: Go ahead and bring her over. Fine. Whatever is best for you. The barking was so close now that for an instant she was certain that Nuri was with her again and would jump at him and bark. She wished he would finally leave, she wanted to be alone. She thanked him out of habit, just in case, and he asked in astonishment: Whatever for? Now I really did go and forget to bring you my book after all. A phenomenal success. I'll have it sent.

Well then, thank you so much my child. Send it over, but unfortunately your dumb old mother can hardly read anymore and doesn't understand much anyway.

She let him embrace her and found herself alone again surrounded by the barking. It came from every garden and houses in Hietzing, an invasion of the beasts had begun, the dogs came closer, barking to her, and she stood erect, as always, no longer dreaming of the time with Kiki and the Greeks, no longer thinking of the day when the last ten schillings had disappeared and Leo had lied to her. Instead she redoubled her efforts to hide things better, wishing she could throw them away, especially the brooch and the photograph, so that Leo wouldn't find anything after she died. But she couldn't think of a good hiding place, maybe the bucket with the scraps, but she trusted Frau Agnes less and less, too, because she would have had to give her the rubbish, and she suspected that the woman would rummage through it and find the brooch. Once she said, a little too harshly: At least you could give the bones and the leftovers to the dogs.

The cleaning woman looked at her in amazement and asked: What dogs? To the dogs, of course, insisted the old woman in an imperious tone, I want the dogs to have them!

She was a suspicious looking creature, a thief. She probably took the bones home with her.

To the dogs, I said. Can't you understand me, are you deaf or something? No wonder, at your age.

Then the barking diminished, and she thought: someone has chased the dogs off or given them away, because now it was no longer that same powerful, recurrent, barking. The fainter the barking, the more adamant she became: she was only biding her time until the louder barking resumed. One had to be able to wait, and she could wait. All at once it was no longer a barking sound, although there was no doubt it came from the dogs in the neighborhood. It wasn't a growling either, just now and again the great, wild, triumphant howling of a single dog, then a whimpering, the faint barking of all the others fading into the distance.

One day nearly two years after the death of his sister Franziska, Dr. Martin Ranner received a bill from a company by the name of Pineider for taxi services listed separately by date, for which Frau Franziska Jordan had made a downpayment and signed a contract. But because only very few trips had been made while Franziska was alive and the majority after her death he called the company for an explanation of this mysterious bill. Although the explanation actually explained very little, he had no desire to call his former brother-in-law or ever see him again, so he paid the fares, in installments, for a woman he had never known and never had anything to do with. He came to the conclusion that the old Frau Jordan must have passed away some time ago; the company had let several months go by since her last trip, perhaps out of reverence, before asserting its claims.

Three Paths to the Lake

There are ten trails on the 1968 edition of the hiking map for the Kruezbergl Region issued by the Tourist Office in cooperation with the Land Survey Office of the provincial capital of Klagenfurt. Of these ten, three lead to the lake: Ridge Trail 1 and Trails 7 and 8. Thus the origins of this story lie in topography, for the author has faith in this hiking map.

She always arrived on track 2 and departed on track 1. Herr Matrei, who must have known this after so many years, wandered around track 2, nervous and anxious, doubting that the information he had received was accurate and the announced arrival time correct, as though he could possibly miss her at a station which after all had only two tracks. And then they were facing each other, someone was already handing down her other suitcase, and she absentmindedly showered a stranger with profuse thanks; it was time for the ritual embrace, they hugged each other and she was forced to bend down to Herr Matrei as always, but this time a pang of alarm shot through her: he was smaller, hadn't exactly shrunk, just grown smaller, somehow, and his expression had become childlike and a little helpless, and now she understood this first pang of alarm: he's grown older. Of course Herr Matrei had grown consistently older over the years, but Elisabeth had never noticed it. The father she encountered every year at the platform was always the same, and every year she was aggravated that he hadn't hired a porter but instead carried her suitcases himself so that she, exhausted from the trip, didn't need to carry anything, but since this time he had aged, she refrained from putting up an argument or tugging at one of the bags as usual; she allowed him to carry them both, proving to her that he was strong, healthy and unchanged and that lugging two suitcases didn't bother him in the least. In the taxi she felt more like herself again; she laughed and talked as always, laid her head on his shoulder, threw an occasional glance at the new facades in the Bahnhofstrasse and registered the Lindwurm at the Neuer Platz with a sense of familiar recognition: it too had grown smaller, and only after that, when they came within view of the theater and turned into the Radetzkystrasse, did she let out a sigh of relief, for now everything indicated the proximity of the Laubenweg and the house which had been her home. No, today she didn't want to talk about the trip and why she'd had to fly via Vienna, nothing of the horror of the past few days; the main thing was that she'd finally arrived, after so many days of waiting and those telegrams which always filled Herr Matrei with consternation, and when she had cancelled yet again, he nevertheless drove to the airport and waited there, although she telegraphed so often just to prevent him from driving there and waiting.

She paid the cab fare and they walked through the front

garden, Herr Matrei wanted to show her all the newest changes but she headed straight toward the house and said: Later, please, tomorrow, please! and in the house they sat down in the living room; first she needed a cup of coffee and a cigarette, then she would take a bath and change. They drank the coffee he had kept warm, a somewhat thin, tepid brew which nevertheless tasted good to her after that English tea-drinking from morning to night, and they indulged in a little mutual grumbling about those young people—namely Robert and Liz—and Herr Matrei declared, almost in earnest, that he couldn't quite grasp why Robert and Liz hadn't come to Klagenfurt but instead had chosen Morocco of all places. After all, Klagenfurt was much healthier and less expensive, and hadn't Liz, who was an orphan and had never known a real family, enjoyed it here from the beginning, finally been able to experience what a home was? Elisabeth's defense of Robert was feeble, because there wasn't much to say or explain. She couldn't imagine her brother in the Laubenweg with his pent-up exuberance, particularly not now, and Liz was itching like a child to see something of the world, particularly now, because the two of them lived such a reclusive life in London all year long. They both came home from work dead tired every day, each taking a separate route, a long ride on the Underground, spending their Sundays in Robert's one-room apartment like an elderly married couple even before they had ever thought of marrying.

Elisabeth avoided this awkward topic and jumped up, she finally wanted to get her suitcases unpacked, and her face took on that inscrutable expression which only her father knew; he would have to be patient. In reality she unpacked only a few things and then began to walk back and forth between her old room and the bathroom on the second floor, but this wandering about was enough to change the house, it came to life because one of the "children" had returned, it didn't matter that instead of a child, a woman was walking through its rooms, a woman who felt herself to be both guest and co-owner. Elisabeth wanted to keep her absence as brief as possible, taking only a shower, she slipped on a bathrobe and quickly found what she needed most that evening, between the books: a small gift for her father which, as every year, had turned out to be modest and paltry because there was nothing, absolutely nothing Herr Matrei needed, and in this respect he made things difficult for his children. It wasn't just something he said, it was actually the truth: you couldn't give him Dunhill pipes, gold lighters, expensive cigars, ties, extravagant gifts from extravagant stores, nor useful things, either; he refused to accept anything, took good care of all he had, from pruning shears and shovel to the few household appliances an old man needed. He didn't drink alcohol, he didn't smoke, he didn't need any suits, silk scarves, cashmere sweaters, or aftershave lotions, and even Elisabeth, who over the years had developed an inimitable imaginativeness in finding the right gift for each and every kind of man, didn't have a clue when it came to her father. His lack of needs wasn't a quirk, it was congenital, and he would hold fast to it until his dying day. But the expression "dying day" bothered Elisabeth now, she blocked it out of her mind and took out the photographs; fortunately they were not bent, because she had checked her impulse to throw out a sturdy old folder. Before she went downstairs, she scrutinized the pictures she had picked out hastily in London, amateurish shots to her experienced eye, but they depicted what interested her father more than her own photography books and journalism. The wedding pictures, taken in front of a shabby Registry Office and the hotel where the reception dinner had been held: conventional, posed pictures which would soon look as old-fashioned as those of her parents and grandparents. Robert with Liz always in the middle, Robert smiling down at Liz; Liz looking up at him, smiling; Elisabeth at Liz's side, almost as tall as her brother, thin, almost thinner than the fragile young Liz. For a split second it occurred to her again that only a slight rearrangement would have created the impression that she and Robert were the couple, although she was smiling into the camera like Robert's friend who stood at his side lanky and youthful. The hotel porter was in one of the photos, had slipped in somehow by accident; another showed two strangers, one of Liz's distant aunts and the young girl with Robert's friend. As Elisabeth sorted the photos so that the one picture of Robert and Liz alone was on top, she began counting. By the end of this year, this coming winter to be exact, she would turn fifty; Robert was sixteen years younger than she was, Liz thirty years younger; the numbers couldn't be changed, only the photographs could deceive: the way she was standing next to Liz, no one would have taken her for Liz's mother. When she smiled that way, she was indefinable, a woman in her late thirties, and Philippe, who had never heard her speak about her age and who was younger than Robert, might have thought or perhaps did think that he'd become involved with a woman who was only a few years older than he was. But today her calculations were precise. Fifty minus twenty-two. Twenty-two years difference. So she could have been his mother, although this thought had never occurred to her and was quite alien, even now. At any rate it was all meaningless—only the arithmetic was correct.

On the way down to her father, who had since turned on the heat for the evening even though it was July—it was too cold in this lonely house for this time of year, for this summer which threatened to be none after all, nothing like the warm summers of her childhood—she tried to read something in the smiling faces, searching for what she had missed, for something must have escaped her notice in London. There had always been another quality to the air, something besides the humid, cool onset of summer, the drizzling rain, the chill permeating every room; it must have been something more, but the prints contained no evidence after all, although she had reexamined them like a detective trying to get on the trail of something elusive. Where had her keen nose gone, where her lightning capacity to get to the bottom of a situation or of herself or others? Either it had to do with Robert and herself or with Robert and Liz. Now we have another Frau Matrei, they had said in London, laughing, so they weren't going to die out after all. Liz would undoubtedly want children, Robert certainly not, no, not Robert, who was too much like herself, he wouldn't really want children. Although Elisabeth had learned to think about it, Robert had surely never given it a thought, but his instincts had been better and stronger than her own from the very beginning. She only knew—and knew only too well—why families like the Matreis were rightly doomed to extinction, knew that this country no longer needed Matreis and that by now her father was a relic. She and Robert had escaped abroad and worked as people do in important countries, and Robert's detachment would increase through Liz. But what made them strangers wherever they went was their sensitivity, because they came from the periphery and thus their thoughts, feelings and actions were hopelessly bound to this ghostly empire of gigantic dimensions. The right passports didn't exist for them, for it was a country which didn't issue passports. It was mere coincidence that they both still were citizens, because Elisabeth had found it too much of a strain in America to go through the tedious application procedures required to turn herself into an American simply because she'd married one, and after the divorce it had mattered even less what she was on paper. She had a work permit and, protected by a number of friends and half-friends, had nothing to fear in any country: in Washington there was an important Jack and an influential Richard; only in extreme cases did Elisabeth take advantage of her acquaintances and when she did, it was on someone else's behalf. Somehow the men she chose had always been failures who needed her for support and advancement; naturally it was the same thing with Philippe.

As she spread out the photos in front of her father, he said that someone had called from Paris, twice now, that must have been Philippe, he would call again if he needed something or it occurred to him to call and say a few friendly words to her. Her father thanked her for the gift with a solemn frown. It was a book she had stumbled upon in a second-hand bookstore in London, "The Road to Sarajevo" with old pictures, and he leafed through the volume in silence because it meant something to him. He had little to say about the photographs and merely kept repeating that Robert looked well and in reality Liz was prettier than in these pictures, but he didn't notice how young his daughter looked, for he knew her no other way and did not add things up the way Elisabeth had today. She was his child, children always looked younger, and Herr Matrei had only one remark for such occasions: You look fine. Or: My, you aren't looking all that well, referring to his children's health. Herr Matrei said: It was time the boy got married, that's a relief to me. Elisabeth knew how annoyed her father had been each time Robert had declared he would never marry, never at any price, and she wondered why he was never concerned that she lived alone; that short marriage with the American which she hadn't told him about until shortly before their separation had either slipped his mind or he had never taken it seriously in the first place. In his opinion, Americans got married and divorced at the drop of a hat, and it was no wonder that someone like Elisabeth hadn't immediately remarried. In the letter about the divorce, which had been more detailed than the one informing him of her marriage, she had told him she was doing well and couldn't blame Hugh for anything, it was better for both of them, they were still the best of friends, etc., everything was settled, there was no question of it being a drama, but she might return to Paris, she wrote. Well, this Hugh person—he hadn't introduced himself to Herr Matrei, and Herr Matrei concealed the fact that he'd found it unbelievable at the time, tactless of Elisabeth, but as long as Elisabeth hadn't been made to suffer, then everything was all right. Her letter had sounded sincerely optimistic, and Herr Matrei said to himself: I know his kind inside out, and the main thing is that this divorce-happy so-and-so didn't make her unhappy. In the streets of Klagenfurt he had brusquely acknowledged congratulations on the occasion of his daughter's wedding, and when he once noted that Frau "Direktor" Hauser, as he ironically called her, had asked him a hypocritical question long after Elisabeth's divorce, he had remarked condescendingly: Aside from the fact that I personally never interfere with my children's concerns, I doubt that an American marriage has any validity here. My daughter is extremely busy; she's in Africa now. I assume that my son will major in chemistry. Unfortunately I can't give you any more information. Good day.

After this episode, no one in the neighborhood dared to ask Herr Matrei about his daughter's private life, and with time so many of these people died—that spiteful, gossipy Frau Direktor Hauser had long since passed away. Now Herr Matrei looked up, astonished on the rare occasions when someone said hello, and returned the greeting politely.

Because the photos were not sufficiently informative, Elisabeth attempted to give an enthusiastic report. Her father had flatly refused to climb aboard a plane for the first time in his seventy-seven years and travel to London for the marriage of his only son, to a country where he wouldn't understand a word and wouldn't even be able to communicate with Liz. Elisabeth needed to embellish those days in London with attractions they hadn't held, and soon she was elaborating vividly: Things had started off on the wrong foot from the evening of her arrival at Heathrow—Heathrow was London's airport, just like Orly in Paris—because she had made a mistake in arranging to meet Robert, they had waited at different places: Heathrow was in fact quite a large place, a little bigger than the airport in Klagenfurt, and then she had gone on to the hotel alone and ended up paying more than double the normal fare. This occasioned fits of roaring laughter from Robert, the fact that his sister, who had been around the world several times, had let herself be taken for a ride by an English taxi driver of all people, that was just too grotesque and would certainly never have happened to even the most inexperienced American or African. Afterward they sat together comfortably and discussed and calculated everything, how much the reception would cost, what still needed to be bought and done, and Liz sewed meantime, Liz didn't make a good story, hers was not at all the popular type these days, she didn't personify "swinging London" or anything else one might expect of a 20-year-old, she had never been in the midst of any commotion whatsoever and her sole pleasure in life consisted in spending time with Robert. Before meeting him, she had had nothing but her work, year in and year out, and a room she shared with another girl, because a place of her own would have been too expensive. On that evening she had been sewing a sundress for a Moroccan beach, and then they had decided to call Klagenfurt to tell Herr Matrei that all the arrangements for the "fatal step" had been settled, that Elisabeth had been accepted as a witness for Robert without any problem and that there was nothing tremendously exciting about it, everything quite simple, and Robert and Elisabeth took turns grabbing the receiver from each other, both professing that they were thinking of him, and in the end they thrust it into Liz's hands and she stuttered into the mouthpiece: "Grüß Gott, Vater, auf Wiedersehen." Those were practically the only words she knew in German. Elisabeth had also taught her "Dummkopf" so that she'd know the right word for Robert at the right time; Liz had often heard the word for "dumb kid"—"Dummerle"—from Robert, but that was a secret, tender expression reserved exclusively for her. Each of them had a glass of beer, dark Guinness, and Elisabeth rejoiced pensively for the two of them: how had Robert ever managed to make the right choice? She would sleep well after the beer. The following two days she went shopping with Liz to Harrod's and a few other department stores and Liz confided to her excitedly that she hadn't told anyone in the office that she was getting married and wouldn't they be surprised; Liz had only asked for her vacation. In the department stores, where Liz enthused in childish delight over everything but refused to get anything that wasn't on the list, repeatedly preventing Elisabeth from buying her presents, Elisabeth had begun to feel sick—and at this point she broke off abruptly and said: Father, we belong in bed. You're nodding off already. And I want to go to the woods first thing tomorrow morning.

Elisabeth felt wide awake again before going to bed and crept quietly into the kitchen and set the table for breakfast so that Herr Matrei could start his day off differently for a change, as in long-forgotten times. But her thoughts were still in London, in those labyrinths of department stores, far removed from fresh rolls and hot coffee, images of familial harmony from some memento album. Why had she felt sick when they rode up and down the escalators, past hundreds of thousands of things to buy; in the coffee shop, where they had taken their places in a long line to get tea and ham and eggs, she had been seized by panic. Fortunately Liz had found two seats together, but they were surrounded by horrible old women whose plates were full of cake and sandwiches and who were devouring everything unappetizing in sight and gossiping and gabbling as though it were the coziest place in the world: old women, many Elisabeth's age but old in a different way, shapeless and hideously dressed. Elisabeth didn't touch her eggs, she must have become extremely pale, because Liz said tenderly: I can tell you're totally exhausted, of course you'd like to relax a little, I'll bring you right back to the hotel. Elisabeth replied simply: Yes, I'm sorry, unfortunately I can't take it anymore. As they were leaving, deliberating what could be put off until tomorrow, Liz said shyly: I know, London just isn't Paris or New York, and we know how much work you've had lately. I think it was a real sacrifice for you to come, but without you Robert wouldn't have been happy, and neither would I. I'd just like to tell you that I know very well that Robert and I—that everything, his decision, depended on you, and I like you, but not only because of that. I really like you.

Elisabeth gave her a quick and grateful hug, because there was some truth in that, Robert had wanted to know if she approved of Liz, and she had said nothing specific but had intimated that she liked Liz, and now she was getting a "Schwägerin," that sounded awful in German, and she reflected that she'd much rather get a "sister-in-law."

She had to be careful when the talk turned to Paris. Liz had traveled to Paris once with Robert for a weekend and found it "super." Elisabeth listened to her with a smile; her own Paris was far from being "super," but once she had been in Paris for the first time, too, and although she wouldn't have described it like that, she couldn't help thinking that Paris must have been wonderful twenty-five years ago, when it didn't yet have the power to bury her various lives and so many others. There wasn't a place in the world which didn't hurt Elisabeth somehow, but this young, sweet woman had cities in her future to admire, and in her enthusiasm would find them all exciting and beautiful.

The next morning she didn't have to take the path to the lake, that might be too much, but she could go to the Waldwirt or at least climb up the Kalvarienberg. She hadn't breathed fresh air for weeks, hadn't walked anywhere, and Herr Matrei was familiar with Elisabeth's habit of getting some "real" exercise whenever she came home, of avoiding the city and entering the woods right behind the house. In the past they'd often hiked together, and even now she took a second walk with him, but she took her morning walks alone, running more than walking, in Herr Matrei's opinion, and he was no longer able to keep up with her pace.

That night Elisabeth awoke with a start, believing she was still in London; she must not reveal to her father, and never to Robert, what a bad time she'd had, particularly after they had both left; she had gone half-crazy thinking she'd lost Robert now, and when she wanted to leave a few hours later, something went wrong with her reservation; the information from the hotel travel agency was no help in deciding what to do, because everything had been booked far in advance. July, tourist season, charter flights were cited as reasons. Entire hordes must have taken control of these planes, and she was forced to stay grounded in the hotel for another ten days. Most of the time she lay on the bed in her room, reading and ordering an occasional cup of tea and a sandwich, men were whispering incessantly in the next room and once she saw a Pakistani emerge; then at night, because she thought she'd heard a knock at the door, she made a cautious attempt to find out what was going on, but it had only been two Pakistanis for her neighbor, and the whispering resumed. Spanish women stood around in the hallways, lethargic and passive. Room service consisted of Indians, Filipinos and Africans, once there had been an old Englishman, and all the guests, too, were from Asia and Africa, she rode in the large elevators in the midst of silent masses, the only Caucasian; it was all very strange here in the vicinity of Marble Arch and Hyde Park. She had never felt apprehension in Asia or Africa and had enjoyed being alone and leaving the others when she traveled with a group, being "the woman who rode away," but not here. In this place everything was so monotonous, the people were all completely mindless, nothing was right, the guests and employees communicated in an English limited to a handful of expressions, and using one more than the allotted number meant not being understood. It wasn't a living language that was spoken, it was a type of Esperanto, and the inventor of this international language would have been astounded to see that it had already come into use, admittedly in a different way, and she quickly forgot her English, using that confounded Esperanto when buying newspapers or cigarettes or asking again about flights. Once she took a seat in a bar to see what kind of men were sitting around and whether one might be worth considering, but then suddenly the bar was closing, everything was constantly closing here, and though you were offered a seat in a glaringly lit side room that resembled a badly designed conference hall and were given a few drops of whiskey or a beer, the next difficulty was how to pay. Elisabeth had no interest in learning which coin had which value and she would hold out a few coins from her purse and say: Please take what I owe you. She had no idea where her old London had gone to, everything she had once enjoyed was gone. The caricature of a city within a city confused her, on Oxford Street she was annoyed as she pressed her way through the throngs of people and chanting religious groups. Once she took a taxi to Westminster Bridge only to stand quietly on the bridge for a while and then cross it to the other bank of the Thames, where she strolled back and forth, seeing everything as it had once looked, although there was some difference. She felt no urge to see London, she was completely indifferent, she was tired, she wanted to leave and go home, she wanted to go to the woods and the lake, and she telegraphed to her father, hopefully he would understand that she was pointlessly detained here and not get upset. After countless recitations of "I'm sorry" and "I don't know"—the most important expressions in this Esperanto—she had finally obtained a flight, even though it was only to Frankfurt. Sheer elation prompted her to arrive at Heathrow an hour early, and then she waited for hours because the flight to Frankfurt was delayed, and in Frankfurt, rather than waiting, she managed to have the ticket reissued for Vienna, and in Vienna she went directly to the South Station, once again arriving too early, and went to the Salvation Army mission and asked the nurse if she could lie down. She was afraid of collapsing on the platform, so she lay exhausted on an emergency cot and drank a glass of water, no, she didn't have a seat reserved, she had arrived from London and everything had been mixed up, that's what you get, those are the fruits of progress. Elisabeth gave the nurse a hundred schillings for the mission and the woman promised to negotiate with the conductor for a seat; if Elisabeth could spare a little more change for the man, everything would be fine. Elisabeth was relieved, this type of talk was music to her ears, well certainly, that was no problem, and as the train pulled out of the staion she feigned a drowsy nausea for the conductor's sake but felt better immediately. The bad dream was over, and in a few hours the train would be stopping at familiar stations and soon she would be home.

In the morning she slept through breakfast, Herr Matrei was already working in the garden and she gulped down a cup of coffee and called out to him cheerfully: I'll be back soon, I don't want to overdo it on the first day! She tried Trail 2, but no longer liked the "lookout tower" and tried to locate Trail 1 to the ponds. But here, so close to the city, there were other people taking walks and raucous children; that was somewhat disappointing, but tomorrow she would hike the long trail to the lake, taking her suit for the swim afterward.

She ate a little something with her father, and once again he was surprised that she was satisfied at home with so little. He imagined her life with fancy lunches and dinners, champagne and caviar, and when she talked about it he had no choice but to get that impression because her reports always alluded to wonderful restaurants and famous and interesting people. And although all these stories were true, she omitted others which were less worthy of mention, the ones without champagne or famous men, consisting instead of colleagues and intrigues in a confusing and strenuous daily routine with work and appointments, an excess of coffee and gulped-down sandwiches, conferences and suitcases which, barely emptied, immediately had to be repacked. Annoyances unimaginable to Herr Matrei, whose daily routine passed quietly in the Laubenweg and who only occasionally experienced shocks, namely in telegrams and letters from his children, postcards from foreign countries with greetings, phone calls which came just as he wanted to hear the news, and yet Elisabeth explained convincingly that it tasted better to her here with him, that she preferred eating a few sausages and some cheese to sitting in a Chinese restaurant in Paris. Since Herr Matrei had never eaten Chinese food and regarded China as a sinister place, he nodded knowingly, he could understand that. He led her around the yard and picked the first Morello cherries and black currants. The poor child didn't get any sensible food all year long, and fruit from your own yard was more nutritious than this foreign stuff on the market nowadays, but he'd see to it that she'd be looking better within a few days. Because this time she really wasn't looking well. All this tea-drinking in England made him wonder, too, it was certainly pure poison, tea might be good if you were sick or had a cold, but not all day long! Robert undoubtedly was more reasonable and marriage would introduce some kind of order into his life, but Elisabeth paid too little attention to her health, and the pride he felt for her professional success was always mingled with the worry that she didn't take care of herself.

In the afternoon they walked part of Trail 1 together, but Herr Matrei, who knew the woods better than she, abandoned the numbered paths and they returned by a detour she hadn't known; she was fairly exhausted because his pace had been too slow for her and they had, as so often before, spoken about the future. Future to Herr Matrei meant reconsidering how to arrange everything for the children and finding out if Elisabeth had finally changed her mind about the house, but she hadn't, so Robert would inherit the house after all. Herr Matrei stopped and said: Just prove that you haven't forgotten everything. What kind of tree is this, and how old is it? How do you know its age? Elisabeth was familiar with these questions, but the answers had grown increasingly difficult; nature had always bored her, even as a child, and she was simply incapable of identifying an ash tree. Even on the learner's trail, where every important tree bore a sign for schoolchildren citing its German and Latin names, origin and identifying characteristics, she read the inscriptions with fleeting interest but preferred walking fast and thinking about other things. What most appealed to her were the different possibilities the trails presented—the intersections, the turn-offs and estimated walking time, for instance how long you needed from the intersection of Trails 1 and 4 to the Zillhöhe, and since she never needed as much time as was posted, she concentrated solely on the times and how long she took. She would never have entered with woods without a watch, because she checked the time every ten minutes to know how long she'd been walking, how far she'd come and how much she could still accomplish.

This evening she withdrew to her room early and fell asleep instantly, unwinding for the first time, the cramps in her body gradually relaxing, for she had held herself tensed for too long. She was the first one up in the morning and made breakfast, scribbled a note to her father and crossed the Kellerstrasse to the second, more remote ascent to Trail 1. She encountered no one; people stayed near the city when they took out their children and their dogs, no one took hikes these days, they all drove to the lake in cars, like everywhere else. As children they had always walked these trails with their parents, because it would never have occurred to Herr and Frau Matrei to take even the streetcar, except perhaps on the way back or when it was raining, but one went to the lake on foot as a matter of principle, and they had always avoided the large public beach and walked on to the smaller beach at Maria Loretto. The lake and Loretto were inseparable for Elisabeth, although for a long time as a young girl she had refused to go hiking, finding it bothersome, unimportant and uncomfortable, and she began to enjoy it again only after all the "super" cities had allowed her to see the forest in another light, as the only spot on earth which was really quiet, where no one kept pushing her to unearth something useful and no one could come chasing after her with telegrams and all sorts of unreasonable demands.

It was an overcast day and she carried an old raincoat slung over her arm and wore the old shoes she always left behind in Klagenfurt. But she had forgotten to put on a pair of Robert's or her father's socks, her feet kept sliding around in the shoes because of her thin stockings, and she trotted slowly onward.

She wasn't at home in these woods, and had to reread the map over and over again, for she had never known homesickness and it was not homesickness that made her come home, nothing transfiguring had ever taken place; she came back, for her father's sake, and that was only natural for both Robert and herself.

Even when she'd first gone to Vienna and started working she'd already had an itch to travel, a lively impatience and restlessness, and the only reason she had worked so hard and with such determination was that she was working toward a miracle, the miracle of traveling far away. In the beginning it hadn't even been clear what would become of her, but her boundless energy landed her a job answering the phone and typing in the editorial office of one of the many periodicals that had mushroomed after the war and folded just as quickly, and soon she was writing short reports, unaware of the fact that she didn't have any particular talent for writing, but no one noticed because the others were no better. Her radiant enthusiasm was so convincing that they believed she was gifted, and she became acquainted with lots of people, ran around with photographers, labored over a "story" or captions, met more and more people, and was popular. She hadn't learned any real trade and thought now and then in despair that she should go to college, but it was already too late and her faith in miracles was so strong that she grasped things extremely quickly and thus was considered intelligent, although at best she knew a little about many things, she simply picked up whatever was current, things her friends really did know something about. Then once, coincidentally, she was traveling with a photographer who fell ill, and she was so worried about the all-important story that she had begun to take pictures and grasped that quickly, too. This proved to be the turning point in her career, because she took pictures better than she wrote, but had no way of knowing or suspecting that this would help her get ahead, in fact quite close to the top. The decision didn't become final until a German photographer, Willy Flecker, who in those days had already made a name for himself but then lost it again, had come to Vienna and, after a short trial period, taken her with him to Paris and taught her a number of things. Through him she met Duvalier, for decades the one outstanding photographer of international renown, and he took a liking to the little "Tyrolienne," as he teasingly called her. Elisabeth, who had blossomed out of nowhere from a dilettantish Viennese newspaper, soon began to accompany the old man on trips, as his assistant, student, secretary—and then as an indispensable colleague, and the childhood dream she had had in Vienna was no longer a dream but had been transposed into a reality which overwhelmed her at first. She traveled to Persia, India and China with Duvalier, and when they returned to France and finished his next book, although he was the most ruthless worker she had ever known, ruthlessly exploiting her as well, it was through him that she met all the people Herr Matrei always referred to as "Who's Who"; Picasso and Chagall, Stravinsky and Julian Huxley, Hemingway and Churchill stopped being mere names to her and became people you didn't only take pictures of: you went out to eat with them, they even called you, and after the first few times when the cautious, even miserly Duvalier had allowed her to participate, she had understood that it was better to have three dresses from Balenciaga or another famous couturier who afterward took a fleeting liking to her and studied and accentuated her individual style than to have twenty cheaper dresses, and although she was obsessed by work and had only one thing in mind, namely to improve constantly, she did in fact develop her own style, "Klasse," as her German friend put it, because now she only wore and did things that really suited her. The scrawny beanpole, the little Matrei girl who hadn't been judged particularly attractive in Vienna, was transformed by the Parisians into a "personality" who was only much later thought interesting and pretty, for it had been her misfortune that, in Vienna, she had merely been popular, considered by men a creature without gender. By the time she reached the age of twenty-three and was still gallivanting around as the cherished friend of important men, not having yet provoked a single twinge of jealousy from the wives and girlfriends of the men she knew, she resolved to put an end to this embarrassing situation. For some time she debated between Leo Jordan, a doctor just beginning his career; and Harry Goldmann, who was not a doctor but was said to have had any number of women at his beck and call, and then decided on Goldmann after all, because she liked him better. It was a calm, cool decision, and a few months later she heard by way of an indiscretion, but without getting upset about it, that actress X had told her friend Y who had relayed it to Elisabeth's admirer Z that she was absolutely frigid, in spite of being such a charming person. She mulled this over, amazed; in all probability it was true, and even though she didn't believe Goldmann capable of such gossip, there were others with whom she had tried the same thing, but still, these men had no way of knowing that she went to them as if to an operating room to have her appendix removed: not particularly concerned, but not entusiastic, either, merely trusting that an experienced surgeon—or, in her case, experienced men—would certainly be able to cope with such a trifle. Without in the least playing a role, afterward she always treated these men, Goldmann and the others, with neutral warmth, as friends; she wasn't one of those girls who broke up marriages and relationships or clamped on to someone with claims and feelings; for her, whatever had happened the day or evening before was a thing of the past, and it was only when she met Trotta in Paris that she changed so completely that she could no longer comprehend her time in Vienna and her behavior there. The fact that she had gone to bed unemotionally, only, as she had believed, to do a man a favor, not once doubting it was a favor—that was something she could no longer imagine; she had wanted to please Franz Joseph Trotta from the first moment onward and was as nervous and frightened as any woman. She began to play all her cards in order to win and hold him and then, on second thought, she rejected all the games: how could this strange, arrogant man ever be interested in her? All at once she found herself terribly dull and didn't know how to interpret his ironic behavior; for five minutes she interpreted it favorably; five minutes later it was a bad sign. The first few days, the days she searched for Trotta and fled and he searched for her and fled, were the end of her girlhood, the beginning of the love of her life, and although afterward she reflected, from her perspective at the time, that a different love had been the love of her life, on Trail 1 more than two decades later it was Trotta after all who was once again the love of her life, the most incomprehensible and at the same time the most difficult love, burdened by misunderstandings, arguments, lack of communication, and distrust, but at least he had left an impression on her, not in the ordinary sense, not because he had made a woman of her—another could have done that —but rather because he made her conscious of so many things, because of his origins and because he—a real exile, one of the lost ones—had made her—an adventuress who expected God knows what from the world during her lifetime—had made an exile of her: long after his death he slowly pulled her down with him to ruin, alienating her from the miracles and allowing her to recognize this alienation as her destiny.

That had been the most important thing in the relationship, but there had been something else, too. It always depended on where one looked for the most important thing, and back then Elisabeth hadn't paid attention to all Trotta's statements. He was from a legendary lineage "no one could escape" and had told her about his father who had also failed to comprehend the times he lived in and had asked in the end: Where am I to go now, a Trotta, as the world ended once more for a Trotta in 1938: he had been among those who had to visit Capuchin vault again and knew what "God protect us" meant but had done everything to topple the Hapsburg dynasty.* Most important of all was that Trotta made Elisabeth unsure of herself in her work—after Duvalier's death she'd been engaged by the best French illustrated magazine—and began to poison her little by little, forcing her to think twice about her work. Once she went to him, crying helplessly because one of her many "friends" (she didn't know him well but she had friends everywhere) had been wounded in street fighting in Budapest while taking pictures and had bled to death with his camera in his hand. Trotta let her cry and remained obstinately silent. Later, the editorial staff and the better, more conscientious part of France lost three photographers and one reporter in Algeria and two journalists in Suez, and Trotta said: The war you photograph for other people's breakfasts hasn't spared you either in the end. I don't know, but I'm unable to shed a single tear over your friends. If someone jumps into the middle of crossfire to get a few good shots of other people dying, then getting killed is nothing special, considering the sportsmanlike ambition it involves, it's merely an occupational hazard, nothing more. Elisabeth was stunned, for she believed they were doing the right thing, people had to be made aware of what was going

*Trans. note: Reference here is to the old Austrian national anthem, rendered obsolete by the collapse of the Habsburg Monarchy in 1918.

on there, they needed to see those pictures to "wake up" to reality. Trotta's only comment was: Oh, so that's what they need? Is that what they want? The only ones who are awake are the ones who can imagine it without your help. Do you suppose you have to photograph those devastated villages and corpses so that I can imagine what war is like, or take pictures of children in India so I know what hunger is? What kind of stupid presumption is that? And someone who doesn't know would page through your brilliantly successful photo stories for their aesthetic value or the nausea they induce, that should depend on the quality of the pictures, you're always talking about the importance of quality, isn't that the reason they send you all over the place, because you do quality work? he asked with an undertone of contempt. Elisabeth argued vehemently, cleverly, despite her confusion, but for the first time someone had pulled the rug out from under her and she said defiantly: Just so you finally realize that I'm serious, I'm going to go now, out of conviction, and I'm going to ask André to send me to Algeria, until now he's been against the idea, but I can't accept my being spared and not the men. It's not like that anymore with other things, all that changed long ago!

That had been a special time for Trotta: he loved her anxiously and apprehensively as one loves a person one will lose, with the kind of worry which was usually part of her love for him, and he asked her not to go. Don't go, Elisabeth, don't ever go, it's not right, I know what you mean, but it's no use, you'll realize it yourself in time. You and your friends won't end this war like that, it'll be different, you won't accomplish anything, I've never been able to understand people who can bear to look at that poor imitation, no, at the most atrocious unreality of all turned into reality, looking at corpses is not the way to stimulate liberal-mindedness. Once, in Sudan, the only thing that really struck me there were notices everywhere, put up for all the whites, because of course they were the only ones who had no sense of decency, stating that it was prohibited, at the risk of a severe penalty, to photograph "human beings." I've forgotten the Nile and everything else, but not that prohibition.

Although Elisabeth insisted on the importance of what she and others were doing and discussing and what measures they took to protect those in danger from attacks and to bring the Algerians over the border into a safe country, especially to Italy, at that time she unconsciously began to change her attitude to her work; her head had always been so full of daily events that she had never devoted any thought to the more intricate forms of right and wrong, as Trotta had, and the suspicion stayed with her that there was something offensive about her work, that Trotta, who was not right, was right in one respect: what made the photographs sent in from all the theaters of war so very different from the pictures of plunging suicides, train wrecks, crying mothers, and gruesome slums? And even if so many photographers hadn't really photographed those wars, a clever forger could have made them just as easily without running the risk of not succeeding and with the simple goal of forging well. Published photo series were rarely forged, but now Elisabeth saw them through different eyes, especially the last photos taken by Pedrizzi, the young photographer who had been blown to bits shortly afterward together with a few Algerians and another Frenchman who were mourned only incidentally: Pedrizzi alone was known to the press and they idealized him in a number of obituaries. Again and again Trotta mocked her fresh, strong faith. Sure, let the people read it, they know everything anyway even before they've read it. You do the same thing, as if you didn't know it, you read all those reports about torture, one is as good as the next, you read them and you know that it's true, inhuman, that it's got to end, and then perhaps you even want to take pictures so that hundreds of thousands are able to see what it's like to be tortured. Simply knowing it isn't enough! Elisabeth took the book she'd been reading—its contents had shaken her—and threw it at him, missing his head but grazing his shoulder. Trotta took her in his arms and shook her. You misunderstand eveything, but you of all people, you can't afford to misunderstand. I'm only saying that it's too much to expect, it's humiliating and despicable to go so far as to show people other people's suffering. Because of course in reality it's different. To do something like that, just so someone else will put his coffee down for a second and murmur, oh, how awful! and a few will vote for a different party at election time, but they'd do that anyway; no, my dear, I'm not the one who believes that mankind is inherently bad, utterly incapable of comprehending anything, lost forever; but you do, because otherwise you wouldn't think that in addition to a few commandments they need newspaper stories and what your Willy calls "the hard facts."

Elisabeth said, I'm telling you once and for all, he's not "my Willy" and people have to see reason. I'm doing what I can, even if it's not much.

What reason, what reason; if they haven't seen it by now, in all those centuries what ever made them come to reason, and how much will it take to make you come to reason?

Still, I admire them all, all the French who fought with

them for liberty and independence . . . I mean the most important thing for Algeria is liberty . . . Trotta's laugh made her begin to stutter out of rage and impotence, and he said: Don't forget that I'm French, and I don't think there's anything admirable about that, my dear, I wouldn't hesitate to go, I'll be happy to wash the dirt off my hands along with those damn French who are only products of your admiration, but I certainly don't want to be admired for it. And you talk about liberty—if it comes at all, liberty hardly lasts a day and is always a misunderstanding.

Then you aren't a real Frenchman, Elisabeth said in exhaustion, you don't understand their predicament, you just don't understand it.

No, I don't understand it because I don't want to, who can expect that on top of everything else I understand it? It's quite enough for me that I have become one and am once more called upon to take on a heritage not of my own choosing.

You're living in another time, she said bitterly, I can't live and talk with someone who has merely stumbled into the present by mistake and doesn't really live in it.

I don't live at all, I've never known what it is to live. Life is something I look for in you, but I can't even delude myself that you could give it to me. You make a lifelike impression because you run around and wear yourself out for all the things people will have forgotten a few years from now.

Even before the war in Algeria ended, Elisabeth and Trotta had separated, and when everyone else had long since resumed their "daily routine," Elisabeth remained depressed and watched what was threatening to become of that freedom, and she returned from the new Algeria despondent and dejected but made a point of telling everyone that it had been fascinating, and she wrote all sorts of positive things with cautious reservations and reread her captions for hours on end before releasing them, her first conscious defection to the land of lies, but she was no longer able to talk to Trotta, who one day had changed hotels without leaving a forwarding address. Years later she happened to read an essay entitled "On Torture" by a man with a French name who was Austrian and lived in Belgium, and afterward she understood what Trotta had meant: for the essay said what she and all journalists couldn't say and what the surviving victims, whose testimony had been published in hastily-written documents, were unable to put into words. She wanted to write to this man, but she didn't know what to say or why; obviously it had taken years for him to penetrate the horror of the facts, and in order to understand these pages, which few would read, one needed more depth than that induced by a passing scare, because this man had attempted to discover what had happened to him when his soul was destroyed and to learn how a human being could change and continue to live, defeated, with that knowledge.

She never got around to writing that letter; she merely avoided a few assignments. Once André asked her, amused: Are you scared, Elisabeth? And she said, avoiding his gaze: No, but I just can't, and I can't explain it. It will probably pass, but I have my doubts, that seems to be something to be ashamed of these days. André, who had already lifted the telephone receiver and hadn't noticed her embarrassment, had lost the thread after the phone call and said: The best thing for you to do is take it easy, because if you want to hear my opinion—but forget it afterward so it doesn't go to your head—you're much braver than our gentlemen here; all the while they're pretending to be brave, but in reality they're merely ambitious or put up a courageous front. It'll pass with you, I've just put you under a little too much pressure, you know I'm a canaille and exploit you where I can, but I know it, and if I weren't one, what would become of our brilliant magazine?

Thank you, canaille, Elisabeth said with a smile, and I've known for quite a while that you're one, but it doesn't bother me to work for canailles like you; but about taking it easy— just now—I'm not sure. I'll sleep on it and let you know.

Elisabeth left the path and cut over to the Zillhöhe, to the benches set up for the tired, rest-seeking hikers who no longer came. She looked out at the lake lying below in the mist and over the Karawanken in the direction which, farther on, must have led to Sipolje, where the Trottas originated and where some apparently still lived, since that colossal, cheerful Slovene had once come to see Trotta. Franz Joseph had told her that he was a cousin whose father was little more than a peasant. She could only remember how unusually tender Trotta had been with this nephew, even though he had taken refuge in irony again, not wanting to show that something had touched him, and she said absently: I'm sure I met him in Vienna once, as a very young man, but perhaps I'm mistaken, he always looks at me in such a way that I don't know what to say to him, could it be that he's a little stupid? No, Trotta said, not at all, just so damn healthy, I don't know how they managed, down there at home, to keep on the right track and stay healthy. I'm too nervous to look at you as he does, I can't even look at myself. That's why I don't shave for

146

days on end, because I could shoot myself when I see myself in the mirror.

She stopped thinking about it on the way home, it wasn't a good day, not a day for swimming, either, but tomorrow the weather might clear up, and she walked home, somewhat dis-appointed, because she had planned to do more but had turned back. Before dinner—Herr Matrei always ate very ear-ly in the evening—she said she wanted to slip over to the Einsiedler and pick up a beer, just this once he should allow her a beer, she pleaded teasingly; Herr Matrei had never for-bidden anything to his children, but he liked to hear them pretend that it was up to him to allow something or forbid it. She left quickly once more, by way of the Teichstrasse. But before she reached the Einsiedler inn, she hesitated: in front of an old, run-down Volkswagen parked at the first or last house in the Teichstrasse stood a young woman who gave her a look of surprise and said hello. Elisabeth stopped and returned the greeting in confusion, they shook hands, she knew the girl but couldn't place her, and the other said in embarrassment: I was just, I'm just visiting my Uncle Hussa, yes, thank you, my aunt and my uncle are fine, but right now I have to . . . all at once Elisabeth remembered who old Hus-sa's niece was, Elisabeth Mihailovics of course, whom she had met a few times in Vienna. So she was here on vacation, hopefully that wouldn't mean complications, she had no desire to meet anybody and talk about mutual friends in Vienna. The two women assured each other that it was a sur-prise and unfortunately the weather this summer was no cause for celebration. Elisabeth noticed that there was also a young man behind the car, putting something in the trunk and locking it, and now he was waiting in the background;

the woman made no effort to introduce her to the young man who was dressed like a woodsman and looked somewhat crude, so she said in a friendly tone: If you feel like it, just give me a call, and say hello to your aunt and uncle, they'll hardly remember me, but my father, yes, thank you, he's doing fine. Since the woman seemed increasingly embarrassed, Elisabeth tactfully let her go. I'm so sorry, but I need to rush and pick up something at the store, have a nice vacation! She walked on in annoyance, hoping she wouldn't call, and she turned around carefully before entering the inn—they were both climbing into the car, which looked as if it were on its last legs, and as she emerged with her beer they were just driving by and Elisabeth, who was smiling and about to wave, refrained, because the other Elisabeth was making a point of staring straight ahead and acting as if she hadn't noticed her. At dinner she asked her father how the Hussas were doing, and Herr Matrei answered indifferently that he had no idea, quite respectable people, by the way, and Elisabeth sketched her encounter with this niece from Vienna, a nice person all in all, somewhat colorless, she must have met her in Vienna, at a friend's, and she couldn't quite understand what she was doing here with some peasant, the woman had made a completely different impression on her in Vienna, seemed more of an intellectual, but she couldn't remember the situation, and of course here people dressed for the woods, just as she did, and not for the city, but there had been something so shabby and pathetic about Elisabeth Mihailovics, of course she came from an impoverished family but they had to have a few social connections, and then, because Herr Matrei had little interest in the details, she closed with the remark: It's not that important anyway, I just hope she doesn't call, in any case you can tell her I'm not at home. As she was dozing off the thought crossed her mind that it was a little too much to meet yet another Elisabeth, she had been confused enough at the Registry Office when Liz had been called by her full name, Elisabeth Anne Catherine, with a last name that Elisabeth could forget immediately: she hadn't known it before and now it was no longer of any consequence for the new Mrs. Matrei. She started, already half-asleep, she had fallen back through the years and lay there with her eyes open, hearing it all again: she was at home and nevertheless in Paris.

Look, your Willy! Elisabeth said angrily; he is not my Willy, so stop it, would you? Trotta continued in a leisurely tone; take this Willy, for example: when he speaks English he becomes human in my eyes, it sounds natural when he says "okay," but they shouldn't speak German, that's the only thing I hold against them. Somewhere along the line they lost the feeling for how the language should be spoken. Younger, exculpated ones like Willy are no exception at all. I don't want you to think that I cultivate so much hate, it's more complicated. Although I could never touch a German woman for fear that she might open her mouth.

Because you want to be complicated! (And he knew that she only said it because she didn't allow herself or the others any discrimination whatsoever as a matter of principle.)

Not me, I'm not complicated at all, but I've met with so much that is complicated. You think I hate them, but there's no one I like, do you think I like the French? Never in a million years, I only want to say that it was wrong to first dismantle everything the Germans had, punish them every

149

which way and then to split the country in two, and hand weapons to both sides so that they would become well-behaved allies.

Well, what would you have done, Elisabeth asked aggressively, you would naturally have had a better idea. Of course, Trotta said arrogantly, I would simply have decided in Yalta or wherever it was that they would no longer be allowed to speak German, that's all, and the whole problem would have been solved. I would have had them learn English or Russian, some language in which one could communicate with them.

Elisabeth said: You're just a fool, a dreamer. But Trotta was completely unruffled: But just think of the consequences this tiny, incredible idea would have had. Your Willy, excuse me, that Willy is likable or at least not embarrassing when he says in English: *have a nice time, darling,* it even sounds normal. But in German: Halt die Ohren steif, Mädchen, dann liegst du richtig. Über den Daumen gepeilt. Acht Uhr plus-minus—I can't help it, all that unbearable blabbing makes me think that someone is talking from his gut, they don't have a language and that's why they falsify everything. Komm mal rüber! Why do they always have to say "mal"? Strange, but of course you know better and say that only comes from the jargon they've learned in their thousand years, I don't believe it, I think it's part of them.

Franz Joseph Eugen Trotta, the world really lost a political genius in you, Elisabeth said grimly. Perhaps, Trotta said, but nobody thinks of asking me. And have you noticed that this Willy is constantly running around acting so important, but he never really does anything, you do it all for him.

That's what you think, Elisabeth replied, laughing, and

you don't do anything at all.

I don't do anything, but that's different, I'm not putting on a farce for myself like a German who keeps everything on the move all the time, himself above all.

Once I was stationed in Heidelberg, it doesn't matter, anyway, I was in a few cities because I had had to run around in that French uniform and had already become a winner by the age of twenty, me of all people, a Trotta, although we're born losers, in any case I was suddenly a winner, and that I could bear cheerfully enough, better than other things. The interesting thing was how the other French, but not only they, believed the Germans were diabolical, particularly those V.I.P. murderers, of course. And the whole time they were nothing but completely dumbfounded and conventional, the middle class personified, so close to lunacy that things are prone to snap without warning. When they were questioned, interrogated, and I had to act as interpreter, two of our own people had their turn, too.

Elisabeth interrupted him, astonished: What do you mean by "our own"?

Trotta said impatiently: The Austrians, of course, and their baseness, the enjoyment they got out of every kind of brutality imaginable was written clearly all over their ugly faces, and their answers reflected it, too. Those were, so to speak, the only two diabolical figures I encountered; they welcomed an order as an excuse, whereas for the Germans orders were orders, and that was why they were so bewildered that a few million victims were held against them. But our French, with their "logique française," had decided once and for all to see the diabolical in places it wasn't, and as a result they sent the two criminals on their way because they seemed more harmless. After all, they came from the land of the operetta, which had been victimized along with all its operetta characters. Yes, a victim, but I didn't want to explain to them why and how, the procesess and the history which made a victim of this amputated country are simply too complicated to put into words. I've encountered so much that is complicated and have remained too uncomplicated to understand it completely.

In the morning before the news, Elisabeth and Herr Matrei each read a section of the paper. Suddenly Elisabeth was curious about in the local papers, and she read the amateurish reports and badly written features not with condescension but rather with a stirring of compassion. She liked the local news best, they were better able to capture the Church Congress in Rosental and the dignitaries attending it, even though it sounded unintentionally amusing; the gala opening of an "International Lumber Auction," which the people here believed to be international, wasn't uninteresting at all; they hadn't forgotten the missionary element, either. So missionizing had established itself even here. The world was the only thing they couldn't deal with, and Elisabeth asked herself with that undercurrent of contempt which had always been characteristic of Trotta and only later of her as well, whether it was of any significance that people in this corner of the world were given distorted news to read and whether it would have changed them at all had they been fed a less garbled idea of events outside their own country. Probably not. Even Vienna was a highly suspicious, foreboding place to them, and since they were suspicious anyway when something leaked out of parliament and ministers delivered statements, perhaps they shouldn't be made even more suspicious about the rest of this complicated age called the present. Meteorological catastrophes and plane crashes were the favorite topics—a heat wave in Italy causing deaths—although they were far removed from the storms and heat and never boarded planes, and from afar, even if the comparison wasn't quite fitting, it reminded her of the many magazines in Paris devoted to the Third World which had much more to say about Bolivia than about things within reach of the Parisians who dragged themselves back and forth between satellite towns or the banlieue and the city, increasingly exhausted. Most of them were exhausted not because of the atrocities taking place in South America or Asia but rather by their own plight, the rising costs, the fatigue and depression that paled pitilessly in the face of major crimes; and they no longer noticed that something spiteful and cold was becoming increasingly prevalent in Paris whenever one asked for something—even for directions—and spreading to people who hadn't yet become that way. What was wasting away inside them, even in Philippe, and survived only in empty rituals, was still enough to infuse some of the younger generation with a love of humanity, but it no longer extended as far as one's neighbor, or to someone walking next to them on the street, sobbing or about to break down. The telephone rang and she jumped up but lifted the receiver too late. It could only have been Philippe, as if he had known in Paris that she was worrying about him just now, because he had used up the fire of youth, the aggression, and charm he'd had back in May 1968 and was now at the end of his rope, bitter and sick with self-pity, even though he was less sick since she'd been there for him.

On Trail 1 she came to the Zillhöhe with its benches where she sat for a moment, gazing down at the lake; but then she looked up to the Karawanken and, beyond, to Carniola, Slavonia, Croatia, Bosnia; once more she was searching for a world that no longer existed because there was nothing left of Trotta except the name and a few sentences, his thoughts and tone of voice. No presents, no withered flowers, she couldn't even imagine his face anymore: as she came to understand him better, the most real part of him receded, and the haunting sentences drifted up from below, from the south: Don't try to get ahead, keep your own name, don't take me, don't take anyone, it's not worth it.

Oh, that old story about being grateful, is there anyone you're not grateful to? Willy, because he brought you to Paris, Duvalier, because you were allowed to work with him, and two people in Vienna, because they let you work, and André, because he thinks you're good. There's no end to it, all the people who discovered you, but this gratitude will wear you down, it stops at a certain point, everyone gives someone else a hand sometime, but that's no reason—since it's no longer true, because you're making your own way—for you to cling to debts that have long since disappeared.

That Trotta was right about Willy Flecker was something he would never learn because only months after the separation, while she was putting enormous effort into something for Willy because things weren't working anymore, although occasionally people did him favors for her sake, and also because he was drunk constantly and the young hope of photography in Germany had become a wreck. He had insulted her, stone drunk as he was, before a couple of friends who, like herself, listened at first in surprise and then in horror, but what burst out of him was not, as many thought, boundless jealousy or an attack of delirium because she was swimming and he was sinking; for Elisabeth, it was instead the hour of truth between them, but she couldn't explain to herself what she had done to warrant such hate, and she thought helplessly of Trotta, put up with it for another few hours and tried to be polite before she finally stood up, left, and then took a few sleeping tablets for the first time because she was incapable of falling asleep in that pool of hate. Willy sent her a last short letter—containing no apologies—telling her to settle something for him immediately, and because she had the material she spent an entire day searching for negatives in the lab. She sent them to him without a word. During this time a number of friendships ended in a similarly grotesque way, none of them quite as violently and cruelly, but more out of indifference, in silence and spite, and she didn't know what it meant, because Franz Joseph couldn't tell her anymore; he had merely said once that at least no awkward feeling of gratitude would be able to come between them because neither of them had ever done anything for the other, but one day she would remember something. At first she didn't remember but weighed a job offer from New York, gave notice to André who wished her luck and said that a telegram would be enough, he'd take her back any time, and she worked in New York with a certain relief, because her first Paris—now disintegrated into hostile relationships—had shattered around her. In New York she met many people and traveled even more than before until she met Hugh, another failure but not someone who wanted to fail: he was exhilarated when he began things but when people disappointed him he became depressed and paralyzed. Hugh had tried to get into business after finishing his degree in architecture but couldn't get any jobs, thank heavens he was better suited for interior design, and she put her hope in his hopes and introduced him to a few of the many people she knew. On the day he got his first job he asked her to marry him, and she said yes instantly, although she had never for a second thought of marrying a homosexual and he was only living with her on a temporary basis, but they believed, excited and happy, that it could work out very well, each would have his own life and never disturb the other, and perhaps a friendship was a better basis for a marriage than being in love. She also knew the boy Hugh regarded as his most significant relationship at the time, and three weeks later it was someone else, she accustomed herself to the ever-changing succession and complications, since Hugh's relationships overlapped occasionally and then she was the one who straightened things out when his confused feelings and promises got the better of him and money was short, even though there were times when she earned quite a bit, but Hugh on the other hand was often hard up because once a young man from Brooklyn and another from Rio had had extremely expensive tastes. But they had a small, cheerful home which Elisabeth really enjoyed, she and Hugh always understood each other well, and when there were three of them—there were often three, never four—things went well then too, because all the boys were particularly nice to her. Perhaps they were really all so nice and tactful, but occasionally Elisabeth suspected that Hugh was behind it, that he was the one who strictly demanded of each boy that Elisabeth not only be respected because she was his wife but also admired beyond bounds because he admired her and wanted her to have the esteem he

156

could never achieve with his boys who were, on occasion, calculating and humiliated him or made him suffer; above all, no shadow was to be cast on Elisabeth, although he told her everything, and the respect they gave her was a substitute for Hugh's own self-esteem, which was damaged and wounded often enough.

But one evening in Paris—she never had to conjure up this memory, for it accompanied her everywhere—she couldn't forget it even long after she had been back, had left New York, it was the fault of a Viennese journalist who had been passing through and given her a call to say hello or give her some news or ask a favor. She no longer knew why she had consented to see this man at all, she had probably said yes on the phone by accident and they had met in a small café on the Boulevard St. Germain, and it certainly hadn't been anything important, the young man from Vienna had been anything but important, he had wanted to meet her because he knew some people she also knew in Vienna, because he was a journalist, a certain Mühlhofer or Mühlbauer, and then he had suddenly asked: You knew Count Trotta, didn't you? Elisabeth said irritably that there had never been a Count Trotta, and if he was talking about the legendary Trottas who had been ennobled by mistake, they had long since died out, in 1914, and of course there were branches, but they weren't nobility, and supposedly a number of them still lived down in Yugoslavia, and one here in Paris. The man from Vienna gave her a brief, searching look and said: In Paris after all, then he's the one! Elisabeth's impatience increased noticeably; she didn't want to speak to a stranger about Franz Joseph and this business about Count Trotta had already gotten on her nerves and she called the waiter. They began arguing awkwardly about who would pay, and before she could get away the man from Vienna made one more remark: in that case it must be the Trotta in Paris and did she know that he'd shot himself a few months ago in Vienna, there had been quite a fuss because no one had been able to find any relatives, no clues at all in the small hotel except his passport, and then someone had voiced the suspicion—he'd done some research—that it could have been the great-great-grandchild of the hero of Solferino about whom he'd tried unsuccessfully to find some information in the archives. Elisabeth, who was not yet shaking, said vehemently: What nonsense, his grandfather was a rebel and not an obedient servant to his masters like the Solferino line.

But since she no longer knew why she was telling these things to this pushy man, she stood up, started to hail a cab distractedly and said, shaking: Would you mind helping me find a taxi, please, I have an important appointment!

That evening she had been invited to the Bateau Ivre, and as she lay on her bed and thought about her only great love and the news whose import the man from Vienna could not comprehend in the least, she didn't cry, she was simply too weak to get up, not even capable of getting a glass and drinking something. She tried to call him by all his names, Franz Joseph Eugen, the names on which his father had staked everything, a real fortune and the misfortune of never being able to forget. Her friends Maurice and Jean Marie called and she tried to say that she just couldn't, she was dead tired, but they took turns at the phone, already in too much of a good mood, laughing and saying they would come right over, and before Elisabeth could protest, they had hung up. She deliberately put on a certain dress, for the first time not to please, but rather so as not to forget, a crumpled old wool dress which had been lying in a drawer, and she made a weak effort to smooth it out on her body, remembering how Trotta had once gone shopping with her and had paced back and forth in front of the store in wild impatience because, in his opinion, it was taking much too long, although she had decided on the first thing in her size, and now it was her dress of ashes, her mourning dress, her Trotta dress in which she went down to the car where four people were already waiting. No one introduced her to the girl who climbed into the front seat with a blasé air, and the man at the wheel, whose name no one told her either, turned around for an instant and said: So that's you. Her friends, squeezed in against each other in the back seat, were talking nonstop. Maurice said: Be careful, Elisabeth, he's dangerous. Jean Marie said: Watch out for yourself, I've got to warn you about him, everyone falls for his act. She didn't answer and remained silent throughout the meal, only after a glass of wine did she begin to talk, trivialities with Maurice, and then when the stranger stood up—he had to get something from the checkroom for the snobbish girl and leaned over to ask if she needed anything—she took a coin from her purse and gave it to him, saying rather harshly: Put this in the jukebox for me! No, she didn't have any particular request, she had no requests at all, he should just press any old button. As he returned, bowing once more to her in exaggerated politeness as though he found something about her amusing, her record dropped to the turntable and a melody began, neither a chanson nor a current hit, there was no voice crooning or wailing to the music; it was something she had never heard, but afterward she often heard it, for a whole year they played it everywhere, a muffled, jazzed-up version of an old piece she didn't recognize. She listened, paralyzed and absorbed, keeping her eyes to herself and simply feeling that the girl was moving her shoulders in time with the music, moving only for this stranger. Elisabeth stopped eating, she couldn't eat during a Requiem Mass, and she waited politely for a moment and then said she had to go home immediately, she asked Maurice to call a taxi for her, she didn't want to disturb the others, not to mind her. But no one had heard; they were all discussing in loud voices whether or not they should take a nightcap at Sascha's or somewhere else and finally, exhausted, she waited alone in the car with the stranger while the others argued nearby, half-drunk. Neither of them said a word, and then he remarked that he would see what was going on and she said, once again too harshly: No, find me a taxi first, I'm not in the mood to sit at Sascha's! She couldn't comprehend why, a bit later, she was there with everyone after all, drinking champagne and dancing, and she stood up and danced with this man she didn't like and during a short break she looked at him carefully for the first time and said: You're not a Frenchman, not a real one anyway. No, a fake one, he said with satisfaction, from Zlotogrod in Galicia, a place that doesn't even exist anymore, but surely she'd never heard of it. Elisabeth said pointedly: No, of course not, no idea, I wouldn't even know how to pronounce it. But after that she really tried to dance instead of shuffling about, and although she had never liked to dance, for once she succeeded in really dancing. Now all of a sudden the others had had enough and they left, he brought her home first and at the door said decidedly: I'll be back right away, I just have to get this gang off my back.

Although she had drunk more than she should have, had a headache and thought she would fall asleep waiting, she dragged herself into the bathroom, brushed her teeth and had just begun to freshen up when the bell rang; he had returned more quickly than she thought possible—it was three in the morning and there was hardly any traffic. She opened the door and he closed it softly, and she wasn't sure whether he had taken her in his arms so swiftly or if she had been the one who pressed herself against him so swiftly and until dawn, desperate, in an ecstasy she had never known, exhausted and never exhausted, she clung to him and only pushed him away to pull him back to her again, she didn't know if the tears came because she was killing or resurrecting Trotta, if she was calling out to Trotta or to this man, didn't know what was meant for the dead or the living, and she fell asleep, having arrived at an end which was also a beginning, and whatever she later thought about this night, in numerous variations—it was the beginning of the greatest love of her life, sometimes she called it her first real love, sometimes the second love of her life and sometimes, because she still often thought of Hugh, the third love of her life. She never spoke to Manes about the reason that had driven her to him, the reason behind that ecstasy which they never experienced again. In a few days he was no more than a man she was in love with, a changing man, who came to wear a face and a name for her and, in the space of two years, a history and a mutual history with her which had taken shape to such an extent that, in time, she believed she could clearly see her life with him, a future together. When he suddenly left her she was more shocked by the abruptness—which had not been heralded by any cloud—than by the brutal wound it inflicted and the fact that she was alone once again. She suffered more from that separation than from Trotta's death, sat by the telephone for days on end waiting for a call, but she didn't try to locate Manes and wasn't able to discover the reason for his desertion because there was none. She avoided the few mutual acquaintances they'd had, not wanting to hear things from third parties. After many days of senseless waiting, she needed to talk to someone and traveled to Vienna to a doctor she had known previously. In Vienna, she avoided all her friends and checked into a small hotel, spending her days comfortably at the offices of this man who had once been an insignificant intern and now had a reputation and prominent patients, and she talked far less than she had expected; she expressed herself in precise terms and answered his questions, patient, sensitive questions not without humor. He twice attempted a narcoanalysis without success, but Elisabeth found it quite interesting and after a few days he said to her that he had never, thank God, had a more sensible patient, and that her problems, if one could call them that, were an integral part of her personality. He congratulated her on her "lucidity," and then they talked only about things which had nothing to do with her, quite like old friends and with a complete liking for each other. She took her certified "lucidity" back to Paris, full of optimism, for nothing had happened to her which did not inevitably, happen to everyone else. The next day she suddenly broke down, overcome by a state of panic because her clearsightedness couldn't change the fact that a person she had come to think of as an integral part of herself had discarded her, that she was incapable of overcoming such a simple loss after a much more difficult major loss. She suffered as though from an amputation, once more in a daze, sitting helplessly by the telephone for days on end.

One day she began to work again, to surface among people and do the things she used to do.

Don't take him, don't take anything, a haunting voice said. Sometimes even the simplest ideas were a help to her. For instance that Manes would have gotten older, that then he wouldn't have been enough for her, that a sudden end was better than the slow dying out of feeling, and one day it helped her, too, to go out with a few men again, with Roger and another Jean Pierre and Jean and Luc, and she slept with some of them and listened to all of them for hours about their problems and difficulties. Roger's dilemma was that he felt obligated to an older woman, whom he called "A" and still loved; on the other hand he had now met a younger "B" with an illegitimate daughter, he couldn't simply keep B dangling because of his own doubts, and he was most tempted to seize the bull by the horns because he was incapable of making a decision. Elisabeth carefully weighed her words of advice, nearly certain that he was debating the alternative of seizing Elisabeth, who did not like the thought of being a last resort, and then just after she had returned from a trip to Africa he suddenly called and said: Please don't laugh! And whether or not she could understand him, yes, yesterday, he had gotten married yesterday, the younger one, "B," with the daughter, the daughter had been the decisive factor, and Elisabeth accepted his invitation for a cocktail that same day and met Roger's "B" and her small daughter. Roger approached her radiant with joy and pulled her to one side after she had greeted the many people there, he would call her tomorrow first thing, but then he didn't call her the next day, or the day after, and once again, like years before, she sat by the telephone for days on end, desperately searching for an explanation and sobbing uncontrollably and once again many months later, unexpectedly, for the same reason, because it seemed unbelievable to her that someone to whom she had been so good had simply stopped calling. The only thing she had realized was that "A" and "B" must have been very determined women: one wouldn't even barely tolerate the other and of course least of all a third who understood both "A" and "B."

She thought of Manes only rarely now, and since she had stopped searching for the reason for his disappearance, she remembered that he had once told her he had never had anything to do with women of her kind, everything had probably been Maurice's fault for having gone into raptures about her intelligence ad nauseam, and intelligent women weren't women for him, he had simply been so irritated by her, the way she had sat in that restaurant in such arrogant silence.

Elisabeth did not tell him about the monstrous misunderstanding underlying that evening or that it was true that she'd been silent but not that she'd been arrogant. And it remained concealed from him, how her parting from Trotta and her ascension through him and a word like Zlotogrod had all become bound together.

This time she took the trail past the Zillhöhe although it was raining again intermittently, and she walked down to where the path led to the lake, but when she emerged from the woods the path disappeared into a field without a trace; there were no signposts at all and she walked to the left and to the right, and finally a long way straight ahead to see where the path resumed. At the last moment she stopped: lost in thought as she was, another step would have sent her over the edge, and she took a careful look at what lay broken off before her, at the very edge of the field, a steep slope which had never been there before. She realized immediately that a part of the mountain had not broken off but rather had been carted away by bulldozers. The fresh, damp earth was still visible and beneath her stretched a gigantic construction site, this must be where they were building the new highway which Herr Matrei, who could no longer walk such distances, had mentioned in passing, with disapproval, because it would surely take years, at the snail's pace they worked at around here, until the highway was ever finished. She paced the rim of the abyss, searching for a way down but everywhere she tried to get a foothold and slide down there was nothing to hold on to, no bushes, no trees, the dirt was loose and bare at every turn and she would have fallen at least a hundred yards. Then she examined the terrain of the construction site, which bore no evidence of activity; in the distance—too far away to hear a loud shout—two workers trudged along the mapped-out route, but she couldn't shout to them and ask how to get to the lake. She sat down in front of the abyss and debated and then, disheartened, returned to the ridge trail, barely recognizing its little-traveled end. All right, this trail didn't work, no. 1, tomorrow she'd have to try Trail 7 or Trail 8, they must have left one of the trails, at least one way down to the lake from the woods. She hiked back, blinking into the weak but piercing rays of a sun that had suddenly appeared between the trees, and in the early afternoon, when Herr Matrei had awakened from his short afternoon nap and anxiously asked her where she had been for so long, she told him that it was no longer possible to descend to the lake by the ridge trail and that they were building a road there but hadn't even thought to put up a warning sign. It was really dangerous, she said, if someone ran up unsuspectingly, expecting to take the trail down. Herr Matrei said that it was just another typical outrage and that he was relieved that she was back. She had overdone it, too, of course; he'd already been worried about that long walk, much too long for the first few days, but she could try it using the other trails, and then they drank coffee in the garden and talked about the old days, mainly about the ones he remembered most vividly. They spoke too about the honeymoon in Morocco, amused; then, after his own wedding, Herr Matrei had simply taken a hiking trip through the Rosental and over the Loibl Pass to Bled with Frau Matrei, and it had been wonderful even if it hadn't been a big trip, and Elisabeth once again imagined Robert's plans, Robert's future, and sometimes she thought wearily of her own plans. A vague suspicion crossed her mind that Robert and Liz had no future, they had only their youth but not the future. Elisabeth had not had her future and her parents had not had theirs, there was nothing to this so-called future which was always promised to the young. This time she didn't invite her father to dinner, to the Sandwirt or even to Paris, she no longer wanted to show Paris to him: since his refusal to attend the wedding she had realized that her father would never go out or travel anymore. He had taken his last trip alone, to Sarajevo, when he was seventy.

Herr Matrei said he didn't understand why Robert and Liz still hadn't sent a postcard, and Elisabeth reassured him: of course the young people wouldn't write immediately, and the mail took longer all the time, and anyway it took longer now than it ever had since post-coach times, though now, there were such fast planes and the trains were faster all the time; she saw no reason to get upset, surely the postcard would arrive by Christmas. Although they spoke of Robert's future without being able to envision it, something strange occurred to Elisabeth: she was thinking about Manes and had once said to him, laughing, that everything had happened to her in reverse: first she had loved a child and then, only much later, a man. And if a woman experienced one before the other, it could hardly be expected that she would be totally normal. Elisabeth wasn't certain and wanted to speak with her father about it once more, and she asked if he could still remember when, years and years ago, she had made such a scene about Robert and treated Mama so badly. Herr Matrei, who was contentedly drinking his coffee, enjoying his favorite time of day after his afternoon nap, said absently: Of course not, I don't know anything about it, I don't understand you, what should have happened between you and your mother? Elisabeth warmed up to the topic: You mean you don't know that Mama and I hated each other, of course only because of Robert. Mama couldn't comprehend why a sixteen-year-old girl whom she had already told at least three times everything there is to tell a young girl suddenly screamed at her and demanded to know whether Robert was really her child, he could just as easily have been hers, Elisabeth's child. And Mama must have lost control at one point, because she slapped me in the face for the first and last time, and of course that only enraged me even more, and I said that one thing was certain, I would never have a child because I wouldn't be able to stand the fact that mine would never be as wonderful and unique as Robert. Mama must have been in a terrible state in those times; we practically fought over the baby, and Robert, who of course could have no inkling of how he had come to have two mothers, drove Mama to despair, too, because he refused to fall asleep unless I was with him, you know, back then after his first illness.

Herr Matrei wasn't angry, he was indignant. He said: You're getting things all mixed up again. Mama was very fair and liked both of you equally.

Elisabeth became agitated: I don't doubt that at all, I only mean that she knew very well that I begrudged her that child, and it's no wonder that, in spite of my feelings to the contrary, I've always held to my first promise, a childish promise never to want a baby because Robert had already been born. And much later something else happened, too, but I don't know why Mama told me about it. Once I was coming home from Vienna and neither of you knew that I was coming; that night, Mama found Robert crying in the dark on the steps, and when he stopped crying and she had put him back to bed he said to her, I know I'm right, I know it, she's coming, I dreamed that she's coming, and "she" meant me, of course. To this day I still think sometimes that Robert is the only person in the world who ever woke up in the middle of the night and was happy because of me and cried and knew that I was on my way.

Herr Matrei shook his head and said: Unfortunately that's going a little too far for me, how was Robert supposed to know what we didn't know, but you two, you and Robert, you've always had a vivid imagination, you certainly didn't inherit it from your mother or me. I only know that once Robert told me—he was a real rascal—that he didn't want you to get married, your royal highness of a brother didn't want to allow it, and of course I told him a thing or two. Excuse me, I really didn't mean to talk about your marriage and hurt your feelings! Elisabeth, who was thinking about something completely different with a sense of relief, comforted him and said, laughing: You aren't hurting my feelings at all, my marriage was really quite a joke, practically the only funny thing in my life, but I know that you've never really been able to get over poor Hugh.

Elisabeth lay down on top of the cliff which dropped off to the highway at the end of Path 7 and, because the sun's scorching rays had returned, she took off her jacket, shoes and socks; she had never been so thirsty and would have liked to drink the lake she couldn't get down to, but she would have to get used to the idea, and she got over the lake as she had gotten over so many things. She focused her gaze on the spot where three countries touched each other, she would have liked to live over there, in an isolated place on the border still peopled by farmers and hunters, and the thought occurred to her that she also would have begun her address with: To my peoples! But she would not have sent them to their death and caused these divisions; after all they had lived together, although trapped in misunderstanding, in hate and rebellion, but people simply could not be expected to be governed by reason, and then she thought of her father with a smile: he had stated in all seriousness that back then everything had been completely unreasonable and strange, and that was the only thing everyone understood, because they themselves were all strange people, and even the revolutionaries had been shocked to realize that this gigantic, pointless empire which was more hated than loved no longer existed. She would never again be infected with this disease which was slowly dying out, but there was one thing she naturally couldn't deny, and that was her moral code: it was from here and not from Paris and had nothing to do with New York and very little with Vienna. She had always visited Vienna once every two or three years for a week or so, always exuberant, always with a different escort, sometimes with two, and her Viennese friends—who devoured her visits greedily—knew as little as she what to make of the latest escort. The sole mishap which took place in the jungle of Viennese gossip was brought about by the discreet Atti Altenwyl of all people: he had once expressed the opinion that people were being enormously unfair to Elisabeth Matrei, because no one was more suited to live with another person—but then his imagination had failed him because the others were gaping at him in astonishment, he couldn't explain the reasoning behind his notion of her, and his wife thought the obvious thing, namely that he had had an affair—sometime in the past, of course—with the slightly older Elisabeth, and Antoinette looked at Atti with a glance full of affection; essentially she was proud of this accomplishment. She discussed Elisabeth's visits with a dozen people in the strictest confidence, and that meant only that the secrets would have been better kept if they had been published in the paper: at least then one might have overlooked them. Knowing Elisabeth was a big plus for Antoinette; after all not everyone—not even in the Altenwyl circle—had constant contact with famous people and not only on a professional basis, but rather with someone who really mixed with those remote personalities, painters and movie stars, politicians and the Rothschilds for a picnic or dinner, and Antoinette, who like many Viennese, truly admired actors and even enjoyed extending warm invitations to Fanny Goldmann, had of course never met any of the real movie stars for whom she had the greatest regard. But precisely for that reason she had a childish interest in asking what happened at the parties in Hollywood or how Liz Taylor looked and acted in person, and that surprised Elisabeth somewhat, because people like the Altenwyls would naturally never dream of setting foot in that demimonde or associating with people whose private lives were the stuff of gossip magazines, and even if all sorts of actresses and models succeeded in marrying into the aristocracy, that sort of woman could hardly comprehend that an Altenwyl would have preferred sweeping streets to being seen with a model, and Antoinette remarked about the Princess of Monaco: I'm not trying to say that she doesn't do justice to her role, but an actress will always be an actress! She would never have dreamed of aiming a similar remark at Fanny Goldmann, who warranted only praise: Fanny in the role of Iphigenia is simply divine.

When Elisabeth talked casually about her life between Paris and New York or rather about incidents she had witnessed—she never spoke about her own life—then her Viennese friends and anyone who happened to be listening could easily have had the impression that they were catching a glimpse of that different world, a shimmering and fascinating place, for Elisabeth's accounts were told well and with a sense of humor, but at home, with her father, the stories crumbled into nothing: not only because Herr Matrei wasn't in the least interested, but also because she noticed that, although she had actually experienced it all, then again she hadn't, there was something bleak and empty in all these stories, and the bleakest part of all was that she had really watched it happening, but her life had run a different course, had often passed her by as though she were a spectator, a member of the audience going to the movies day after day and letting herself be drugged by a counter-world. She never said a word about the things that really upset her, because they weren't fit to be put into any words at all. What could she say, for instance, about one of her latest reports which had received a prize she mockingly dubbed "The Golden Lion"; the report had dealt, like so many others, with the problem of abortion, with all those shocking accounts many women unfolded so readily and in a tone of condemnation. This time she had been fighting on the legal front and needed to interview doctors and lawyers who were all authorities on different viewpoints, but their accounts struck her as no more precise than the women's, and she was well aware that it was another one of those extremely important "storylines," but the end product had nothing to do with it and was merely a horrible accumulation of pat sentences she could have invented at her desk. But Elisabeth, who no longer believed anyone, had to manufacture a report with terrifying photographs and captions, knowing the whole time that none of it had anything to do with her, especially not those women and those doctors. Once, while conversing with an elegant gynecologist of refined sensibilities, she was suddenly seized by inexplicable rage: she wanted to jump to her feet and shout that she didn't give a damn about all his sympathy and careful wording. What did she care about all these women with their problems and their men and their inability to say one single true word about their lives, and she suddenly had the urge to ask this doctor: Why doesn't someone ask me for a change, why not ask someone who thinks independently and dares to live, what have you done to me and so many others, you with your insane empathy with every kind of problem, hasn't it ever occurred to anyone that you kill people when you deprive them of the power of speech and with it the power to experience and think.

Of course she hadn't screamed, but instead thanked him politely and submitted a brilliant report which disgusted her, and the report had been long forgotten and buried in the wastebasket by the time she was awarded the prize.

After turning forty, she was increasingly overcome by boredom; Jean Pierre, her latest, had told her that he once lived with a woman from Vienna, an unbelievably ambitious woman, a simultaneous interpreter, but luckily for him there still were women like Elisabeth who wouldn't leave a man for the sake of their work, and in his opinion, they were both in similar situations: ostensibly she had always been abandoned by idiots, and it was a shame, for both of them, that his affair had left its mark, and ever since the thought of marrying—even her—made him gag.

She got along best with Claude Marchand, who was a primitive, dangerous, but sincerely cynical man who had unscrupulously worked his way up in the Parisian movie industry from the underworld and who was involved in shady deals. He had an unbelievable amount of energy which sometimes infected her, he was so thoroughly corrupt that she experienced him as a liberating change from all the scrupulously proper and enervated men who had made her sad, and even if those around her were at a loss as to how she could fall for someone like this small-time gangster, she simply ignored them; by the time they were meeting less often, others were already kowtowing to a man they no longer held to be a gangster: by then he had bought up two film-dubbing companies and shortly afterward toppled first one and then another producer. Occasionally he took Elisabeth out to dinner to celebrate old times, when he had "pulled off a few jobs."

Her increasing success with men was directly related to her increasing indifference to them: what she now, in retrospect, jokingly called sojourns in the desert and dry spells were things of the past, those days when she had cried after each loss and isolated herself in defiance, going on with a sense of pride because there was nothing else she could do but keep working. She could no longer understand what had been so tragic: now she was calm, well-balanced, and it was only a question of time, of opportunity, when she would finally end this relationship with Philippe which had already gone on too long. It wouldn't do to return to Paris and tell Philippe he should take his pajamas, his razor and his few books and get out, it wouldn't be that easy, and there were still things which had to be done for his sake. The phrases—I don't need you, I don't need anyone, it doesn't have anything to do with you, it's just me, and I don't feel like explaining it!—were easy to think but not easy to say, just like that, in Paris, just as she couldn't very well say: My brother has gotten married and it's over between us, I hope you understand. There was only one hope she didn't and wouldn't allow herself to hold on to: that if, in almost thirty years, she hadn't found a man, not a single one, who was exclusively significant for her, who had become inevitable to her, someone who was strong and brought her the mystery she had been waiting for, not a single one who was really a man and not an eccentric, a weakling or one of the needy the world was full of—then the man simply didn't exist, and as long as this New Man did not exist, one could only be friendly and kind to one another, for a while. There was nothing more to make of it, and it would be best if women and men kept their distance and had nothing to do with each other until both had found their way out of the tangle and confusion, the discrepancy inherent in all relationships. Perhaps one day something else might come along but only then, and it would be strong and mysterious and have real greatness, something to which each could once again submit.

In the evening, after the news, the phone rang and Elisabeth ran down to answer it without hearing what Herr Matrei was saying with a shake of his head: this phoning around was one of the real problems of today's youth. Philippe said he had been trying to get through for hours and was worried, and then they talked about everything under the sun, today he'd really missed her, because this morning the decision had been made, he was going to work as Luc's assistant, Luc was already beginning the preliminaries for his new film, and what did she think of that? Elisabeth said that's wonderful, and then repeated a few times that it was the best news for ages, and how they would celebrate, together, after she came back; at the same time she was thinking, it had materialized after all, in spite of her skepticism, and he had a happier disposition than he himself believed: he'd already forgotten that she was to thank for this, but she warmed up anyway so it wouldn't occur to him and only asked herself why Philippe couldn't think of anything better to call her than "mon chou" or "mon poulet": that had been bugging her for years, with Claude, with Jean Pierre, with Jean Marie, with Maurice, with the other Jean Pierre; she was always a "chérie" or "mon chou." "Oui, mon chou," she heard herself answering, with an edge of malice in her voice, and then she spoke cheerfully about her vacation, how marvelous it was, tomorrow she would go swimming, and Philippe, who had already unloaded his big news, said she should finally gain some weight, he found it scary, the way she'd been wasting away lately, but out there in the country she'd eat well, and they both said, okay, see you soon, and once more, see you really soon!

Here, "in the country," as Philippe put it, she and her father ate only a few cold cuts and some salad and fruit and drank milk or buttermilk—from the county dairy, not from a cow. There was nothing rural about this place, located at the edge of a provincial city that was also a capital and could even boast connections with the international railroad and airplane network via one train and one plane which one could take—for no apparent reason—to London via Frankfurt. There was no particular relationship between Carinthia and England—connections to the south and east would have been more appropriate but, strangely enough, these flights were always sold out, although the English seemed to disembark in Frankfurt and the Germans come on board, for only Germans arrived in Carinthia, and when Robert took this flight he was always the only passenger who flew all the way to Klagenfurt. All the connections were bad for Elisabeth, she had to stop over in Vienna, Milan or even Venice, and then she still had to spend hours in a train to get home, and she said to Herr Matrei: Please understand, it's not for lack of wanting to see you, it's simply such a strain, and I hate travel because I'm always on the road; Venice is not the same for me as for others. For it's just a pain, all those trains being pushed back and forth, and Milan is a catastrophe, not to mention Vienna, for hours on end in the city express I have to listen to those conversations which I understand from the mouths of people I completely understand. It's much easier to travel back and forth between Dakar and Paris because you don't understand every single word all the way to its roots, every misusage, every falsification, every vulgarity. How many people could you find who spoke like Herr Matrei and Robert, one of these days she'd stuff wax in her ears to escape being so insulted, for hours on end, on a train in Austria.

Herr Matrei didn't quite follow but nodded in assent: That's why I don't travel, and I don't like to talk to people anymore. He too loved phrases in dialect, playing them into a sentence at the right time and intoning that old civil-servant German, always appropriate to himself, his idiom and his mood, and he enjoyed reading sentences from the paper aloud, finding fault here and there and dropping remarks such as: Where in the world did that come from? "A certain amount of uncertainty," you don't say! Are you listening to me? Herr Matrei was proud of the fact that Elisabeth and Robert could speak so many foreign languages. He had no idea where their talent had come from, certainly not from their mother—she had spoken that harsh Slavic German—

nor from him, because he had never learned another language, not even Slovene. Elisabeth preferred not to tell him
that Robert wasn't really very gifted in languages after all; his
job had forced him to learn two and his English had become
quite passable thanks to Liz; in reality she, Elisabeth, was the
one who was gifted, although she had seemed to demonstrate
the contrary in Vienna when she wrote in German, strangely
enough she could write English and French but had never become bilingual as Trotta had, and hers was not a genuine ar-
tistry, she was merely more adroit and adaptable than Robert,
had more intuition and was more cautious, never attempted
to speak a certain kind of English: her accent was neutral and
she didn't copy the idioms of her English and American
friends; Trotta had once complained that she would never
speak French as well as he did but had added that he didn't
wish it upon her, it would be better if she didn't end up in
that state of disintegration, for languages had also made him
go to pieces. In the beginning he helped her occasionally
with corrections when she was unsure and then one day he
said it would suffice for her "trade," as he mildly put it, and
in America someone had helped her, and she had learned it
faster because many of the people there had already developed a more readable language; there she wasn't even a sen-
sational exception as she had been in France. Trotta spoke
German like a foreigner, from a foreign German land, and
French like a Frenchman, but he placed no importance in
this or in the fact that he spoke two or three Slavic languages
like someone who has merely been away for a long time, and
once he said to her: I've found out that I don't belong anywhere anymore, I don't long to be anywhere, but I used to
think I had a heart and I belonged in Austria. But one day

e was telling her about his first depressing experiences
ool, above all how the others talked, about the
s," and he confessed to her that he had had to pretend
e knew a lot about broads so the others wouldn't think
d no experience, she did give him a little advice and
ted his belief that the others needed to brag: if they
had had experience with "broads," they wouldn't talk
it; once again she had felt useful, as she had in the be-
g, when the diaper-washing and the sleepless nights
en the most important thing, for his sake: as a baby
d often awakened at night and cried, not for Frau
, but for Elisabeth—only then did it occur to her how
eous it was, what she'd said about her father, that com-
At least then he'll have something to think about—
e almost stopped listening to Robert, she couldn't take
, she could only hope that he hadn't caught it, preoc-
with the problems of puberty and school. Of course
e at the top of the class in chemistry but you don't like
then—and she didn't exactly deliver a lecture, but be-
the first aperitif Robert had ever had, in that gentle
which descended on the Place du Tertre, between gen-
tences which reassured him that it wasn't an absolute
e that, at sixteen, he hadn't yet slept with a girl and
verything was just stupid boasting after all, and
th, being open-minded and experienced—if there was
thing as experience—knew more about these things
ll wasn't one of those "broads" who played such a big
school. Her thoughts returned again and again to her
with tenderness and passion, and she promised herself
o say anything again that hurt her more than the per-
e was speaking about in that way. That evening she

it all comes to an end, you lose both heart and soul, and now there is something bleeding to death inside me but I don't know what it is.

Elisabeth understood now, as she talked to her father, that Trotta had been an Austrian after all, by way of negation, like her father who didn't contradict but rather disapproved of everything which acted "as though," as though there were still such a thing as this soul, this spirit, and he persevered obstinately in his belief that an error of history had never been corrected, that the year 1938 had not been a turning point: the split had occurred much earlier and everything that followed had been a consequence of this older split, and that his world—which he had hardly experienced after all—was destroyed for good in 1914 and he had never known how he had come to land in this time, a civil servant in an age in which civil servants no longer existed, in which nothing existed he could link to it. He liked talking, with critical respect, about the time before, he knew each error by heart and never overlooked one, as though he had committed all of them himself, and Elisabeth listened to him with increasing enjoyment as he grew older; before it hadn't interested her much. The future was all she had ever cared about, and she knew that, although he was not a Socialist at heart and couldn't be one without betraying himself, he had always voted for the Socialists. He said grumpily: To accelerate things! To put an end to this hypocrisy, because he didn't like this back-and-forth business with the memories, because what he remembered was something completely different and was no one's business now. He had only smiled when Robert, coming back from his second semester of college, had told him triumphantly that he had voted for the Communists, and he had said: What a scoundrel, voting for the Commies, of course that's Elisabeth's fault with all her enlightened talk from the big wide world, isn't it? Once the world actually was almost big and wide and more progressive, but I won't explain that to you. Just keep it up, it's all right.

At the time Elisabeth had been quite embarrassed and had yelled indignantly: I've only told stories and have always said what I think, and I've never given anyone any advice, why of all people am I supposed to be the one who has influenced this rascal. He's old enough to know what he's doing, and you always stressed that we should think for ourselves and not try to talk our way out of it with the excuse that we're young; that there was to be no childish behavior, not even at an early age: a child who isn't capable of comprehending something at twelve or thirteen certainly won't understand it later. You and your policy are at fault, not me.

Strangely enough, Herr Matrei was loved equally well by both his daughter and his son, which must have been due to the fact that he had never said or done anything in order to make himself popular, not even with his children; never had he made a point of stressing the sacrifices—and there had been many—he had made for his children, never how he had made a downpayment on the house in the Laubenweg and paid installments for decades; he expected thanks neither for that nor for the fact that he had never remarried because it violated his principles to expect that Elisabeth and Robert would become accustomed to a stepmother, and he had been right in assuming this, for both of them had been unconsciously merciless after the death of Frau Matrei and unbearable when they felt that a woman was within their father's proximity.

Elisabeth had once invited Robert to P[
still in high school, and it occurred to her [
ever realize, have you ever really understoo[
everything, he's a great man, and we're awf[
thanked him. Just imagine: had he marri[
have had every right to, we would have [
would have been opposed to his being wit[
Today we'd understand, but I'm not sure [
accept it. Sometimes I think that he w[
Frau Jonke, that pretty teacher of yours,[
liked him, because she was always co[
though everything depended on me and r[
was a good woman, they would have [
together. But can you imagine us with [
Laubenweg? I can't. And we leave him all [
will only go home for quick visits, and [
to do with the house, Robert, if I may [
day, this time he talked with me about i[
it will belong to you, but I could reser[
one room when I get old, for my old ag[
to subject you to my old age, and soon I'[
ment and perhaps one day I'll get marri[
But when you get married it could [
maybe your wife won't like me or I wc[
everything he's done for us would have [

Elisabeth closed the tiresome subject[
told Father that he should think abou[
least then he'll have something to th[
your bad grades in Latin and my visi[

Only when she was sitting at the [
Robert and explaining something he [

threw Robert out of her bed: he was somewhat tipsy from the first Pernod of his life and had begun to stroke her hair and face: that had to be nipped in the bud immediately, or better yet, it should never get started.

When they took their short afternoon walk to the ponds, Elisabeth mentioned that Trail 8 was also blocked by the construction site, and Herr Matrei said that nothing surprised him anymore, his pessimistic premonitions about what these construction planners were capable of had always proved right in the end. But if she went far beyond Trail 1, beyond the Jerolitsch Inn, a steep track must still be there, a way down to the lake, but if all else failed he would make an exception and drive her to the lake early in the morning, before they ran the risk of meeting other people, tourists and crowded buses. He didn't resume swimming until September, when he was safe from the summer residents, the heavy traffic and the noise at the lake. He couldn't understand how she could find the Laubenweg so quiet. All in all there was sometimes more noise than in her apartment in Paris, although of a different kind: a dog barked, a car drove around the corner and ten minutes later the next one drove by, those intermittent sounds really startled you more than the concentrated, steady roar of a big city. Herr Matrei flew into a rage when someone drove by inconsiderately, and once someone even had the nerve to leave a car parked at the front gate all day long, yes, and one night two cars had stopped nearby: doors were slammed, they had all talked in loud voices, just before midnight; he had lost his patience and had yelled something out of the window. He remarked with satisfaction that things had quieted down immediately, and the incident, an outrage, hadn't been repeated yet. Occasionally he heard the neighborhood children, not many, but all the more distinctly; even more audible was the young woman who shrilly called to them from the window: Laaadie! Laaasie! Laaadie!

In spite of everything it was quiet here, but the quietness came from the muteness of the houses; in Elisabeth's youth the entire neighborhood had been bursting with life, young couples with children had made downpayments on all the houses and now only a few elderly people lived there. Herr Matrei mentioned calmly: Frau Jonas—you remember, the one from Styria whose nephew is said to be famous now, they even talk about him on the radio, a poet who writes all kinds of incomprehensible stuff, but I can't presume to judge—she died last winter. Frau Vuk's children have gone to Canada. Edmund—let me think, he must be a little older than Robert—he went to America. Herr Arrighi passed away a month ago. You mean you don't remember? He used to work at the Kelag.

Elisabeth was used to the news about the latest deaths, she heard about different ones each year and changed the subject, asking about the "neighborhood children" from the old days. Helga had married and gone to Scotland, yes, a Scotsman, Lise had moved to Graz, was already divorced for the second time, she gave piano lessons there. Jolanda, who sometimes came back from Vienna in the summer, had stopped saying hello and Herr Matrei would be damned if he'd say anything to a silly goose who pretended not to know him. The grocery store across from the army barracks still had the same name, but the owners were newcomers trying to transform it into a "supermarket." Herr Matrei had trouble pronouncing the word, he stumbled into it with an ironic touch and explained to Elisabeth what a superwhatch-amacallit was, now you had to take a wire basket and walk around the tiny store and then pay at the cash register, even though five people were hanging around doing nothing except being thankful for every person who came in. Elisabeth offered to do the shopping the following day so she could see the change and was immediately recognized by the new people she didn't even know, and she wandered about in awkward embarrassment: Gnädige Frau, back home with us for a visit, Minni, now go and help the gnädige Frau, she doesn't know her way around yet, oh my, what a surprise, your dear father will be so delighted, your dear father is doing marvelously, so sprightly and always here first thing in the morning! Elisabeth nodded and expressed her thanks, they all helped her to find the milk bottles which really were hidden in the farthest corner, and from then on everything was the same as always, and in principle she could have dispensed with the basket and stood there while they brought everything she needed. The new owner, Herr Bichler, added the items up with an elaborate, important air which gave him time to cleverly ascertain that Elisabeth lived in Paris. Yes, Paris, he sighed, he and his wife could only plan on Paris next year, this year they had already been to the Canary Islands, Teneriffe, in low season. At first Elisabeth didn't recognize the woman at the stationery store where she wanted to buy a notebook and postcards, shapeless and with a large-pored face, but then they shook hands: they had both been in the same class, this was the young girl who had, with a few others, been mixed up in a scandal with the stationery store: a number of fifteen-year-olds had secretly visited the stationer, who had kept an entire harem of minors, but this

one here—Elisabeth had forgotten her name, Linde or Ger-
linde, he had had to marry. The woman breathed heavily
from under her fat, three years ago her husband had died, she
hadn't had an easy time of it, he had been old enough to be
her father, and today the fact that some of the others were
jealous of her because the handsomest man around had married her didn't help her. The woman said with a groan: What
a life, like a novel, I tell you, but not a happy one, and yourself? I hope you've been spared this kind of thing, but you still
look the same, we always called you bean-pole, remember?
Elisabeth laughed a little and promised to come back, but
she would certainly never set foot in the shop again and
returned home in an uncommunicative mood.

At lunch she tried to tell amusing anecdotes of her conversations in the shops, then fell silent and left out the woman
in the stationery store. Her father wanted to lie down, and
she said: I think I'll go out after all, even though it's late,
please don't wait for me to have coffee!

She took Trail 1 again, undecided whether to try one of
the three paths again and then went north toward Falkenberg
castle on Trail 10. The path narrowed and was dark and
damp, but at least she wasn't walking in the direction of the
lake. There were a number of German cars parked in front
of the castle, which had ostensibly been turned into a guest-
house or a hotel, but the grounds were empty. No one was
sitting at the brightly-colored tables which looked so incon-
gruous next to the castle; the guests were either sleeping or
had driven to the lake, and she sat down at a table, smoked
a cigarette and made sure that she had twenty schillings with
her, because if someone came she'd have to order a coffee or
a tea in order to legitimize her presence here. Her biggest

mistake had probably been abandoning New York so quickly; when she married Hugh she had no longer believed that she loved Trotta and that he had been the right man, and this afternoon, gazing at the forest, she believed one last time that, unfortunately, there was something she'd done which had been completely wrong, she never should have consented to the divorce, in response to a letter, she should have followed him immediately, because the letter had probably not been meant seriously: it had contained a series of confused self-reproaches that he never, never should have gotten her into this mess and something to the effect "it's more than I can take, trying to explain it to you, you deserve better, I hope that you'll find your prince charming and forget me . . . ," but her memory of that guilty letter asking her to file for divorce had faded, and even today she couldn't comprehend what had been more than he could take; they had gotten along together so well. On the other hand, she could remember exactly—because she'd constantly drawn strength from it in New York and even afterward—how his first letter to her had begun "Uncrowned Queen of my Heart!" and she loved the opening to this letter longer than she loved Hugh, who must have misunderstood something or been in one of his confused states of mind when he arranged to flee to Mexico with a young Italian and left her frantic with worry for three long weeks. She had written him a grandiose, emotional letter, saying that of course she respected his wishes but failed to see why he alone wanted to take the blame, because she couldn't see that there was any, that he could always depend on her and that she was willing to wait, but perhaps because her letter was just as confused as his, the reply was confined to a short request not to wait, he had to weather this crisis alone, he had only one big favor to ask, namely that she forgive him, and the second big favor that she get a divorce. Gino was suffering horribly because he, Hugh, was so far away in his thoughts, always with her, and above all from the fact that he was the cause of this separation. The trials and tribulations this Gino, whom she had seen only once, was made to suffer due to Hugh and herself remained forever a mystery, and once again Hugh had succeeded in endowing someone with secrets and a sensitivity she was unable to discover, but Hugh was really the sensitive one, not the Ginos. Everything should have gone well with Hugh; he was the only one who had succeeded in making Elisabeth happy even today; he had been truly generous and good to her. Once he had received an order and an advance of one hundred dollars, and of these first priceless dollars he'd earned he bought so many flowers for her that they didn't fit in all of the vases and pots and swam around in the sink and the bath, and he'd given her an expensive perfume, a huge bottle, and Elisabeth was stunned, not out of sheer happiness, but rather more because the phone bill hadn't been paid and she was barely getting by, but now, standing up and taking a last parting look at the castle which was no longer a castle—no waitress had come and thus she had been spared German coffee—she saw herself with her arms full of flowers, between laughter and tears like in a movie where the man sent the diva so many flowers that the starring actress collapsed under the load, and she heard herself saying, even now: *You are a fool, oh Hugh, my darling, you must be crazy!* Today Elisabeth would certainly not remember a paid phone bill, but one which was almost impossible to pay stuck in her memory like the flowers and the money out the window, everything that Hugh had done for no good reason. That was what he had become for her, he lived on in her, glorified and perhaps—in Mexico or whatever place was now fashionable for "starting all over again," in those days Mexico had been the "in" spot—perhaps he had completely forgotten that hour when the little apartment had been buried in flowers and he had said, beaming, that Bandit was the only perfume for her. Maybe he was thinking of something painful, in South America or back in New York, something she knew nothing about, or maybe of something pleasant, a pleasant moment she could no longer remember. Before the junction with Trail 5 she sat down, from here she had a view of the Freyenthurn castle, but only up to the Plattenwirt, and of course that was the solution. It was only a short walk from that point, which was still part of the city, to the promenade—but she didn't want to go that way because she'd have to walk down open streets, the Villacherstrasse had to be avoided at all costs, she couldn't allow herself to be seen in this outfit, of course she could, she didn't really care, but the intersection of Trails 5 and 6 bothered her because it came too quickly, and she descended after all but stopped at a field, she should have spent more time looking, she couldn't even glimpse the lake from where she was, in a level clearing, there must be a continuation somewhere, but cross-country hiking wasn't allowed, and after roaming around looking for a new path she turned back and took the ridge trail home.

Herr Matrei had put up a long fight about the telephone: he wouldn't tolerate one in the Laubenweg and mocked the way his children talked on the phone, at these calls from men who couldn't speak German and asked for Elisabeth, and each time he said write down how much you've wasted on calls, Robert has to pay the bill. Although Elisabeth had initially tried to convince him to have a telephone installed, believing that she could wrap him around her little finger because she was his daughter, Robert's coaxing had succeeded in the end. But he had to pay the bills, and Elisabeth in turn had to pay him for the calls she made. Herr Matrei sat back with a smile and let them pay only because he had not wanted the telephone; he would gladly have paid it all, but they were going to learn a little lesson and make symbolic amends. At first he hadn't liked the contraption because it bothered him, ringing when he was resting in the afternoon or in the garden or when the news was on. And the children were always calling at the most inappropriate times, from foreign countries. In the beginning he had only been annoyed and said curtly: Write instead, write me a letter, you haven't written for three weeks and the news is on.

In time he was glad that Robert had had his way, for it really did cheer him up when the children called. Only once had he been horrified: Elisabeth had called from New York and he thought she was deathly ill, but she only wanted to ask if he could get a copy of her birth certificate for her, she didn't have all her papers and couldn't find that one. Later he was forced to admit that this silly daughter of his had simply lost all sense of perspective, calling only because she couldn't wait to get married, and a letter would have been quite sufficient.

The next morning it was raining, and Elisabeth and Herr Matrei sat together at breakfast. The paper hadn't come yet, and she said: I don't know, this summer is turning out to be no summer at all. Herr Matrei apologized for the Carinthian summer and said that they might risk driving to the beach today because many would be discouraged by the rain, and then walk to Loretto. She didn't mind the rain anyway, and neither of them wanted to meet anyone. They took the bus and changed at the Heiligen-Geist-Platz, boarding the bus to the lake.

They no longer had the old streetcars with their open cars in summer and the hordes of children hanging on the running board and the adults sitting on facing benches. Nowhere in the world had there been prettier summer streetcars than in Klagenfurt. Now you simply took a bus that looked like buses everywhere. They proceeded to Loretto on foot and were the first and only ones who had come to go swimming.

Elisabeth had already put her suit on under her dress and threw her clothes on the bridge. Herr Matrei changed painstakingly in the booth and then they swam for twenty minutes in relatively cold water. It was so marvelous that neither wanted to return home, she froze and swam vigorously to get warm, but she must have gotten really thin lately. She went in once more anyway, her father swam again, too, and they met at a tree trunk which was turning in the lake like a buoy. *Daddy, I love you,* she shouted at him in English, and he called back: What did you say? She shouted: Nothing. I'm cold.

On the way home they passed the huge camping ground and Herr Matrei made one of his biting remarks, not without some satisfaction, that these people were so crammed together by choice. This was the reason he would never come here alone, although he enjoyed swimming as much as before, but you simply couldn't go to the lake anymore before fall, it was so full of Germans. Herr Matrei brooded: Every-thing is full of Germans, now they've finally managed to buy out, and they didn't even put a stop to it, those fools in the government, they should have seen it coming. And now, in his old age, he was forced to look on while the Germans took over Carinthia. The farmers had sold almost all of their land to them, the new owners acted like lords and masters, not like guests. There wasn't an Austrian to be seen during the tourist season and the menus abounded with idiotic names no Austrian understood, once he'd read something like Käsesahnetorte for a simple "cheesecake" and promptly stood up and left and would never set food in the Ronacher again. Herr Matrei exclaimed indignantly: And our people knuckle under and believe it's good for the foreign exchange and the tourist industry. But this, he said, has nothing to do with the tourist industry, it's more like occupation. Elisabeth was aware that, for quite some time now, half the population of the Rhein-Ruhr district had been invading Carinthia, of course not the rich, they wouldn't be caught dead visiting such a poor country, but as her father—who voted for the Socialists—said, it was the workers with their huge, stinking cars who were ruining the country, and that was simply too much for him. Constantly hearing these workers who began yelling and drinking at nine in the morning and were always washing their cars and then speeding down to "Fenice." Elisabeth, not wanting to upset her father even more, thought to herself: This lake isn't the lake that once be-longed to us either, its water tastes different, swimming in it isn't the same. It only belonged to us for half an hour in the rain. Herr Matrei began repeating himself while they drove back through the city: now the Germans had everything, and he hadn't wanted to live to see that. They had lost the war, but only on the surface, and now they were really conquering Austria, now they could buy it, and that was worse, in his opinion a country that could be bought was worse than one that had gone astray or been cursed. One mustn't sell out.

Elisabeth didn't know why she suddenly had to think of the Trotta who had been a district officer during the monarchy; to her he was only a legend, but she thought: he and my father, they have so much in common. More than half a century later someone existed who was so similar to someone from another, submerged time and place. And perhaps that was the reason why, during these days, her thoughts kept returning to Franz Joseph Trotta, whom she had rarely thought of in this time. In essence, Trotta had meant the same thing father meant when he spoke about the Germans: I mean, it literally left me speechless, ever since I was in Germany with the French Army, I know what it means to be speechless, because there were so many people around me who deluded themselves into thinking that they were speaking German and the French even believed it, though not much else, but they believed that.

They had to wait for a connection at the Heiligen-Geist-Platz, and Elisabeth said: I'll get a few papers! On the front page of one she was shocked to read in a small article that one of her friends had plunged from a cliff near Sorrento and the Italian police had not yet determined whether it was an accident, suicide or murder. But this paper, like the others, sported huge headlines which she skimmed distractedly. She was out of breath as she came back to her father, who was standing in front of the Landhaus waving to her because the

bus was coming. She gave him two papers, although he usually read only the one he subscribed to, and then, in order to
calm down, she began to read slowly: Jealousy Leads to Tragedy on Millionaire's Mansion. "On" was good. That didn't interest her much at all, but the next one carried the same
story: Bloodbath in Millionaire's Hunting Lodge. Against her
will she began to read. Just then the bus came, and they
climbed in. During the ride home Elisabeth labored through
the text: she was too much of a journalist and the writing was
so convoluted that initially she couldn't understand a thing.
When one knew the provincial press and its amiable inability to write about something outside its domain, one really
needed imagination or professional insight to find the facts
in the jumble of sentences. Elisabeth looked up once and
said as they were driving past the Theater: Bertold Rapatz
shot his wife and some Slovenian assistant forester and then
shot himself, isn't that unbelievable? Herr Matrei didn't answer; he was engrossed in his newspaper and remarked:
Rapatz? Never heard of him. Elisabeth said in surprise: But
Father! After all, he's one of the three richest men in Austria,
if not the richest, and he keeps some hunting grounds here.
She couldn't quite understand the article: the sixty-two-year-
old certified engineer Bertold Rapatz had shot his thirty-
three-year-old wife Dr. Elisabeth Rapatz, presumably out of
jealousy, first her lover, in front of whom she had tried to
throw herself, a certain Jaslo So-and-So. The local police in
Eisenkappel had been called to the scene of the crime by a
Radmilla So-and-So, who was the housekeeper in the millionaire's villa. Elisabeth now took her father's paper, it made
her too nervous, these awkward, long-winded reports. Any
two-bit journalist working for the popular press in Paris or

New York would have known how to report this, but here they simply had no idea. Jealousy Leads to Tragedy, it had the provincial ring of haylofts and penknives, but in spite of it all, the husband was Bertold Rapatz. For a while she even tried hard to go on: "Certified Engineer Bertold Rapatz, whose father is descended from the illustrious family of the Noblemen von Rapatz upon whom a title was bestowed for the great service rendered in gaining access to the Gail Valley for purposes essential to the war effort. . .," and Elisabeth thought at first that these poor little journalists who were so good at reporting lumber auctions unfortunately had no idea what had fallen into the hands of the local police, and that Bertold Rapatz's illustrious title wasn't worth a penny because Kaiser Karl had bestowed titles on just about anyone who crossed his path before the end of the war, and that it was of no consequence whether Bertold Rapatz was a certified engineer like his father, the Nobleman von Rapatz. It was, however, of some consequence to know that Rapatz was not only a millionaire—there might even be a number of millionaires in Carinthia—but that he was a power to be reckoned with, money personified, and that a hunting lodge was not a mansion but rather something else, and that, as a sideline, Rapatz owned a third of Carinthia's lumber industry and hunting grounds. The fourth paper, which Elisabeth finally captured from her father, also featured the bloodbath and jealousy aspects, and after a moment she stopped reading and let the paper drop. Rapatz's third wife, "Dr. Elisabeth Rapatz, née Mihailovics," it said, and she thought of the short, strange meeting in the Teichstrasse and said to herself: No, that can't be possible, but it must be true, that shy, little, poor Mihailovics had become the third Frau Rapatz, but what did

195

it all mean? She wasn't the type of woman who was after a rich man, and this young Slovene she remembered must have been the "forestry employee" they mentioned, but surely there was nothing going on between them, she would have noticed it in a second, it must have been something completely different that had so embarrassed the Mihailovics woman. She said to her father in a choked voice: It was Elisabeth Mihailovics he married, imagine that, and our well-mannered local police will never find out what was really going on, all the nonsense they cook up in their tiny brains doesn't add up to anything, it makes no sense whatsoever. I know what I'm talking about!

Herr Matrei, who could not realize why Elisabeth was so upset, merely said: The poor woman! These older men today with their much too young wives, it's doomed to go wrong.

Oh, come on, she said impatiently, it's not like that. There are much more complicated things than tragic cases of jealousy. I'd like to know what that poor thing got herself into and what kind of man that Rapatz really was. Hardly anyone ever saw him, not even in Vienna. You never see people like that.

Herr Matrei was amazed, because he had always thought of the important people as being completely different. To him and probably to most people in the country, those who appeared in the papers, senators, the mayor, above all the head of the province, were the V.I.P.'s. That there were people like Rapatz who wouldn't even have allowed such public figures in their houses—that didn't fit into his concept of a hierarchy at all, and neither did the fact that someone like Rapatz, if he really was the famous man Elisabeth seemed to think he was, would have refused to allow himself to be photographed or to talk on the radio: that was even less comprehensible to him. I think you're grossly overrating this man, Herr Matrei stated firmly. He's never been in the public eye.

I believe it, Elisabeth said with a smile, and if he hadn't killed himself and two other people, his presence here would never have been publicized. At least not here in Klagenfurt. The initial statements of the housekeeper and the other employees contained so little information that one could almost interpret it as deliberate silence and concealment, and she could imagine how Rapatz had erected a wall around his life and, for that reason, later no one would talk about them because people like Rapatz chose their personnel well; and it also occurred to her that they were almost exlusively Slovenes, a few Croatians, and that meant another protective wall against the curious, even after his death.*

After the first week, although she had originally planned to stay for two, a restlessness took hold of Elisabeth and she became increasingly nervous with each passing hour because she had to control herself in front of her father, who had noted: You're already looking much better. The restlessness came from the long hikes through the woods and from the lake which she no longer wanted to see, but today she had tried once more to descend via the Jerolitsch Inn, knowing all along that it wouldn't work. She came home with a deeper tan but exhausted and, pretending to be very tired, she left her father to eat supper alone and went to her room where

*Trans. note: Baachmann's unfinished story "Gier" ("Greed"), which was originally intended as part of the *Todesarten* cycle, relates the details of this murder and suicide. The story was published posthumously in *Der dunkle Schatten, dem ich schon seit Anfang folge*, ed. Hans Höller, Vienna and Munich, 1982.

she read one of Robert's old adventure stories until midnight and then, when she was certain that her father was asleep, quietly called the long-distance operator and asked for Paris. The connection took only a few minutes, she was relieved to hear Philippe's voice and asked him in a whisper to send her a telegram to the effect: very urgent, work required departure. The next morning the telegram arrived from Paris, and Elisabeth professed indignation, mumbling: It would have to be just now, when I'm finally starting to relax.

For a second she looked down, for she was afraid of disappointing her father but was relieved to detect no note of sadness or despondency because she wanted—or, as he believed, was forced—to leave him so soon, and they took the next bus into town to the travel agency, no, he would take charge of getting the ticket and would not tolerate Elisabeth's paying the fare to Vienna. He gave her these presents, in overabundance, to compensate for his request that she pay for her phone calls, and on the way back he grumbled about the horrible traffic Elisabeth could not detect. They spent the evening before her departure quietly together, listening to the evening news and taking turns reading sections of his paper which once again contained reports of the bloody tragedy "on and around" millionaire's hunting lodge without citing a single new fact. Still no postcard had arrived from Morocco, and they talked a little or maintained a thoughtful silence, and this time it was Herr Matrei who insisted that she go to bed early. Alone in her room, she didn't feel like lying down obediently on her bed and instead rummaged through her things and began to pack her suitcases. She was a little startled when her father knocked and entered, but he didn't comment on the fact that she wasn't in bed yet; he shyly pressed an envelope in her hand and kissed her on the cheek, saying: Just so I don't forget, it's a little something for the trip and to help you manage in Vienna.

Elisabeth was at a loss for words, it occurred to her that the envelope would contain the usual thousand shillings so that she, the little, girl, would be able to manage on the road, and she said, as always: How sweet of you, so that he smiled and was reassured, knowing how much she needed him. No feelings of guilt plagued her as she drove to the train station with her father the following morning, where Herr Matrei once again went to great lengths to make certain that the train was really departing from track 1 at the stated time. Letting him go ahead, she bought newspapers, magazines and cigarettes at a stand and strolled to the track, where Herr Matrei was waiting with a stern expression: he firmly believed in arriving early as a matter of principle, and now unluckily there was another half-hour to wait, and they stood next to the suitcases and talked, she promised to write immediately, she might call some friends from the airport in Vienna, oh, some friends Herr Matrei didn't know, insisting that she preferred a night flight to Paris to a flight during the day, that she had no interest whatsoever in seeing anything from the plane. Finally the train pulled in and she hugged him and boarded and took a place at the window, yes, her father had grown smaller and here, when he wasn't at home or walking with her through the forest, he once more had that childlike expression, the wizened look of an old man left behind, left alone, and although it was too late, Elisabeth had the urge to get off and say something to him, but what? whatever could she say? not knowing how frightened she was when the train began to move, frightened that she would never see him again. She shouted, but perhaps he no longer heard her: I'll write immediately, thank you for everything, I'll write! She smiled and waved and hoped that the train would pull out more quickly than usual, she waved as though she were not upset, a radiant woman, his daughter, a child, Robert's sister, someone who left and traveled and always traveled on.

At the airport in Vienna, after having mechanically completed the formalities and disposed of her suitcases, she went immediately through the passport control because there was no line at the moment. She considered going up to the restaurant but then decided on the more deserted café, a huge room with tired people sitting and waiting at plastic tables. After she had drunk the first cup of coffee—unfortunately, no longer Viennese coffee—she paged through her address book. Perhaps she should call the Altenwyls or the Goldmanns, no, each of them had quirks, that was too tricky, and she turned page over page, maybe the Jordans, or Martin or Alex . . . No, it was completely useless, no one would be in the city at the end of July.

A man had passed her table at least two or three times only to retreat, and when she involuntarily turned and looked at him, he came back and asked with clumsy politeness: Excuse me, are you Elisabeth Matrei? She stared at him without replying, and he repeated: Excuse me, you probably don't remember me.

He was her age but seemed younger, although all men of that age usually seemed older to her, and he spoke that harsh German familiar to her, but she simply couldn't remember what was so familiar about it, how he knew her and whether she knew him. She made a cautious gesture, he took a seat, and at that moment it occurred to her: he must be that cousin of Trotta's, Branco, one of those who had stayed in Yugoslavia, the son or grandson of peasants or merchants, (or had his ancestors roasted chestnuts?), from that very same Sipolje which no longer existed, and since this Branco could hardly live there anymore, she hesitated and asked. So, he lived in Ljubljana. He ordered a coffee too, and now she didn't know what to talk to him about; he would know everything there was to know about his cousin's death, and then again it had been so long ago. She listened inattentively and half-heard him talking with difficulty about Ljubljana and that he had a visa for Moscow and was flying to Moscow now. Then he said, quickly and effortlessly, causing her to glance up in surprise: I've waited for a long time. A very long time. But you were always surrounded by so many people. I mean you were always so busy and there were always so many people around you. She said lightly: Really? So many people? He added disjointedly: I married a year ago, yes, down there, and I have a son, he's two months old. She laid her cigarette on the saucer and said warmly: That's nice, I'm really happy for you. But it seemed rather strange to her and she looked at him more closely, he already had a few grey hairs on his temples. But so late, I mean. You waited so long to get married? It was intended as quite a normal question and sounded normal. Yes, he said and then gazed fixedly into her eyes: You were always surrounded by so many people. I saw you once in Vienna and then with my cousin in Paris, and I'm sure you know all about it, but then I never heard anything else about you. I don't even know if you know about Franz Joseph and me, we weren't only related, it was more than that, but I couldn't do anything more, and we stayed home.

Elisabeth said softly: That was probably better, but you say "home," then it still exists after all. The man said: Franz Joseph didn't feel at home in Paris or in Vienna in the end, he always liked to say paradoxical things, above all that he was ex-territorial. Don't be upset, he was beyond help. His flight was called and he stood up, listening uncertainly to the voice coming over the loudspeaker, there was no longer any doubt, the passengers to Moscow were being called, and not waiting for her to extend her hand in farewell, he said softly, hurriedly in leaving: May God protect you. She watched him go, not able to say "goodbye" to that, and stayed seated, flustered and noticing too late that her cigarette had turned to ash and fallen from the saucer and the glowing butt was lying on the plastic tabletop, she burned her fingers, not knowing how else to estinguish the cigarette in this public place. She was in a daze because she couldn't understand what he had meant about so many people and why he had kept repeating it. Another flight was called, once again in three languages, and then she was startled to hear another voice, again over the loudspeaker; it didn't call passengers but rather was a polite monotone announcing that the flight to Moscow would be delayed for approximately two hours due to technical problems, the passengers to Moscow were re-quested . . . When he returned she had already stood up, having sensed his approach from behind before she heard his steps, and she turned to him, they stood facing each other, gazing at one another. Gently, and then with increasing pressure, he took both of her slender, overly thin hands in his massive ones. They each began to smile at the same time and didn't say a word. She didn't ask him why he was flying to Moscow and what he was going to do there, and he didn't ask her if she was still living in Paris and what she had lost there. They merely looked into one another's eyes, and a very light blue swam in them which darkened when they stopped smiled. Thank God he was no longer saying that she was always surrounded by so many people, and she forgot all the other people in her life, the people at the airport and in this dreary café. But time passed so quickly, more quickly than ever before, and suddenly she felt she was fainting, but at the same time she had the impression that he, so much stronger than she, had begun to pale and that he, too, was suffering from this high tension, this abandon. At that moment the flight for Paris was announced and, as if delivered from an unbearable anguish, she gently disengaged both her hands. She took her leave like someone who has memorized every detail, the direction of the glass door she had to pass through, her senses were concentrated solely on the gate number, as though it were extremely important to concentrate solely on that. He followed her slowly to the glass door which would divide them, and she was afraid he would say something, but he only stood still, pulled out a small notebook and pen, ripped out a page, wrote something on the sheet and folded it. She was still afraid that something might be destroyed, and her glance at him was an urgent plea, hopefully he hadn't written down his address in Ljubljana or Moscow, but he returned her gaze calmly, his face no longer showing that pain and that pallor, and tucked the folded page into her coat pocket. She turned and walked through the automatic door.

She didn't read the note on the plane, but when she was waiting for her luggage at the claim area in Orly and was looking for a handkerchief in her pocket, she pulled out the

note opened it and read numbly, without comprehending:
I love you.
I have always loved you.
She held the handkerchief in her hand and no longer
knew why she had wanted it, oh yes, there was a draft and
she had been about to sneeze, but then she hastily stuffed the
note and the handkerchief back in her pocket, frightened to
death at seeing Philippe approaching her. First he took her
suitcases and energetically loaded them onto a cart and then
pulled Elisabeth to him and gave her a long, intense kiss, in
the middle of all the people passing by, as though they were
alone, and his tongue was so deep in her throat that she
pushed him away, feeling as though she was suffocating. She
said breathlessly: But really, you know that wasn't necessary,
why did you come out to Orly just because I've come back!
Philippe pushed the luggage cart to the exit, she walked with
it and repeated: I just can't understand why you rushed out
to Orly, we could have met afterward in the city . . . Philippe
looked for a taxi and actually found one, and in the taxi he
kissed her again, with the same greed, and she stopped pro-
testing. Then he began to talk, with the same intensity: Now
come on and tell me what happened, why I had to send you
that telegram, I went half-crazy with worry! She straightened
and said in amazement: What do you mean? It's all quite simple, I was bored to death, I should have expected that, it's
boring in the country, that's the only reason I asked you to
do it.

But Philippe wasn't stupid, not in the least, and he looked
at her in disbelief and insisted: But something must have
happened. Come on, don't try to fool me.

She gazed out of the window and didn't reply, as though

she had suddenly developed an interest in the streets at night with so many cars and neon lights.

Philippe said: I can tell something's wrong just by the way you act.

He was mystified when still no answer came and finally began to talk about the movie, because he had wanted to talk about it and, after all, he didn't have to let everything be ruined by one of Elisabeth's moods, but when they stopped at a light and he had totally exhausted the topic, he said once more: Something did happen.

She said in a firm tone of dismissal: For heaven's sake, first of all, hardly anything ever happens and even if it did, a lot of things have happened to you, and I'm really, really happy for you, but—she paused in mid-sentence—but the real things, they never happen or they happen too late.

Have you fallen in love with some Tyrolean? Philippe asked. At least she was talking now, but she thought with disgust of Jean Pierre who had once whined about someone who wasn't a real "tyrolienne," and then she thought sadly of Duvalier, who had so often said with pride and in jest: That's my talented little tyrolienne! To Philippe she said: No, not at all, unfortunately, mon chéri, not even with a Tyrolean. And she added casually: Only, I don't know how to tell you, now when I've just arrived, but I think I'm going to have an awful lot of work coming up, you know how it is, please don't look so disappointed, please, not like that!

Philippe said tenderly: No, ma chérie, it's only that I was so concerned, that's why I called so often, because every night I felt so miserable without you, without your advice, I've never needed you so much as in the past few days. (Elisabeth thought detachedly, now he's really exaggerating, in fact it wasn't the first time that he had needed her as never before.) I would feel so cheap lying to you, I think I've done a really stupid thing, and I have to tell you about it right away, I couldn't go into it on the phone because I noticed how happy you were, enjoying that exhilarating country life. It's about Lou.

Elisabeth now really felt that she was back in Paris. She began to recognize streets and knew she was on the way to her apartment, asking with absentminded sympathy: Isn't she doing well, is she sick, is she in trouble?

No, not that, Philippe said, it's just so idiotic, she refuses to understand a thing, first these girls act so modern and free as though they were superior to bourgeois morals, and then they want to get married after all and set their fathers after you like in a slapstick farce from the last century; old man Marchand, excuse me, I mean Claude, he stormed in like the avenger of his daughter's honor, you know him, I mean you know him better than I do. (For a moment Elisabeth and Philippe exchanged a look of conspiracy, but only for an indeterminable space of time, for each of them knew what the other associated with the name Marchand.) I can only imagine that all men revert to being old-fashioned when it comes to their daughters! Elisabeth interrupted him: Well, what's wrong with Lou? Philippe said simple: She's pregnant. Marchand hates me, you know, and of course I didn't want to look like an idiot in front of that stinking rich capitalist, I said to him that I wouldn't dream of shirking my responsibility, because after all, and although I don't have much to show for myself. . .

It was the first time Elisabeth had heard him use the word "responsibility," and she hoped he wouldn't notice her smile in the half-light of the taxi. She said: Chéri, you can't simply shirk a responsibility of such magnitude, you know, I would never want to give you a lecture, but since you brought it up yourself, I can only say that I've seen all of this coming, and about us, you know, we really had a wonderful time together, at least I did, and I'm infinitely thankful, but I don't want to stand in the way of responsibility, mon chou, the thought would never occur to me.

Now he had his exit, and a very good one at that, combined with admission into a world he had sincerely despised, even long after his May euphoria and the time Elisabeth had pulled him out of his depressions, out of his drinking and the increasingly pointless discussions and outbursts of rage directed not at the regime, capitalism and imperialism, but at his comrades who had disintegrated into splinter groups and were battling against each other. In spite of all her follies, she had always had a knack for choosing the best of the shipwrecked. Once Philippe had come to see her after the May revolution and asked for a favor, he had behaved somewhat arrogantly because he saw her as one of these detestable creatures of luxury, not exactly a capitalist, but at least a capitalist's whore. That had changed gradually and he had come to see her more and more often, talking to her for hours and dragging in groups of young people with him who consumed unbelievable amounts of food and drink and hardly left her any time for work, and one day he began to think about her and was astounded. She hadn't wanted to go to bed with him, perhaps she only did that with someone like Marchand who could buy her expensive dresses, but then he found out that no man bought her dresses, that perhaps no man ever had, and although it was true that she earned money, she worked for it. One day he had deluded himself into thinking he was in love or at least unable to live without her, and after he had explained it to her she had said, between laughs, No, but one day she stopped resisting and they moved in together.

Now, in this taxi which was taking so damn long, he kept watching her anxiously, no, she didn't look deathly pale, but she was almost always tan, in the winter she traveled to countries where it was hot, but she hadn't broken out in tears, either, or thrown herself into his arms and begun to burden him with accusations. He wasn't sure how to act, she was being tactless, heartless, and he really needed to talk about Lou and the idiotic course things had taken over the past few days. It wasn't easy for him to marry this woman Lou just like that, he desperately needed advice. But she simply smiled, and he prepared himself for a scene, because you had to be ready for anything with an older woman, he'd consulted a friend about that, the last friend he still had left from the battles at the Sorbonne, for he didn't want Elisabeth to have a breakdown because of him, maybe commit suicide because of Lou, he at least was not a Claude Marchand or another one of those characters she'd been involved with before, at least he admitted to himself that he had lied to her and used her more than once. But probably Elisabeth hadn't yet realized the full impact of the changed situation, the breakdown might not come until she got home, or tomorrow or the day after, he could see it coming clearly enough. Of course she had marvelous self-control and that refined allure, otherwise he never would have become involved with her in the first place. About the money, Philippe began, it's certainly not the right time, but I want you to know that I know how much I owe you and how thankful I am. I think pretty soon now, when the movie. . .

What did you say? Elisabeth asked absently. But that's simply absurd, I don't know why you're in such a hurry, it's not as though I were starving; actually I've earned a lot of money in the past few months. No, the money, you know, don't worry about that, I've had so much good luck, over and over again, and what role could money play between us, anyway? I really can't understand you.

Philippe thought in despair: Oh no, now she realizes it, she's going to break down now. Marchand had simply had money, but Elisabeth worked for hers.

They got out, she paid but gladly allowed Philippe to carry her bags upstairs. She had never liked carrying luggage, but today she really was too weak. In the apartment the situation became unbearably awkward: Elisabeth had totally lost the thread. She began incoherently: In case you can't get along with Marchand, who certainly envisioned a quite different catch for his angel—Philippe cut her short impatiently: You know as well as he does that Lou is no angel, besides, she's a drug addict, and I don't want to marry a woman who's an addict, the main thing is that she should regain her health and get away from that crowd she spends her time with.

Elisabeth said rationally: It's already settled that you're getting married, it wasn't my idea.

Philippe stood awkwardly in the room in which he had so often sat and moved with casual ease. Elisabeth said: Excuse me, I'd just like to check my mail, and she ripped open a few letters. Philippe, who at first had merely watched her in dismay, sat down next to her and kissed her hand, asking: Are you angry, are you sad?

She looked at him in surprise: Do I look angry, do I look sad? I'm dead tired, that's for sure. But that's natural after a boring stay in Austria and a wedding in London and other such pleasures.

She began to push letters and printed matter to the side and leafed through the mail in search of telegrams. The first one was completely incomprehensible. It opened with "merde," closed with loving words and was signed by André. But André never sent garbled telegrams with unclear messages. The second telegram was uninteresting, the third three pages long and once again from André, he must have sent it before the other, between stop and stop and stop there was something about Kemp and ulcer. So what of it? it was common knowledge that Kemp had long had some kind of complicated stomach problem, she didn't need to be told about it by telegram. But after the next stop she realized that Kemp required an operation and thus couldn't go, and when she had read the second half of the telegram once more it finally dawned on her that André was asking her to fly to Saigon in Kemp's place. It was the longest telegram she'd ever received, but the people on the editorial staff didn't cut corners when it came to quality reporting.

Elisabeth pored over this telegram for an unnaturally long time, laying it on the table but continuing to stare at it, and Philippe, who felt more miserable in this apartment with every passing minute, asked whether it was some important news, and she looked at him with relief and said with more animation: Yes, I think so. Would you do me a favor, go to the kitchen and get some ice and mix us two drinks, we have so much to drink to. To all these changes! Never before had she seen Philippe so considerate or timid, never so young, and she was a little sad because he was no longer the un-reasonable, presumptuous, self-confident, failed rebel of two years ago. Now he looked like any other young man, an un-certain lover who was on his guard today not to irritate her. Philippe placed the glasses on the table and filled them, do-ing everything as he always used to, and they smiled at each other and touched glasses.

Is it something good or at least not something bad? Philippe asked. She said: Good or bad, those aren't the right words. But I'd like to have another drink with you. Apparent-ly Philippe was still thinking she might break down and that he would have to stay the night with her and have no oppor-tunity to call Lou this evening. All the same, he was willing to do anything today, for he had a responsibility, even to Elisabeth. She casually pushed the telegram over to him and said: Read it, it's better if you know what it says. He too read it twice, taking a few sips, and said nothing for a while. He put his glass down on the table and said: André must be cra-zy, it's out of the question, you aren't going, I forbid you to go.

She looked at him closely, amazed, what did that have to do with him, he had such a big responsibility now, but that was for Lou, not her. But she couldn't tell him that now, she was too tired and merely said compliantly: I can only promise you that I won't call André today, I'll let him pine away until tomorrow morning, but then I'll go. I know for certain that I'll go, I don't need to make a decision, I know it already. And now please leave. Okay?

She didn't kiss him or allow him to kiss her, she evaded him, only giving him a fleeting kiss on the cheek and a quick hug at the door. Philippe was incensed and helpless and said angrily: You can't go, don't do it, you just can't!

But his sentence had nothing to do with Trotta's sentence, his voice held nothing of Trotta's voice, which had echoed inside her for almost twenty years, and she had come to believe only her own voice now and the completely different voices of her Trottas which were, for once, not against her. Philippe was still standing at the door with an angry, aggressive look on his face, and once more she loved him for a second, and he almost shouted: That clown is out of his mind, how can he send a woman out there, he must have some men in reserve, that canaille.

She had to laugh and shoved him out the door, promising to call him the next day.

Elisabeth, who had never felt at all sorry for Philippe, was suddenly overwhelmed by pity for him, and while she undressed, too exhausted to take off her makeup, she thought, everything had turned out well in the end, between the two of them, he was safe. But where had the May gone? She emptied her glass and threw herself onto the bed. She must have fallen asleep instantly, when her first dream catapulted her out of her slumber and she reached out her hand to the telephone, mumbling: Hello! It could only have been André, but she replaced the receiver instantly, reaching for the tiny, crumpled scrap of paper and tucking it under her pillow as she dozed off again, struck by another dream at the edge of sleep, and clutching at her head and her heart because she didn't know where all the blood was coming from. Nonetheless she kept repeating: It's nothing, it's nothing, nothing else can happen to me now. Something might happen to me, but it doesn't have to.